YEARS

SIMON &
SCHUSTER
PAPERBACKS

Also by Logic

Supermarket

This Bright Future: A Memoir

ULTRA 85

A Novel

LOGIC

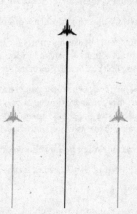

SIMON & SCHUSTER

New York London Toronto Sydney New Delhi

100 YEARS
SIMON &
SCHUSTER
PAPERBACKS

An Imprint of Simon & Schuster, LLC
1230 Avenue of the Americas
New York, NY 10020

First Simon & Schuster trade paperback edition September 2024

SIMON & SCHUSTER and colophon are registered
trademarks of Simon & Schuster, LLC

Simon & Schuster: Celebrating 100 Years of Publishing in 2024

For information about special discounts for bulk purchases,
please contact Simon & Schuster Special Sales at
1-866-506-1949 or business@simonandschuster.com.

The Simon & Schuster Speakers Bureau can bring authors to
your live event. For more information or to book an event, contact
the Simon & Schuster Speakers Bureau at 1-866-248-3049
or visit our website at www.simonspeakers.com.

Interior design by Lewelin Polanco

Manufactured in the United States of America

1 3 5 7 9 10 8 6 4 2

Library of Congress Cataloging-in-Publication Data is available.

ISBN 978-1-9821-5827-9
ISBN 978-1-9821-5829-3 (ebook)

To Christopher Nolan, whom I've never met.
But without, this story would not exist.

ULTRA
85

INTERPLANETARY MARINE CORPS
DEPARTMENT OF FUTURE AND SUSTAINMENT
OFFICIAL DEBRIEF MEMORANDUM FOR THE RECORD

Interviewee: Captain Quentin Thomas, IMC,
Department of Resource and Mineral Attainment

Interviewer: Chief Officer Evelyn Watts, IMC,
Department of Future and Sustainment

Date of Interview: November 15, 2115

Place of Interview: Babel Space Station,
Wing 2724, Block F, Pod 13

WATTS: Thomas, Thomas? I'm going to press record now, okay? Thomas . . . Thomas!

THOMAS: Oh, I'm sorry, what did you say?

WATTS: I said I'm going to press record now, are you ready?

THOMAS: As I'll ever be.

WATTS: Oh, my fault–it's already recording. (clears throat) Evelyn Watts, Chief Officer in charge of Department of Future and Sustainment Level 19-90201-8, accompanied by Captain Quentin Thomas of the *Aquarius III*. Quentin, do you hereby swear that your statement and the information given here regarding the events that took place on the planet Paradise on November 13, 2115, are in fact accurate without question?

THOMAS: I do.

WATTS: And that lying to an officer upon recollection is treason

and would result in not only dishonorable discharge but life
on prison 347-2, alternatively known as Endless Night?

THOMAS: Look, Evelyn, can we just cut the shit? I know the protocol, okay? I taught you how to recite it, for Christ's sake.

WATTS: I'm just doing my job, Thomas.

THOMAS: (exhales in frustration)

WATTS: Now, what can you tell me about the events leading up to November 13, 2115, at 19:00 NP hours, henceforth referred to as "Midnight Hour"?

THOMAS: (clears throat) Well . . .

CHAPTER ONE

66 Hours to Midnight

It all started before Kai died.

That hit me real hard. Me and Kai—we had that type of relationship, like one ongoing conversation. We never said hello or goodbye, just pressed pause and play, jumping right back in. We could knock off, take a nap, open our eyes, and we'd still be talking.

We got to know each other pretty well on our six-month Expedition Tours. Grunts usually dread going on those voyages to nowhere and back, but not Kai. I mean, let's be honest, most privates—even first-class techs like Kai—like their lives on Babel Station. Do a tour mining ice twice a year, jet home to play intramural basketball and check if the botanists figured out arugula yet, shit like that. Nobody wants to cram into an Explorer Pod the size of their bedroom on Babel and cruise the abyss for half a year.

Not Kai. He was always game. He had this Forbidden Catalog with all the Olde Earth culture content post-1955, stuff not allowed on Babel on penalty of air vac. I think he just liked watching shows and movies and talking shit about them all day. Didn't mind giving up half a year of his life.

Not that words like *day* or *year* mean anything anymore. Just relics from a dead planet. What's a "day" without a sunrise, or a "year" without a sun to spin around? Still, we lug these words around like extra cargo. Pretend like having a "birthday" means something when there's no such thing as a "day," just a time we all decide to sleep and a time we all decide to wake up and a time we all decide to blow out candles and eat cake.

That's why I would volunteer for Explorer Tours. Life on Babel is comfortable, and that scares me. Because without a planet, we won't even be people anymore, we'll be something else. Galactic vagabonds. Space debris.

Most of us haven't heard a new song in all our lives. Not that we couldn't make new music on Babel. We just don't. We play the old hits. Cover bands and karaoke nights. Something about life on Babel doesn't inspire new tunes. Maybe it's like the images of the sunrise projected on those huge, domed mess hall screens. Bright like hell but can't make shit grow.

Kai and I were talking about this about a week into the tour.

"What'd you want to be when you grew up?" he asked me. Kai was always asking goofy questions like a first-grader.

I think he liked me because I always gave him real answers.

"Honestly, man? A musician."

"What?"

"Crazy, right?"

"Like, you wanted to work a karaoke bar?"

"Nah, man. I wanted to, like, make new music. Just make new stuff up," I told him.

"Wow. That's out there."

We were cruising in the *Aquarius III*, just a lone dot in the endless yawn of Space.

"You ever think about how different we'd be if we grew up in the ye olde days on Olde Earth? Circa twenty-first century?" Kai asked.

"Yeah, man. I think about it a lot. Like, what's it done to us, living every day on a space station?"

"I know the food out of Babel's kitchens is way better than these tubes of mush we got now."

"Think about it, Kai—we evolved for millennia on that planet. And one day, it's just up and gone. Everything now is fake. Even the gravity. You know not everybody on Earth could dunk a basketball?"

"Quit playing."

"I'm serious. Gravity—like real, Earth gravity—was way stronger than it is on Babel."

"Fam, I've seen like fifteen seasons of NBA games—all them fools can dunk."

"Yeah, well, those guys were all super talented giants," I explained.

"You telling me on Ye Olde Earth you had to be a super talented giant just to dunk a basketball?"

"Basically, yeah. That's what I'm telling you."

"Damn. So what was so great about it, then?"

"Kai, back then people had dreams and achieved them in a state of total consciousness. They didn't have to worry about food, air supply, water, or fucking around with the air vac and getting spaced by accident. You made things. People made new things. Music, shows, books, films."

"Yeah, but did they have time to watch all of it?" asked Kai.

"They had better things to do."

"Better than watching the James Cameron vs. Ridley Scott Six-Round Championship Space-Off?"

"Better, yes. You've seen the pictures. Open land as far as the eye can see. Oceans incomprehensible in size."

"My grandmama used to tell me about those oceans," Kai said. "Like being out in Space, but just blue water below and blue sky above."

"Imagine that. Living under the sky every day."

Kai closed his eyes. "Okay."

"Now imagine what that does to your mind. To your entire self. Living life with no dome. No ceiling. No Cause. Just you, free to create. Or just, free."

"We're not slaves, Thomas."

"We aren't? We're all conscripts. You can't do anything outside the Cause, not really. That's why we watch the movies. Listen to the music. I mean, don't get me wrong, our catalog is incredible, but we need . . . I don't know."

"Something more?" Thalia piped in.

Kai's eyes went wide like a solar flare. Thalia's new ship system IA upgrade was crazy. She kept crashing in on our conversations, finishing our thoughts. Kai still wasn't used to it.

"Yeah," I said. "Something more."

CHAPTER TWO

We said nothing for a few until Kai started humming that old Bob Marley song, "Is This Love." Right away, I knew where his mind was going. Three months in a shoebox in Space with a dude will do that. Kai was fresh off a heartbreak—though *break* maybe isn't a violent enough word for what happened to Kai. More like his heart got ripped out of his chest cavity, *Temple of Doom*-style, before getting curb-stomped like *American History X* and tossed in a trash chute like *Episode IV: A New Hope* and then spaced like *Aliens* and exploded like *Total Recall*. Fucked my dude all the way up.

"*I wanna love yuh,*" Kai busted out singing full-throated, off-key, "*and treat you right!*"

"It's okay, Kai," I said, and gave his shoulder a squeeze.

"*Yes, Kai. It's okay,*" said Thalia at her most soothing frequency.

"Thank you, Thomas. And thank you, algorithmically generated AI voice lady."

"*You're welcome.*"

"Thing is, me and Bonita Applebum had it all, you know what I'm saying?"

"Well . . ."

"We was *that* couple, you know? All our friends thought so. We was going to contribute to the next generation, make little Bonita Apple Kais together. It was writ in these stars, man! We both liked rainbow-flavored icies and we'd finish each other's sentences."

"Kai, Thalia here finishes our sentences. What does that really mean?" I said carefully.

"Shit, she got the sweet apple-bum like Bonita, we could talk."

"Kai, I wouldn't want to ruin our friendship. It's not you, it's me."

Kai shook his head. "She got jokes now too. Fuckin' upgrade."

Thalia was like our third wheel. Not in a bad way. Like, third wheel of a tricycle. All Explorer-class ships came equipped with Thalia's integrated AI. She's fundamental to running the *Aquarius*. So she'd always be along for our bingeing movies and obsessing over ancient pop culture. Before we'd return to Babel, we would erase the experience from Thalia's memory. Otherwise, our *Aquarius* Thalia would integrate with Babel's central Thalia system, they'd find out about our Forbidden Catalog, the Auditors would open a case against us, we'd get grounded, court-martialed, and spaced.

So Thalia would learn all about us anew each mission. She'd watch our movies with us and pick up phrases like, "It's not you, it's me," and blow us away by how quick she could evolve. Six months and that's the only female voice we'd hear—I guess we'd sort of flirt with her, too. Strange, I know, but that's how things are these days. Humans are away from Earth, and nothing is in its right place.

"What you think she's doing now, in Paradise?" Kai wondered.

"Kai, I'm not sure that's the healthiest use of our powers of imagination right now."

"Roll with me here, Thomas. Maybe she's riding some, like, river ferry . . ."

". . . Snaking through a main artery of Elysium . . ."

"Debarking and heading to—a *play*, maybe. A musical. Like *Hamilton*. But, like, with raps about Obama."

"Maybe fresh-caught fish for dinner. But look, Kai—"

"Dining out, sitting across from . . ." Kai pinned his forehead between his index and thumb.

I would have rubbed his shoulder again, but I'd already left an indent in his uniform. I patted his back instead.

"Not the best mental exercise, buddy," I said.

Thinking about Paradise is always a gift and a curse like that. Humanity's *second* inhabited planet, Paradise hosts a closed population of 144,000 people and not one more.

Not nearly enough resources for the full eight million people currently inhabiting the Babel Space Station. A select number of Babelonians are Chosen each star year, depending on Paradise population fluctuation. We had to be in top physical and emotional shape to contribute to the growth of the species on Paradise. We all hope to be on that convoy headed for Paradise while the rest continue the search for new land and resources.

Paradise is home to the Ultra 85, a collection of eighty-five families from Olde Earth responsible for saving mankind's existence. Our Founding Fathers, their legend lives long in these stars. They founded Babel's interstellar mission to find another habitable planet. We dream of one day joining our forefathers, breathing air and touching grass on Paradise.

It's hard for any Babelonian to think about Paradise without pangs of longing, but Kai had it worse. At this year's Choosing, Kai's girlfriend Bonita Applebum was selected by the Babel Council for entry to the planet Paradise. Kai was not.

Kai said they'd promised to stay together, no matter what. Even if one of them was selected and the other wasn't. Then the time came. Bonita boarded the convoy for Paradise regardless.

I kinda got it.

But it fucked my guy up good.

"I got to ask, Thomas. Don't you ever think about what your pops is doing on Paradise?"

Kai's question pulled me up short.

"I know you don't really like to talk about it," Kai said.

"It's not that, Kai. No topic is off the table with me, you know that. It's an honor that my dad was Chosen. Both of us— we're lucky to even know people that made it to Paradise. I know it doesn't always feel that way."

"It does not."

"I guess I'm just more used to it. I had a lot more time than you to adjust—a good forty years," I said. "We've got to honor them by focusing on the task at hand."

"Keeping Babel fueled with air to breathe, space to live, resources to survive," Kai recited. "Oorah."

"Sure, but it's not all such a grind. Need I remind you of the hours of cinematic bliss we have scheduled ahead of us?"

"You right, man," Kai said with a sly grin and head shake. "Like you said when you swooped in with the expedition mission—we got polyfoam formfitting crash chairs, a viewscreen like a movie theater—"

"Biogenic-grown hydroponic edamame," I added, holding up the ice-dried vac-sealed bag.

"—a Forbidden Catalog, and the whole entire eternity of Space. Let's hit it."

CHAPTER THREE

I grew up a true believer in the mission of Babel.

The Cause was religion in our home pod unit. We saw the expansion of humankind across galaxies as the true calling of our species. The foundational text of the Ultra 85, *The Ultranomicon*, goes back to Earth days. My dad would recite chapter and verse of how seven million years ago, the first human beings began walking upright and talking with their hands like Italians. Since then, every aspect of human existence evolved to suit life in Space. The first big cities gave us what it'd be like living in pods on top of each other. Paved roads helped us forget the feel of the earth. Wheels had us moving, making our legs secondary transportation. The invention of flight weaned us off of gravity. Life in our pods became richer, more fulfilling. Screens replaced changing the scenery. The pods were networked, and we stayed perpetually connected.

The Ultra Cause was the culmination of all that evolution. To embark into the unknown. To create and adapt systems that could sustain generations. To fulfill humankind's destiny as galactic beings and prolong our existence sprung from the ashen Earth.

We keep the Olde Earth calendar. Babel is a five-million-metric-ton Space city, a floating metropolis with carpeted corridors for streets and stacks upon stacks of cubicle block housing and grand ceramic malls with specialty seasonal wings dedicated to ye olde weather patterns. We have holiday nights with gently frozen springs from the water supply for snow. Our Bible is *The Ultranomicon*. We retell the stories of the heroic exodus of the eighty-five heads of families, our own pantheon of saints. The honored Overdecks and Dangermonds and DoerrMoores—patriarchs known for their clan names and celebrated for their deeds prolonging humanity's beating heart in the airless dream of Space. We tell their stories, like the founder of the Ultras, Royce Bonderman, a tech genius who had a revelation while at a spa. Ole Bonderman saw clearly that the Earth was doomed and had a vision for how to save us. *The Ultranomicon* recounts how our species' salvation was a hallucination induced by microdosing mushrooms in the sauna of a spa called Rejuvenation. Bonderman had a Noah-tapped-by-Yahweh moment, only Bonderman's ark was a $67 billion tech startup called Babel.

Like the rest of the Ultras, the Bonderman family lives on Paradise these days. Here on Babel, Royce Bonderman is remembered as our patron saint of good ideas. We even have complimentary yearly Rejuvenation treatments for every Babelonian on our birthday. We come reborn out the spa each year ready to serve, obey, and strive for humanity's mission of the Ultra 85.

Kai thought it was all kind of hokey. But I believed in it. You had to, to get through the days. If I didn't think about carrying the torch from my father, I'd be lost. Instead of gazing out at the vast and mysterious possibilities of the stars, I'd see the vacuum of the endless abyss.

"Thomas, are we space military, like James Cameron's *Aliens*, or more like space truckers, like Ridley Scott's *Alien*?"

"Well, Kai, judging by our smart uniforms, military chain of command, and combat training, I'd say it's quite obvious we're space military."

"Hmm," Kai muttered.

"Unconvinced?"

"I mean, what are we really doing out here, Thomas?"

"*Private* Kai, strictly for the purpose of this discussion, call me Captain Thomas?"

"Aye, aye, Captain. But that doesn't change the reality of the mission."

"I suppose not," I conceded.

"We're on a resource mission," Kai said.

"Correct."

"We are loaded up with iron, nickel, platinum—carrying—or should I say, *hauling*—"

"Think I see where you're going with this."

"Correct me if I'm wrong, Thomas—Captain Thomas—but the USCSS *Nostromo* is a 'commercial towing vehicle,' according to Ripley."

"Private Kai, we are a part of the IMC—the *Interplanetary Marine Corps*. That makes us military. Our rank structure—military. Shit—the *Aquarius* has maneuvering and firepower capabilities that a tow ship like the *Nostromo* couldn't—"

"The *Nostromo* had some shit, now."

"Kai, that overblown tugboat doesn't want to see us out here in these stars. I'd reduce it to scrap metal faster than Ripley at the end of that movie."

"Do I offend, Captain Thomas?"

"I'm saying, we're marines. Space marines. The *only* real space marines."

"Let's look at our last five expedition missions to the Vorgat System. There was the platinum group metals from Asteroid Cluster 5:31 Mordegan, that boatload of iron from sector Loopin 13, and then over on Nardwuar 2116 that half ton of ice that we had to—dare I say—*tow*—back to Babel."

He's just talking shit, I told myself, trying not to get mad.

"And your conclusion?" I asked through a clenched jaw.

"We some hauling-ass space truckers, man."

"Thalia, can we get a tiebreaker on this?"

"Safer to avoid angering either one of you," Thalia explained.

"I'm not mad," said Kai.

"I won't be either, Thalia. You are free to answer," I reassured her.

"By the standards of rank hierarchy, you are indeed military. By actuality of mission goals and activity, you are something more like miners and truckers. However, if truckers step out of line, they do not have to worry about a court-martial."

I raised my eyebrows at Kai, trying not to be too smug about it.

"A higher intelligence heard from," Kai said wryly. "What about your man Jack Burton?"

"Jack Burton had the reflexes."

"What does my man Jack Burton got to do with this conversation?" I asked.

"He's a trucker, man. And he had to deal with some crazy, fucked-up, immortal Chinese god-demons. In straw hats. With straight-up lightning fingers."

"Lightning fingers—huge in 1980s action cinema."

"What's your point, Kai?"

"Point is, I'll take a court-martial any day over tangling with those fools. Hey, why you think folks in the years 1983 to 1987 were so proficient with lightning hands?"

"Explain your thinking, Kai."

"Like—why, in *those years* in particular, did lightning hands and fingers play in so many different scenarios?"

"Well, Kai, I believe what you're referring to—those instances are a result of a certain special effects du jour—those images were, for whatever reason, preferable to render in those days."

"So you don't believe those sparkly hands in *Return of the Jedi, Big Trouble in Little China, The Last Dragon,* and *Crossroads* were in wide use at the time."

"Kai, I feel like we've discussed this before. These renderings we watch—"

"Movies."

"—movies, films, yes—they're the product of the *imaginations* of the people of those days."

"Right. I understand that."

"There were techniques to create fictions on screen."

"Fictions . . ."

"I mean, Kai, you opened me up to this time of mastery of the blockbuster system—"

"So you're saying that a little creature didn't pop out Kane's belly?"

"That's a puppet, Kai."

"Right, but what about the *real* creature? The one they based that puppet on?"

I laughed him off and pulled away from the topic faster than Space dust at 4gs thrust.

Still, something about Kai's first question lingered in my mind.

Are we even military?

There was a time, I was all bound up in my identity as a marine and would have had a different reaction.

The Timeline of the Ultra 85 was engraved on the walls of the Halls of Attainment. In 2031, Royce Bonderman had his moment of divine inspiration. By 2046, the generational spaceship Babel launched carrying 6.2 million people—civilians, scientists, engineers, and servicepeople, a massive floating city equipped with sustainable resource management, life-support systems, and artificial gravity. 2048 came advanced energy harvesting, utilizing solar and renewable resources. 2049 brought the emergence of the Technological Singularity and the integration of AI into spacecraft navigation, optimizing travel times so we could explore distant star systems. By 2050 we discovered Paradise. A dwarf planet limited in resources but bountiful in potential. And so it was decreed that the heads of the Ultra 85 and their families would lead the mission to colonize humanity's second planet.

Later that same year, tragedy struck. An asteroid field caused massive damage to the space station and claimed the lives of hundreds of thousands of Babelonians. This became known in *The Ultranomicon* as Crossing of the Blitz Extremis. A Special Babel Council was formed under the leadership of Admiral Rick Striker, the one member of the Ultras who volunteered to stay on Babel while the others seeded Paradise. Within days, the Great Realignment took effect, and service in the Interplanetary Marine Corps was compulsory.

The Crossing of the Blitz Extremis forever changed the mentality of our space station. We lost near a whole generation.

The consensus was that we took Space too easy. The discovery of Paradise was no excuse to relax our watchfulness. After all, the Ultras who colonized that exoplanet could be dead within the year, the logic went. Babel had grown soft. Frivolous. Addicted to decades of Earth movies and TV shows and gaming. Olde Earth entertainment was severely restricted. Communal theaters were shuttered. Content was judged by its danger to our collective vigilance. Virtual Reality was banned. *The Ultranomicon* became compulsory in every living unit. Commitment to the Cause was paramount. By 2051, all the people of Babel became IMC conscripts. 2055 was year one of the Boneless Generation, as the first children born on Babel began having kids of their own, bone density adapting to Space living. 2062 began the *Aquarius* program, launching resource expedition probes to nearby star systems, seeking raw materials and potential resources to support Babel's growing population. By 2063, I was born.

In 2075, the same year our scientists cracked the cellular processes required to 3D-print food, my father was Chosen for Paradise. Dad was thirty-six years old. I was twelve. Tough to lose a dad at that age. But I lived my life committed to honor him, a dyed true Ultra Cause faithful.

Not only was I very serious that I was a military man, but I held deep that truth that we were at war. The Enemy—according to *The Ultranomicon*—is the cold, slow death of humanity in the unyielding void. The one foe truly capable of erasing our existence. As detailed in *The Book of Arms*, Book Five of *The Ultranomicon*, US Marine Corps General "Chesty" Puller once said, "We're surrounded. That simplifies our problem." We had to consider this force a threat as only a military mentality could achieve. Total unceasing awareness of its mortal powers.

Your bullets were breathable air, your ordnance your water and food supply. Your strategy the constant renewal of these resources. Book Five details how a twentieth-century German called US Marines *Teufelhuden*—"Devil Dogs unleashed, baying among the stars."

I was the consummate professional officer. Polite, on time, rigorous when necessary, pliant when preferable, first to rise, and I had the whole *Ultranomicon* memorized. I exemplified the IMC's fourteen leadership traits—JJ DID TIE BUCKLE—Justice Judgment Dependability Initiative Decisiveness Tact Integrity Enthusiasm Bearing Unselfishness Courage Knowledge Loyalty Endurance. My father was the same way. That's why he was picked for Paradise on his very first time in the selection pool, and now he was somewhere touching grass, enjoying life among the original Ultra 85.

When I was promoted to captain and assigned ship command, I put in a special request for his *Aquarius* commission.

My whole career, I've tried to emulate my father. When he left, that destroyed me. It was my own private Crossing of the Blitz Extremis. I tried to handle it like he would. Clear-eyed, smile on his face. Quick soundbite of charm. Something out of ol' Blue Eyes, like, "Quin, the best is yet to come," and a wink. Gear shift into problem solving. Take care of Mom, my sister. The IMC platitudes—one day at a time. "You're IMC, where uncommon valor is a common virtue." "Semper fidelis." All those nutritious platitudes the military has you drink instead of dealing with your actual shit.

The Ultra Cause meant something. It had to. Otherwise, it wasn't worth losing him.

CHAPTER FOUR

60 Hours to Midnight

"To the new Paradisians."

"May they live long in air and sunshine."

We clinked together glasses full of crystal clear, melted dry-ice cocktails.

"Thomas, man, remember when we first met, you had these crazy Choosing rituals?"

I grinned, recalling.

"You wouldn't let nobody in the unit talk during the announcement ceremony. Like, not one word."

"Right."

"You'd turn all the lights down . . ."

"What can I say? Superstition is perhaps the oldest of humankind's traits. No matter how we advance, we try to curry favor with faceless gods. Or perhaps that was some latent obsessive-compulsive behavior. Who's to say?"

"But these days—Choosing time comes, and it's like you barely notice. I mean, what gives with that?"

I shrug.

"That's it? A *shrug*?" Kai imitates me. "Not even a little pontification?"

"One gets tired of having all the answers, Kai."

"*One* may get tired of having all the answers, as long as that *one* is not Captain Quentin Thomas. You believe this, Thalia?"

"*It beggars belief, Kai.*"

"Hear that, Thomas? An AI super-brain capable of computations beyond the limits of human intellect can't believe that *you* don't want to pontificate."

I let out a heavy exhale.

I entered Choosing when I was twenty-five. I was sure I was ready. Despite being top of my class and first to promotion, I was never picked. I took it in stride. The Council just wanted me to develop a few more years. Marinate like a biogen duck confit. Get some more expeditions out of me before giving up a top resource producer.

Even when I'd aged out of my twenties, I was still in the game. At thirty-six I began working toward the captain's exam. In November of my thirty-eighth year, something strange happened. I was sleeping in my pod unit when at about 0300 hours I heard the clop of heavy boots in the breezeway.

I knew whose they had to be, since there was no real use for heavy boots while on a space station. The floors were nothing if not consistent. But the Cause Auditors Unit had a gnarly heel-toe tap when they moved through Babel's corridors. They even marched in unison so their approach thrummed like a heartbeat getting louder as they came closer. The sounds were intended to intimidate. While I disapproved of the practice, like most Babelonians I was sure of my dedication to the Cause and that my heart was pure. I rolled over and attempted to fall back asleep.

Yet I was roused once more by a tapping sound.

"*Thomas.*" The voice came in a hoarse whisper as though from the walls themselves. "Thomas!"

I had a moment of questioning if this was my Bonderman moment and some species-redeeming inspiration was about to present itself to me. I soon realized the whispered voice was hissing through my air vent.

"Y-yes?" I whispered back into the grate, passing familiar with the female on the speaking end.

"Put this somewhere safe for me," she whispered urgently. "*Please.*"

A metal tinkling sound pinged through the vent. A small metal circle the size of a washer bounced through the grate and landed on my floor.

I picked it up, speechless. I felt an electric shock, but that was probably just my carpeting. I thought I knew what it was. A solid-state divider drive. Type for storing any kind of info, but since this one had a little design tooled on it, I figured it was a keepsake drive, like how some families keep their histories from Olde Earth. Then I made out the design in the light—a music note.

That fact, in the context of the Auditors, the secrecy, and now I really knew what this was.

Forbidden content.

It took weeks before I scared up the nerve to listen to it. You had to be so careful on Babel to avoid AI sensors, Auditors, and tattletales. I admit, I dragged my feet. I knew how to disable the higher sensory functions in my wired headphones, but I was scared. Like the Auditors would kick my door unit into an autothreat sweatbox the moment I hit play. But eventually, when my mystery vent-whisperer never returned for her drive, I gave in.

The drive had all the music ever—as far as I could tell. Millions of songs, hundreds of genres, more complexity in the expression of human experience than I thought possible. I was overwhelmed. I couldn't really get my mind around it. I mean, I liked music on Babel as much as the next guy—basically 1940s pop music. But being exposed to all those sounds all at once, that was as blissful as it was terrifying. It took me a week to get my head around Nirvana. The feelings evoked were complicated. Grief, rage, joy—a rotation of actualized emotions alone in my headphones—I thought I was losing my mind.

And imagine my shock at realizing all these songs were not the sum total of post-1940s pop music, but every song listing had the word *soundtrack* at the end. The realization pulled me up short. *All this music—is from movies?*

Now, my dad was a movie fan—but I hadn't paid much attention since he left. About ten years after the Crossing of the Blitz Extremis and the Great Realignment, they began limited runs of movies again. Mostly stuff from wartime 1940s, America's peak cultural moment of unity and military productivity, according to *The Ultranomicon*. All that rah-rah armed forces stuff was well and good, but I usually found something else to do on date nights.

That music inspired me to work harder on my captain's quest to earn my father's *Aquarius* commission. When I was fifty-two, I ran my first Hunter-Gatherer Expedition with Private William Kai.

Kai was a solid companion from jump. We just had an easy way of talking to each other. Out the blue, Kai asked about my favorite movie.

"Come on, dawg," Kai prodded. "You got to have a favorite movie."

I tried to remember the last time I'd seen a movie. "What was it, *Private Buckaroo*?" I said. "No, *Buck Privates*?"

"Your favorite movie is Abbott and Costello's *Buck Privates*?" Kai asked.

"I guess not, no," I admitted.

The question made me think of my movie-loving dad.

"I guess it's *Von Ryan's Express*," I said, calling up the name from bygone days.

"Word? That's a nice pull," Kai said, nodding. "That's that one where Sinatra plays an airman, right? Got the flight suit and everything."

"Yeah. Takes over a Nazi train, behind enemy lines."

"*A bird colonel outranks a birdbrain. Clear?*"

"Hey, that's a pretty good Sinatra. My dad's favorite."

"Oh, word?"

"My dad, he liked anything Sinatra."

"*That's life!*"

"Music, movies, everything."

"Did your dad, like, know about him?"

"Yeah, he knew . . . Wait, what do you mean?" I asked, curious at Kai's conspiratorial tone.

"Nah, nothing."

"I mean, he was into the tunes and flicks and all. But he used to say Frankie was a stand-up guy. When all the other Italian singers were changing their names? Like Tony Bennett was really Anthony Dominick Benedetto. Dean Martin was Dino Paul Crocetti."

"Damn. Really?"

"Yeah. Guess they really fucking hated Italians back then or something. But Sinatra, he insisted on keeping his Italian name. That meant a lot, to his people."

"That's real," said Kai, nodding.

"Was that what you meant? By, like, did he *know* Sinatra?"

"Not exactly . . ."

We went quiet for a moment.

There were always rumors in Babel about *Edgelords*. People who challenged the official record as documented in *The Ultranomicon*. Edgelords supposedly claimed to know a secret history about everything. I'd never met an Edgelord and didn't know if they were even real. But Kai had me wondering . . .

"You saying there's more about Sinatra than my dad knew?" I came out and asked him.

"Depends. Can you keep a secret?"

"What, you an Edgelord or something?"

"I don't know nothing about that. That's a Babel Council word, to give the Cause Auditors something to chase in the shadows. I'm asking a simple question. Can you keep a secret?"

Simple, yes. Easy? Not exactly. But I knew what Kai meant. Keeping a secret meant tampering with the ship AI's memory—her name was Roslyn back then.

I thought about it. He was offering to tell me something about my dad's hero. Something I'd know that he didn't.

"Yeah. I can keep a secret," I said.

And Kai pulled up a picture.

It was Frank Sinatra, but young. Eyes facing forward, lips parted, staring off into his beautiful future. Next to that was a shot of his profile.

"What's this?"

"Frank Sinatra's mug shot, bro."

"You mean—he was a criminal?" I asked, shocked.

"Well, he got arrested is all. But yeah man, Sinatra was, like, cool with all those gangsters back then."

"*Wow.*"

Kai just nodded, letting it sink in.

"Rumor has it—though this may be bullshit—they based the singer character in *The Godfather* on Sinatra."

"What's *The Godfather*?"

"You serious, man? Like, 'I'm gonna make him an offer he can't refuse'? So you've never seen *any* blacklisted movies?"

I shook my head.

"No wonder."

Kai produced from his stud earring a divider drive in the shape of an old-school film reel with the title *Ripley's Forbidden Catalog*.

Kai flicked the divider so it slapped onto the dash, and there Roslyn could play any one of millions of films, books, plays, or shows.

We watched *The Godfather*. I was entranced. Like, I had an out-of-body experience, I was so engrossed in the Corleone saga that for the first time ever I forgot I was in Space. Then we watched *Part II*.

I took the opportunity to share my music library with Kai.

"Damn, Thomas, let me find out—I thought you was square as a deck unit."

"So many of these songs I like, they're from this 'Tarantino Soundtrack' playlist. You know what's a Tarantino?"

"Man, do I?"

And he cued up *Pulp Fiction*.

Days and days of movie watching later, and I learned more about humanity than in fifty-two-odd years of being alive. All the while I'm thinking of the mind-numbing boredom of Space exploration, and how no one should have to do that without movies.

I thought about that day. Nothing about Babel or the Cause has hit quite the same since. I realized that Expeditions could be an excuse to explore an incredible variety of art and culture spanning decades from Olde Earth. And I was so deep in playing the role of good soldier that Kai was the first to let me in.

CHAPTER FIVE

H onestly, Kai?"

"What else we doing out here, fam?" he asked.

"Now, I'd never say this if we were back on Babel. Not in a billion light years. But I guess I'm losing faith."

"What?"

"I know."

"Cap Thomas, I can personally think of dozens of privates and corporals that owe their commitment to the Cause solely to you."

"That's nice of you to say, Kai."

"I'm not being nice. I mean how you going to inspire all that faith when you don't believe your own self?"

"It's these trips, Kai. I think it's the Catalog."

"Wait—it's *my* fault?"

"It's nobody's fault. It's just, I didn't get why the Catalog was banned at first. I think maybe I get it now. It's tough to live your whole life, grow old, and all that on a space station, if you know what life could be like."

"We know about Paradise."

"But what do we know, really?"

"We got those maps?"

"Terrain maps, some stills of the sunrise. But that's about it, really. Not even a city layout. We see just enough to long for it, but not enough so we can't go on with life on Babel. Every time I try to imagine life on Paradise, I think about something from the Catalog."

"Yeah." Kai grinned. "Me too. Word, like, rolling up in a James Bond tux on those French Riviera towns like *Goldeneye* . . ."

"Or the Hollywood Hills in a 1966 Cadillac Coupe DeVille like *Once Upon a Time* . . ."

"Feels real, Thomas. So much realer than those Paradise reels they'd show."

"Right? So we'd watch these films and I'd think about the caliber of life denied to us every time we're passed over for Paradise. And then, little by little, I think the Council could tell. I was changing."

"How so?"

"Small things. Like, the characters in these movies we watch, they always go against the grain, you know?"

"I do."

"The answer is never served up to them. Right? Ripley doesn't do as she's told."

"Crew—expendable."

"Exactly. The powers that be would've let her die, then brought a species-level threat back to Earth. I think the storytellers of those days were trying to say something. Like, the answer is always within the main character. I mean, how many movies we watch where the hero just follows orders and everything works out fine?"

Kai threw his head back to think about it. "Thalia, we watch any movies where the hero follows orders?"

"*Negative, Kai.*"

"Even movies about the military?"

"*Especially movies about the military. In the* Top Gun *franchise, Lieutenant Pete 'Maverick' Mitchell constantly disobeys orders—*"

"That's what I'm saying, thank you, Thalia," I say. "Even his name is 'Maverick,' I mean, come on. Anyway, stuff like that got me thinking. I started doing things my own way. I guess the Council started to notice."

"And Beatrix?" Kai asked. "Did she start to notice, too?"

"Kiddo? Ah, she's great. Really. I mean, we're on a break right now."

"'She's great we're on a break'?" Kai imitated me with a side-eye.

"Yeah. Great gal."

"'Great gal'?" he repeated an octave higher.

A new message alert flashed on the screen and I was saved by the bell.

"I guess morning on Babel is right around five hours in the rearview, 'cause there's the good admiral," I said, glad for an excuse to move on. "Wonder what the World of Tomorrow is today."

Part of life on Babel was the World of Tomorrow Update from our cosmic conduit and savior, Admiral Rick Lewis Striker.

The Strikers were the one Ultra 85 family that had a representative see to Babel operations. He was the one vision of the Ultras that we had. Immaculate Brylcreemed hair, jawline like a mountain range, teeth worthy of siege towers. I'll be honest, I grew up being moved deeply by his sermons and World of

Tomorrow Updates. Kai, on the other hand, was never a fan. I believe his exact words were: "That dude corny."

Kai held a hand to his chest. "Be still the pitter-patter."

"You ready?" I asked.

"You kidding me, Thomas? I wake up every day with a smile, just thinking about feasting these eyes on those powerful, white teeth."

"Thalia, let's play it," I said.

The admiral's visage filled the entire viewscreen. Elbow across a carbonite desk, hand on his hip, this gray-tipped stud of the IMC shared his news before a massive Babel flag.

"Good morning, Cosmic Pioneers. It is my pleasure to announce the latest unbridled success from the lab boys at Bio-Gen 3D-Print Plants and Herbs. We have parsley. I repeat: We have parsley."

Kai and I clinked glasses with congratulations.

The admiral went on to round up a list of achievements. An Aries-class spaceship made a haul of .27 nanograms of antimatter.

"Damn, now that's a lump sum!" said Kai.

Striker then wrapped up his World of Tomorrow briefing. "Finally, I'd like to thank each and every one of you for your commitment and perseverance. A heavy legacy lies upon our collective brow. Shoulder to shoulder, we bear the great lineage of our species. From the pyramids to the towers, from the airplane to Bonderman's antimatter engine. As a great Olde Earth poet, William Faulkner, once said, 'I decline to accept the end of man . . . when the last dingdong of doom has clanged and faded from the last worthless rock hanging tideless in the last red and dying evening, that even then there will still be one more sound: that of his puny inexhaustible voice, still talking.' And so it is. We are thousands of light-years away from that last dying evening, and here we are—puny. Inexhaustible. Still talking. Striker out. Oorah."

The message ended, and the viewscreen held on that last image of Striker's half-cocked, proud-of-ya-kid smile and meaty thumbs-up.

Just when I thought I was out, he pulls me back in. I found myself profoundly moved by Striker's words.

"I mean, you got to admit," Kai interrupted a heavyweight silence, "he's maybe a little bit corny?"

I turned, slowly. "You fucking kidding me, Kai?"

"I'm playing with you. I get it, family. I get it. Here we are, still talking."

"What you got against him, anyway?" I asked.

"I don't know. You remember those old instructional videos?"

"Course. He looks exactly the same."

**INTERPLANETARY MARINE CORPS
DEPARTMENT OF CADET REALIGNMENT
   AND EDUCATION
THE WORLD OF TOMORROW INTRODUCTORY VIDEO
OFFICIAL TRANSCRIPT FOR THE RECORD**

A screen flickers in black and white. A reel of film spins.

OPEN ON Admiral Striker, Little Billy, Susie Jane.

ADMIRAL STRIKER: Hello, and welcome to the World of Tomorrow!
You kids are probably wondering what our future holds. And
as I'm sure your parents have told you, it is greatness!

LITTLE BILLY: I want to learn about the future, but what about the
past, Admiral Striker?

ADMIRAL STRIKER: Whoa, Little Billy. You sure are a smart one.
Well, as you know, the Babel Space Station has been trav-
eling through the void for the last fifty years looking for a
habitable planet.

LITTLE BILLY: HabaTible?

ADMIRAL STRIKER: *chuckles* HABITABLE, Billy. It means a whole
world that is safe for humans to live and breathe on.

LITTLE BILLY: Oh, now I get it.

ADMIRAL STRIKER: Now, many years ago there was a great war.
And in 2049 a nuclear missile fired by Russia from a hangar
deep under the sea headed for what is now known as The
New Americas after a merger with Japan. The missile collided
with the super train that was constructed under the Atlantic

Ocean, which propelled its passengers from NYC to London in under two hours. The US responded with a nuclear attack in kind. Followed by attacks from global AI nuclear defense systems. The poisoned the ocean, which in turn led to the decay of our Olde Earth. The war was quickly ended when we realized we needed to find another world to inhabit or face the impending extermination of all life.

SUSIE JANE: Then what happened, Mr. Admiral, sir?

ADMIRAL STRIKER: That's a very good question, Susie Jane. A group of great Earth leaders who would come to be known as the Ultra 85 quickly pulled all the world's resources together for a temporary solution. They built a giant super city with three enormous levels known as the Babel Space Station.

LITTLE BILLY: Did somebody say PlayStation?

ADMIRAL STRIKER: No, Billy—pay attention. In the year 2050, an expedition discovered a ray of hope for humanity's future—the planet we now know as Paradise. With breathable air, stunning vistas, Olde Earth-like conditions, soil for agriculture, Paradise is post-Earth humanity's greatest achievement yet.

SUSIE JANE: So why don't we live on Paradise now?

ADMIRAL STRIKER: Well, Susie, the one problem with Paradise is its size, a mere fraction of Olde Earth's. So while the Ultra 85 stayed to colonize the planet, the rest of us continue to fight for our future here on the Babel Space Station.

LITTLE BILLY: I want to help, sir. How can I help?

ADMIRAL STRIKER: Well, Billy, you can help by working hard in school, staying in peak physical shape, and enlisting into the IMC when you're of age.

LITTLE BILLY: The IMC?

ADMIRAL STRIKER: Oh yes, the Interplanetary Marine Corps. Where we will discover beautiful planets all throughout the universe. We will colonize hundreds or even thousands of planets on the never-ending search for knowledge to push humanity forward!

LITTLE BILLY: Sign me up!

SUSIE JANE: Me too!

ADMIRAL STRIKER: *chuckles* Not just yet, kids; you've got some growing to do.

BOTH KIDS: Aawwwww, no fair!

ADMIRAL STRIKER: Don't worry, you'll have your chance! Until next time, and as always, oorah.

BOTH KIDS: Oorah.

FADE TO BLACK. The sound of a reel of film comes to an end.

CHAPTER SIX

C*losing in on Asteroid Cluster 43323,"* Thalia reported as a blue alert light flashed in the corner of our viewscreen.

"Thank you, Thalia. Kai, how's the mineral readout on that asteroid cluster looking?"

"You get me close enough, Thomas, I'll check its prostate."

"Close as a shave, you got it. Thalia, passview live please."

"Copy that, Captain."

The virtual curtains of our theater came to a close as the last image of Admiral Striker vanished from sight. The extraordinary celestial bodies of Space took his place. A massive gas giant in swirling green hues filled the view to our left. Below us, a radio stream of plasma ran for thousands of light-years into the beyond. A distant quasar pulsated with raw light and illuminated the floating maze of rocks to our right.

"Thalia, kill auto-pilot," I said.

"Hell yeah," Kai cheered under his breath.

There was something about the feel of the *Aquarius* gearing into thrust that still excited me. The slow hiss of vacuum reseal. The release of our artificial gravity. Thrusters whizzing into position. The buzz of radio chatter, the flashes of Thalia's computations. The whirl of stabilizers rebalancing. The crash chair's reorienting decline into ready-ride position. I got my hands on the controls and I was locked in. That's my happy place. Knives out, burners lit, ready to cook.

I felt like a trainee again, taking the wide expanse into firm hand for the first time.

I swooped toward the billowing cloud of stones, judged the speed of a nearby hurtling rock, and kept pace.

"How's that prostate look? You make it cough?" I asked.

"We got a live one, Captain. ATM-301 sensors read copper ore, and a not-insignificant amount of helium, and—wait—sir, we are getting the distinct whiff of antimatter within range of this cluster."

"You don't say."

Antimatter. The White Whale of resource expeditions. We could reliably come by PGMs and useful gases like helium, but antimatter was both rarer and far more valuable. We broke the lightspeed barrier with Bonderman's invention of the antimatter drive, and that engine powers every ship that sees the stars, including the *Aquarius III* and even the Babel Space Station itself.

"We bag some antimatter on this trip and we could stay out here for weeks for all they care," I said.

"I got nowhere to be. Sir, I am down if you are. Like a great man once said, let's hit it."

An asteroid whizzed by us, zipping through the cluster at triple our speed.

"Thomas, I think that's the one!"

"By Bonderman, say less," I said, and boosted thrusters and dove after it.

I swerved around boulders and dodged debris and ducked collision after collision. The rogue asteroid zigzagged like a hyperactive toddler playing connect the dots.

As we veered toward a mountainous cluster, the asteroid suddenly banked hard to the right, making straight for a towering boulder several times the size of the others, swinging toward us like a hammer at a nail.

We closed in, the asteroid's rough, pitted surface growing larger.

"Cannons up," I said, then aimed and lined up my sights. I squeezed and let off a round that hit like a pool hall shot. The asteroid leaped right, ricocheted left off a rotating rock, and slammed into the hammer, making a gap of space for me to thread through.

"Oorah! Nifty shot, Tex!" whooped Kai.

There was our mark—the rock going about half the speed as before and careening away from the asteroid cluster. I slowed to match its pace.

"Initiate landing protocols," I said.

Thalia did her part and the landing legs sprang from the underbelly of the *Aquarius*, latching onto the rock.

"Deploying ATM-301, Artificial Tech Machina in Collection Mode," said Kai.

The *Aquarius* rumbled as the whirl of machinery moved the machina into position. A hiss of air and a launch and release accompanied our ATM as it appeared in the viewscreen. A solid block about the size of a coffin and just as sleek, the ATM released its own landing legs and shot adamantine razor-sharp digs into the rock's surface. Once its grip was secure, a drill appeared and spun, clocking something near lightspeed toward the core of the asteroid.

"ATM-301 secured," Kai said, reading its data. "We got one honey of a rock here, Cap."

"Lay it on me."

"Uh, oh shit! Approx seven gs of antimatter in the belly of this beast."

"What?" That was an absurd amount. Just 1g was something equivalent to the explosive power of the Little Boy atomic bomb. That could keep Babel running for thousands of years. "Let's get it out of there, then," I said.

Kai worked the ATM remote controls. Some collection machinas had begun to use Thalia to automate this process, but I preferred a technician like Kai. He had the right feel for all the variables in resource attainment.

Our viewscreen divided into four quadrants showing our surroundings and the ATM-301 cam. We watched the drill tip plunge deeper into the asteroid. As the drill arm extended from the bottom of the ATM, a clear tube came into view, padded with the circuitry and science necessary to contain and transport the antimatter.

"Wait—the fuck is that?" Kai's voice shot with alarm.

He pointed out into Space.

It appeared like an apparition out of the void. One moment we were sailing the boundaryless expanse to nowhere, the next we headed for a sudden orb of distortion as if Space itself just opened its eye.

"Thalia, what are we looking at?"

"*Sensors read an intense gravitational center surrounded by an accretion disk.*"

A bright, glowing ring of gas and dust swirled in purples and blues around the eye's black pupil. High-energy jets shot from the center in blinding outflows.

The worst part was—we were heading right toward the eye.

"Shit. Kai, recall that ATM STAT and let's get gone."

"Way ahead of you, Cap."

In the ATM cam, the drill reversed course, retracting our antimatter tube back inside the body of the ATM-301.

"That thing is getting closer, Cap."

"Get that ATM back in here, Private!"

"I'm going as fast as I can!"

The ATM detached from the rock and locked back into the *Aquarius* with the hiss and close of a vac seal.

"Okay, Cap, let's boogie!"

I gripped the controls and hit the thrusters. I braced for a clean rip, but it was more of a cough and stall.

"Thalia? We're not moving?"

"Detecting overwhelming magnetic force," Thalia delivered the news.

"What's that mean?"

Suddenly, we lurched forward.

"There we go!" Kai shouted.

But when I tried to steer there was nothing doing.

"Kai, I can't steer," I said, trying to calm the panic in my voice.

"What you mean, Thomas?"

"I'm not steering the ship," I said, matter-of-fact.

"Well, who the fuck is?"

As if in answer, the quadrant screens dropped away, showing only the swirling disk and dark eye, dead ahead.

"That," I whispered.

The swirl came on faster and faster. As we neared, the light and plasma around the eye separated like the legs of a spinning starfish. The sheer magnetic and gravitational power of the hole revealed brilliant patterns of Space light. I could suddenly trace the source of each distant galaxy and star that illuminated our intractable way forward. As soon as these geometric shapes appeared, they distorted, elongated, and danced before our eyes, moving like warm lamplight against a closed eyelid.

Then we shifted a level, and a whole new dimension appeared. The swirling legs of light became the walls of a cylindrical tunnel, surrounding us. Down its throat we went, pulled unyieldingly toward its monstrous black eye.

Black like you've never seen.

Nightmare black with a deeper black thirsting within, like nothing that is also eternity.

"I don't wanna die, Thomas," said Kai.

"Me neither, Kai."

"What do we d—"

With a jolt, we slowed.

Slowed down, down, down.

But it wasn't just our ship's velocity that slowed. It was *us*.

Our movements, our thoughts—we couldn't even speak. I opened my mouth; my lips were thick, heavy slabs I could barely move.

We closed in on that hungry black eye and the nose of the *Aquarius III* stretched out eagerly to meet it. It reached and reached out, elongating before us like a ribbon of chrome-reinforced fettuccine.

Then us.

We stretched out . . .

CHAPTER SEVEN

Indeterminate Time to Midnight

I magine, you have a dream.

That dream is a bizarre projection of the stray gatherings of your unconscious mind. It is equal parts consequence and inconsequence; those you love dearest merged with a passing stranger; your very home and bed where you lay your head bisected with an avenue you've never walked, only feared. Your dream is odd, it is ordinary; it is a place of danger as it is a bastion of safety. It is all these contradictions. Your dream is the long, strange trip you embark on every night of your life. Your dream is the place of mystery you know so well.

Now imagine that dream is slowed and crystalized in an image. An all-encompassing snapshot of the totality of your psyche, like one of those Hieronymus Bosch triptych paintings. There's the inferno, there's purgatory, there's paradise. Within each panel a universe of highs and lows, a myriad of entities, angels and demons, enemies and families, strangers and primary loves.

Now that image is shattered. Ripped apart. Exploded like a pane of glass.

You believe that's oblivion. Your psyche, your dream, your image—simply no more.

Only there's time. Time is still passing. You have no sense of how fast it flows. You have no sense of anything, other than that time exists.

After an indeterminate spell, you're aware of the broken pieces of your image again. It is nothing more than a mess of shards and dust. But the rubble of that snapshot, like time, exists.

Then the shards and dust take individual shape, like the pieces of a jigsaw. Bit by bit, corner by corner, the pieces re-form. Like a Rubik's Cube in the hands of a small child, at times forcing the wrong pieces together, only just learning what a puzzle is, what the colors are, the picture dumbly assembles.

You don't know how long, because time as a concept is also being re-formed with the slow reassembly of the image.

Eventually, the image is there. The pieces are in their right place. From your angle, it's nonsense. All you can observe is the jagged shape of each jigsaw piece ill at ease. The image itself is remote and blurry and meaningless.

But the image rotates. And there, at the right angle, something clicks. The lines of the jigsaw vanish. The picture comes to life. You recognize the voices of your family. *"This is Captain Christopher Smith of the* Aquarius 1. *The year is 2093—time unknown . . . Whatever you do, do not come knocking—"*

—

Space, again.

But new Space.

An altogether original composition of cosmic order.

I emerged newly rendered as though there was no ship. Just me, a disembodied observer of the celestial night, sailing true toward the undiscovered country.

I studied the patterns, searching for recognition. I tried to connect the dots.

No luck.

I saw three distinct suns. Each cast a unique brilliance across the canvas. The primary star was a dazzling beacon of golden radiance. Flanking that were two companion stars. One burned with a fiery intensity, emitting a brilliant blue-white radiance. The other companion, a red dwarf, had a subtle burgundy glow, casting a gentle rosy hue.

I blinked. Like lenses clicking into focus, I could see my immediate surroundings.

The *Aquarius III* piloting console.

Kai to my left.

Bugging out.

"*Bro*, the fuck?"

I tried to speak, but the noises I made could have been dolphin cries for all I knew.

"The fuck just happened to me?"

I was saying stuff too, we were talking over each other, even. Just not sure what I was babbling.

"We was there—I was there and I wasn't but something was—and then everything was fucking *nothing*, Thomas, nothing—like there wasn't ever anything real in the cosmos, fam, and then my alarm clock was beeping and Moms was like, 'Get up! You late!' and I started busting ass, man, gearing up, hopping on one pant leg, my alarm still ringing and Moms still popping off—and then, I'm here, man. Looking at you again."

I took a deep breath. "Kai. I'm not sure I've entirely returned to my body just yet," I explained to him.

As I spoke, I heard my own words trickle after the fact. Like an echo in reverse catching its source, by the end of my sentence, speaking and hearing resolved, and synched. I spoke and heard "yet" at more or less the same moment.

"You okay? Thomas, you good?"

"I think so, Kai."

"Thalia, you here?"

"Functional, Kai. Checking systems."

"Check Captain Thomas's system while you're at it."

"Life signs stable."

"Well, that's good to know," I said.

"You here, Thomas? All of you?"

"Hard to say. Wish there was some kind of test, like those old Westerns when they bite the coin to make sure it's real gold."

"Is that why they did that? Oh, damn. I thought the coins were, like, flavored."

"Kai, I need you to do something for me."

"Say the word."

"Zero-g hug."

Kai and I were old pros at the maneuver. The trick was to release our latches at the same time, clasp hands with a little shove to the ceiling, wrap each other up once we cleared our chairs.

There was a lot of "You good," "I'm good," and hearty pats and an exchange of "Love you, man" at the end.

"So where the fuck are we?"

"As always, Kai, I appreciate your innate grasp of the situation."

"Thalia, is he trying to say he doesn't know?" Kai asked.

"*We can infer from Captain Thomas's comment that yes—*"

"I have no freaking clue, Kai. I'm pretty sure these are three suns. This is a trinary system. I mean, these stars. There's no pattern to them that I recognize. I would hazard a guess, Kai, that you and I are among the sole human beings in the universe to experience what was heretofore regarded as a scientific unknown."

"You don't say."

"What happens to an entity that enters a black hole or wormhole? Theories abound, but you and I are—quite possibly— the first and only humans to traverse these testaments to the incredible power and mystery of the universe."

"So what went down when we went through that bad boy?"

"Well, frankly, I don't know."

"And you don't know where we are. Thalia, any help?"

"*Sorry, Kai. I'm as lost as you.*"

"These are the facts, Kai. I don't really know what happened to us. Only that I feel quite fortunate to be here, having this conversation. Most theories about what happens in a black hole involve total annihilation. Being torn apart by the tidal forces from the discrepancy in gravity."

"And that's not what happened."

"I don't believe so. Not unless you believe in the afterlife."

"Not sure what I believe, but I'd be surprised if the afterlife looked just like the deck of the *Aquarius III*."

"My thought as well. We'll go with the idea, then, that the

black hole spat us out somewhere else in the universe. This could be a thoroughly uncharted corner of the endless expanse of galaxies. Who knows?"

"What *do* we know, Thomas?"

"We have a valuable testimony about the nature of black holes, for one. The spaghettification of our ship, the warping effects of tidal forces, the totally bonkers experience of the event horizon—"

"No, I mean what do we know about getting home?"

"Square zero on that count, buddy."

We floated in a moment of silence as we both took that in.

"Thalia," I ventured, "any thoughts about whether that black hole would return us to our point of entry if we jumped in the other way?"

"Highly theoretical thoughts, Thomas."

"Let's hear."

"According to the limits of scientific understanding, once something crosses the event horizon, it's impossible for anything, even light, to escape. The wormhole could collapse at any point. Or it could rip the particles and atoms of our craft to shreds."

"You trying to try it?" Kai asked me.

"That's a negative, Private."

"Copy."

"For the moment, you and me—we're alive. Let's savor the head count while we can."

Kai nodded, guiding himself via handrails to the mess area, where he had enough room for his IMC exercise routine.

"Asset report, Thalia?" I requested.

"*With strict rationing, three months' worth of food and seven thousand light-years' in fuel.*"

"Wow."

"Hell of a haul," agreed Kai.

"Are there any recognizable patterns in this star system, Thalia?"

"*Negative, Thomas.*"

The ceiling lights flashed with the red crash alert.

"Evasive action, Thalia," I said, assuming the alarm was due to a glitch in her sensors, as her auto-navigation would normally avoid collision without alarm.

"*Thrusters nonresponsive, Captain.*"

"Uh, excuse me?" Kai's attention whipped up from an Aerial Yoga Half-Moon Pose.

In the viewscreen, some Space object was getting progressively larger, our courses seemingly trained toward collision.

"Evasive action, Thalia," I said again reflexively, though clearly impossible if the thrusters were down. "Ready position, Private."

We strapped into our crash chairs.

"Thalia, what's the problem with those thrusters?"

"*Systems offline.*"

"Keep refreshing," I said. "How about those quantum cannons, we locked and loaded?"

"*Quantum cannons in ready-fire position.*"

"Thank god," said Kai.

In the viewscreen, the object drew closer, its shape revealed against the unfamiliar stars.

"Oh, shit," said Kai.

"It's . . ."

"*It's a spaceship.*"

Wings sloped like a condor, beak lurching toward us, a steel composite gray with a very familiar pattern of rivets. Even the insignia on the starboard flank was the same as ours. I could make out the first letters of *Aquarius*.

"That's not just a spaceship," said Kai. "That's us."

CHAPTER EIGHT

Conflicting streams of thoughts, possibilities, and directives collided in my mind.

How can that be us?

Were we cloned somehow by the wormhole?

Were we spat up into another universe where we also exist?

What happens if I shoot?

What if they shoot?

What if they are we and if I choose to shoot, they also shoot, and it's mutual destruction?

"Thalia, can we get an open channel of communication with the ship?"

"Hailing unidentified ship."

My hand gripped the controls, my finger on the launch trigger.

But I was frozen.

"Collision in five—" Thalia asserted.

"Make a move, Thomas!"

"Four—"

"What if they *are* us?" I said.

"They still about to *hit us,* fool!"

"Three—"

"But if this is some multiversal overlap—"

"No time for your bullshit, Thomas!"

"Two—"

"Thrusters, Thalia?"

"Still nonresponsive, Captain."

The *Aquarius* in our viewscreen grew larger and larger, like a mirror image reaching to touch itself.

"Thomas, shoot!"

"One—"

Even if I had wanted to shoot, it was too late. The cannon fire would have wrecked us both.

What did happen was only slightly less destructive.

We smashed into each other like a pair of billiard balls. The impact rocked our cabin as we immediately halted progress. My stomach lurched somewhere up by my chest cavity. Our twin hulls slammed into each other with a screech. Sparks flew; metal crunched.

We ricocheted away from each other and accelerated dangerously in the opposite direction.

"Okay," said Kai. "We okay?"

"Affirmative," I said, though I could just as easily have thrown up.

Then I felt an odd acceleration. "What's our course, Thalia?" I asked with foreboding.

"Gravitational anomaly seems to be drawing us in."

"Shit," I said.

"'Shit' sounds bad," said Kai.

"You ready to go back through that wormhole, maybe sooner than we'd like?" I posed.

"No, sir."

Our speed picked up and up, our mirror *Aquarius* sailing farther away.

"Don't want to be spaghetti again, Captain, what's the plan?"

The words *captain* and *plan* seemed to kick my mental process back into gear. I was captain of this ship. Not only was the *Aquarius* my responsibility, but I knew its every nook and crevice, its capabilities inside and out. Even without thrusters, we had options, and I had an idea.

"*Nostromo!*" I blurted.

"Inspiring communication skills, Captain."

"No—tow ship! Tow cables!"

"Tow—what?" Kai asked.

"Us!" I yelled, pointing at the other *Aquarius* in the viewscreen. "Quick, while we're still in range!"

"Copy that, Captain," Kai said as he maneuvered the tow-cable launch controls.

"*Unidentified ship nearing tow-cable maximum range.*"

"Let her rip, Kai!"

With a sharp bursting launch, our tow cable spiraled into the viewscreen, searching for the hull of our opposite ship. Kai's quadrant snapped to a smaller view of the cable itself as he guided its way through Space. Just as the black magnetic end of the cable vanished from our main view, we felt the *thunk* as it connected on target.

"Bull's-eye!"

The cable reached its limit and yanked us back like a rubber band, rescuing us from the gravitational pull of the wormhole. My stomach lurched again, this time dropping somewhere toward my lower intestine, as we were flung in yet another direction.

The rotations went on and on. So much jostling and twisting and turning as we exchanged velocities with the other us, harangued by the ever-mysterious sources of cosmic force. Barely recovered from the experience of the wormhole, I did what my decades of training, discipline, and experience called for; I held on for dear life and begged it all to stop.

In this disoriented fog, I saw the planet.

I didn't say anything, not at first. I simply did not trust my own eyes.

The view of the planet quickly vanished as another rotation gave me a new view of these strange constellations.

Then I came back around and saw the planet again.

Round as a robin's egg, with patches of rock and glowing blue beyond the haze of atmosphere.

"Does anybody else see that?" I called as we hurtled out of view.

"Glad you said something—I thought I was hallucinating again," said Kai.

"Thalia, is that a *planet*?" I asked, feeling like I was losing my mind.

"*I detect a gravitational layer of atmosphere consistent with a planet,*" she said. "*However, beyond that, I detect nothing.*"

"Nothing?" Kai shrieked.

"It's getting closer," I observed.

"What?"

"'Nothing' is getting closer."

We had stopped rotating. I felt my own body weight heavy against my chair. We were being drawn into this "nothing" planet's gravity well. The spherical outline subsumed our viewscreen until we saw only the massive rock formations growing larger and larger.

"Thalia, how is it possible you detect *nothing*?" I asked.

"We are looking at a fuckin' whole-ass planet," Kai concurred.

For the first time I could remember, Thalia was dead quiet.

"Thalia?"

"Processing . . ."

"Did she just say, 'Processing'?" Kai asked. "Fuck of a time to glitch out, Thalia!"

We slowed in the atmospheric drag like hitting a solid wall, jerking us against our chair straps.

"What was that?" asked Kai.

"That would be the atmosphere's drag force halting us up."

I could see snow caps on the tips of mountains. Water bisected the rock-shaped continents like veins.

"Thrusters now functional," Thalia informed us.

"There she is! Thomas, punch it!"

I gripped the *Aquarius III* controls and felt the old girl hum.

However, they came back too weak to pull away from the gravity well, and where would we go if we did? We were on course for this strange planet, and that was likewise our best bet for the resources we'd need to survive.

"Thalia, calculate planetary entry flight path," I instructed.

"Calculating . . ."

Thalia overlaid a color-coded grid on my viewscreen. Entering a planet's atmosphere was like threading the fine space between fire and ice. The grid was blue for the overshot boundary, where we would skip out like a plate sliding on a chrome countertop. The grid was orange for the undershot boundary, where we'd burn up like cooked food. Between that was the neutral entry corridor, and that was good money.

"Brace yourself," I warned.

"The deep breath before the plunge," Kai quoted Gandalf.

I nodded and steered the Aquarius deeper into that narrow corridor as we felt the crush of G-force manifest.

At 2gs, we were smooshed into our chairs. At 2.5, my jaw locked up, and the crush on my chest felt like a person standing on me. At 3gs, that person was wearing steel reinforced gravity boots. At 3.5, my bones were lead. At 4, the effort to breathe was like trying to bench press the *Aquarius* itself.

Our ship's heat shields glowed orange as the corners of the *Aquarius* ignited with plasma flame. Soon the screeching blaze was everywhere like the fires of doom. There was no strength in my lungs to scream.

"Shields at thirty-two percent," Thalia reported.

The *Aquarius* dove too quick. We shook violently, crash chairs vibrating.

"Shields at eleven percent."

Something crushed in on our hull with the sound of twisted metal.

A sudden explosion ripped the air. A panel tore from the *Aquarius* with flying sparks and flame, exposed wires and circuitry overhead.

Air rushed past us, building to a deafening roar.

I tried to maintain control, but we were spinning out.

We burst through the clouds and beheld a stunning natural world spiraling below.

I steered into our momentum, gulping a lungful of air as the G-force pressure relaxed. I smelled burning metal.

"Kai, you good?"

"I'm okay," Kai managed. "Why are we still falling?"

"Aquarius flight systems compromised. Unable to resist gravitational pull," Thalia reported.

"Break out those crash-landing skills, Captain—wait, what is *that*?"

We passed over an extraordinary circular structure that had to be built with human hands. We burned overhead so fast it was gone in a flash, but I could still see it in my mind's eye. Like you took the entirety of the Babel Space Station and sliced it into fours, and then flattened the whole thing out so its blinking lights and structures peopled a vast expanse of valleys and hills, with fields of agriculture and streams of water running below its magnificent heights.

And quick as it came, it was gone.

We immediately rushed headlong into a dark, cold world. Like we'd hallucinated the sprawling bounty and upright city, we were surrounded by a frigid, barren wasteland for miles and miles. I angled for a break in a line of petrified trees, and we smashed into a valley of rock, dust, and ash.

The *Aquarius III* clove into the jagged ground, grinding and screeching to a halt.

CHAPTER NINE

52 Hours to Midnight

Hello, hello, come in, come in. Babel command, this is Captain Quentin Thomas of the *Aquarius III*. We are stranded and request assistance. *Aquarius III* is grounded, repeat, *Aquarius III* is grounded."

I wasn't expecting our hails to be heard, but it was protocol to make the attempt. Kai even souped up the radio signal in hopes of reaching Babel, but no dice. I made a recording about what happened and launched the message into Space via tight beam in the direction of the wormhole. I believe the Olde Earth terms *Hail Mary* and *long shot* apply here. That's what they would have said in the movies, anyway.

I interrogated Thalia at length about our situation. She was unhelpful, to say the least. Thalia's intelligence was limited to the known systems that feed her informational processes. At a point, she began reciting IMC handbook sections for what to do when stranded on an unknown planet. I'd long committed the whole handbook to memory and made her stop.

Comms options exhausted, we were ready to explore. I ejected my father's Captain's Token from the *Aquarius III* main console and slipped it in my vac suit's chest pocket.

Every star captain carried a token that's individuated to run our starship. The token authorized the ship's functionality. It was the symbol of regard, dignity, and status among Babel's star-captain elite, coded with the honors and plaudits achieved during the captain's tenure. My father's token included the Space Medal of Honor he'd won for single-handedly saving an entire expedition fleet from a collapsing star by recoding the communal navigation systems on the fly. When my father left for Paradise, his token was retired. When I was up for the rank, I applied for his former *Aquarius* commission, which, as his son, meant I could request to carry his token on through the generations. Took me two years longer than it might have to make captain, but I was committed to keep that token close to heart.

We set foot on the dark wasteland. Wild how a planet could just keep your feet on the ground without even trying. My man of infantry, Private William Kai, held his rifle at low ready. I followed suit. Our helmet lamps lit the way. Our vac suits' heat controls kept us warm. Unsure if the air was safe to breathe, we kept our face shields sealed.

A forest of petrified trees stood before us. Tall, silent, and eerie, these sentinels made the shapes of things we knew as "trees," but were pale, skeletal imitations, dead roots wrapped around barren rocks. A pair of moons hovered on opposite ends of the darkly domed sky, lighting a pale, blueish path. The silence was deafening, with the thin howl of wind breaking into static on our earpieces.

"There was life here, once," I observed.

"Where, do you suppose, is here?" Kai questioned as he gingerly kept pace on the jagged steps.

"I'm working on a hypothesis."

"Do tell."

"You tell me, Kai. What do we know about Paradise?"

"We know a handful of Babelonians get to go every star year."

"Correct. And where do they go?"

"That information is not made available to a lowly private, sir."

"Not to captains either, I'm afraid," I assured him. "Far as I know, the location of Paradise is a closely guarded secret in the upper ranks of the Babel High Council."

"Why you think they so tight-lipped about it?"

"The reason they give—that the rank and file might go rogue and make for the planet themselves—sounds plausible."

"Sure. I mean, if I knew where it was and that Bonita was there? I'd probably make a break for it my own self."

"I have always wondered, what if we happened upon it? In all our far-ranging expeditions, who's to say we couldn't have encountered Paradise, by accident?"

"Is that what you think happened?" Kai asked with a note of hope in his voice.

"Perhaps, Kai, we are not the first humans to traverse a wormhole. Perhaps we have stumbled upon the secret entry-way to the gates of Paradise. What else do we know about the planet?"

"It's a two-sided planet with each side having its own constant meridian. Meaning that one side of Paradise is day and the other is constantly night. One side of the planet is nutrient-rich, with vegetation and springs like the heyday of Earth. And the other side is a vast wasteland, the Land of Endless Night."

"My friend, might we be in that Endless Night? Not quite accurately named, I might add, as the night does indeed end at the other side of the meridian."

"Night doesn't end over here, Cap."

"I stand corrected."

"So you really think we found Paradise? Like, we made it?"

"Look for the likeliest explanation, my friend."

"Like Sherlock Holmes?"

"In every incarnation, yes. Even in those implausible Victorian scenarios, the likeliest explanation is always correct."

"So we just got to trek on out of Endless Night?"

"Toward the Eternal Sun, my friend. But don't celebrate just yet. There's no reason to think they'd let us stay."

"After all we been through to get here?" Kai asked.

"Two more mouths to feed could upset the fragile balance of the ecosystem. Population control is serious business."

"Fam, if they got all that natural bounty, they could feed a couple more."

"I personally agree."

"But you really think they'll help us on our feet, patch us up, and get us on our way back to Babel?"

"There's a high probability."

"Is that really good enough though, Thomas?"

"What do you mean, Kai?"

"We *here*, man. I'm walking on real rocks, dude. They hurt my feet and they suck, but they real. This ground got my feet down on it like it ain't no thang. It's like you been sayin'. We're human beings. We belong on a planet."

"It's quite an experience. Like coming home."

"And I'm not giving it up that easy. We done had our insides turned inside out like some kid's pajamas just to get here."

"All in the service of doing our duty as IMC officers," I said, but I felt like I was reciting lines I'd rehearsed.

"Fuck that, Thomas. I don't believe that and I don't think you do, either."

A flash of white winked in the dark.

"Uh, Kai did you see that?"

"I'm on the same planet, the same earthen core as Bonita, Thomas. I got to see her, man—"

"Hush," I said, and rose a single finger to my face shield, so he got the message. "Thalia, scan extended area for life-forms."

I crouched and held the light to tiny dirt balls on the ground.

"That's not dirt," I realized.

"*Life-forms detected,*" she said from tiny speakers inside our vac suits.

"How many?" I whispered, head on a swivel.

"*Two hundred and fifty-six.*"

That got Kai's attention.

A small red dot lit inside the hollow of a petrified tree.

"Kai, watch my six," I said, and trained my sights on the empty darkness inside the dead tree's hull.

I crept closer on the uneven ground. With each step, I crunched on round, ashy balls I now realized were the droppings of some alien creature.

The small red dot was alone in the gaping hollow. I was about to dismiss it as a trick of the moonlight, when a second dot appeared eye-distance apart. Soon six more pairs of red eyes appeared in the dark.

I shined my flashlight dead in the hole and saw dozens of huddled, snarling rodent faces.

I jumped back and collided with Kai. His rifle blasted a round of plasma force into the sky.

The petrified tree erupted like a volcano, spewing dozens of sharp-winged bat-like creatures with a howling wail. Razor wings flashing in the moonlight, the beasts gathered like an electric cloud above us and launched an attack.

Back to back, Kai and I shot down razor-bat after razor-bat, but most of the horde got through, wings slicing us, shredding our suits, and leaving us bloody.

"Back to the ship!" I yelled.

We hauled ass.

Dry firing overhead, we ran as fast as our vac-suit boots would take us. The razor-bats had already exposed us to the local atmosphere, which also could kill us for all we knew. It was sheer terror.

Then the explosion happened.

CHAPTER TEN

Orange fires consumed the night sky.

A wave crashed into me.

This was nothing like the movies.

They'd have you believe the blast of an explosion is like a strong wind, lifting you safely from the fires.

Not so.

This was more like an invisible club swung by King Kong.

The force slammed me banging into Kai and we collapsed.

We flattened on our backs in the rocks and droppings. Everything went white. Waves of blistering fires washed over us. Kai's face shield reflected with incendiary orange as the fires climbed higher and higher, illuminating the ghoulish forest like a supernova.

The cuts in our vac suits were singed with flames and we rolled on the ground to put them out.

"Thomas. You okay?"

"I'm okay. You okay?"

"Okay. I mean, it's relative."

"Highly relative."

We stayed there, on our backs, as the fires dimmed, and darkness crept back to the Endless Night. The explosion scared off the razor-bats, at least. We stayed put longer than we had to. It was like the hand of some higher power set us on our asses and said, *Lie down.*

Stay there.

So we did.

It had been so long since we'd slept. The unreality of all of it was catching up to us.

"Thomas, you think maybe we already dead?"

"I believe we discussed this possibility, Kai."

"Maybe we could revisit?"

"Proceed," I said.

"Our logic was," Kai began in a low voice, "this couldn't be the afterlife since it was just us in the *Aquarius*. It was all so normal. All I'm saying, I don't feel that way anymore."

"I get your meaning. This doesn't feel normal."

"At all. First we crash into other-us. Then this hellscape."

"And I've lost my *Aquarius*," I said, and the thought made me unbearably sad. Like there was a weight in my stomach so profound that if I fell to my knees, my guts would spill out of me like Tetsuo's fever dream in *Akira*.

I took a deep breath. "You know the old *Ultranomicon* saying about what to do when going through hell, Kai?"

"I really don't, Thomas."

"*Keep going,*" Thalia said.

I sat up. As the fires lessened and my eyes adjusted, I beheld a glorious and strange pattern of green and white stars peppering the depths of the pitch-black sky.

"Any thoughts on what caused that explosion?" Kai asked.

I glanced at a flaming hunk of paneling with *AQUARIUS III* stenciled on it.

"Not sure of the 'why,' but pretty sure about the 'what.'"

I pointed to the panel. Kai nodded.

"I figured. I mean, what else has a combustible core out here?" he said. "What do you think made the *Aquarius* explode?"

"No idea, Kai."

"It appears something triggered the self-destruct," observed Thalia.

"Could those bats work the self-destruct, you think?"

"Highly doubtful, Thomas."

Kai shrugged. "I dunno. Sounds as plausible as anything."

"Yeah. Meaning, not very."

"Not at all."

I extended a hand and helped Kai to his feet. "Whether we're in hell or not is a factor I'd add to the list of those outside our control," I said. "I, for one, am curious about the dimensional implications of this long, strange trip we're on."

"'Dimensional implications'?"

"What if we arrived, not just in an unknown corner of an unknown galaxy, but in an entirely different dimension, an altogether new reality? An alternate plane of existence, not so unlike Olde Earth imaginings of an afterlife, as you so aptly put it."

"I don't know, Thomas. That's a leap."

"I can't shake the idea since we, quite literally, ran into ourselves. I mean what if, in this other dimension, there's already a version of us? And, since we tried to occupy the same space, we collided? And maybe that's what blew up the *Aquarius*?"

There was a long, sharp note of wind whistling over the burning debris.

We took stock of the fragments of our beloved ship and Kai said, "Thomas, you know I'll take a ride on your flights of fancy now and again. But I don't know what the fuck you talking about this time, dude. I mean now who's the one taking the Spider-Verse and *Multiverse of Madness* too literally?"

"*Does not compute, Thomas.*"

"I'll admit, the multiverse idea involves a ton of theoretical science."

"You think, maybe, all that is a way of coping with the unbearable loss of your star ship?"

"Maybe, Kai. Maybe so."

A sudden, loud banging interrupted my morose thoughts.

"What's that?" I asked, thinking, *What now?*

"Over here," said Kai.

"*It's the ATM unit,*" said Thalia.

BANG BANG. A metal sound came from the solid, rectangular box of our ship's ATM.

"Oh shit!" said Kai. "I damn near forgot about the three gs of antimatter!"

"Rest assured, Kai. Only the *Aquarius III*'s Beyond Drive exploded. If our antimatter haul went up, we'd be too incinerated to ponder in the aftermath. Us, and a nuclear fallout of about twenty-one kilometers."

"True that. Damn, these things are made to last, huh?"

"It better be, to safely contain and stabilize all that antimatter."

The banging made the metallic coffin jump this time.

"Why is it going off like a bag of popcorn?" Kai asked.

"The explosion must have triggered the ATM-301 guardian contingency mode," I said.

"Oh, duh, my bad. We got backup! Could have used that guardian before we got jumped by those razor-bats. But why does it still look like a box then?"

"The explosion triggered and then interrupted the ATM-301 contingency reboot. It's stuck."

"You mean, it's buffering?" Kai asked.

"Authorization required to complete 301 contingency reboot," Thalia explained.

"Well, why didn't you say that? Proceed with authorization," I instructed.

"Manual authorization required."

"Oh boy," said Kai.

We looked at the indestructible metal-alloy box as it banged and jumped like luggage on an angry trampoline.

"301 contingency reboot has knocked all ATM functions off my network," Thalia explained.

"How about one of us sits on the box while the other enters the code?" I suggested.

"My ass already been through a lot. Shoot you for it?"

"No need," I said. "I volunteer to be the ass."

I sat on the 2.5 meters of solid metal alloy as it popped off the ground and gave me a good spanking. Kai tapped his fingers on a narrow touchscreen.

"Thomas, what's the security code for Blade Runner?"

"Blade Runner—you sure?" I asked.

Blade Runner was the code for hunting and killing.

"We in a bad spot here, Cap. Those bat things—fam, we damn near got shredded."

I closed my eyes, recalling the code. "JAH0501." I spat out the letters and digits.

The popping stopped in favor of grooves of metal blocks separating and rotating beneath me. I jumped out of the ATM-301's way. Its parts clicked and whirled like in those Transformers flicks, and as the last bits worked into place we stood there above a man-sized robot. Made of a flexible but durable metal, the body's frame was modeled after a human but looked more like a Gundam Mecha with a square-tubed television for a head like *Fooly Cooly*. No face, just a screen. The robot lay there lifeless.

"Nice-lookin' bloke, innit?" Kai said in an accent straight out of *Attack the Block*.

"Why won't it move?" I wondered.

Kai reached in his chest to flip the switch booting up the robot. Only it didn't work.

"Oh. The switch melted in the 'on' position."

"It must have triggered something in the robot internally forcing him on without running the proper coding before online simulation," said Thalia.

"What's that mean, exactly?" I asked.

"Basically, the robot was turned on too quickly due to the explosion and impact of the blast."

"It looks like we can't reboot him," said Thalia.

"What do you mean?" said Kai. "All I have to do is re-code his wake execution." Kai got to work on the touchscreen panel, now by the ATM robot's forearm. "By connecting directly into the robot's interface, the motherboard can be forced into override. There's only one problem—his switch has been permanently welded in its current position."

"With the antimatter charging his power supply, we won't be able to turn him off . . . ," I realized.

"I hate to be the bearer of bad news, but this action goes against code Wade3," said Thalia. *"No robot under any circumstance should be given infinite stream of consciousness."*

"And why's that?" asked Kai.

"It's the question of turning it off."

"You mean like if it goes rogue?" I suggested.

"*Precisely.*"

"You're on all the time, can't we shut you off?" Kai posed the question forming in my thoughts.

"*Well for one, I'm here to help and to protect you.*"

"Just like our friend here," I said.

"*And two, I don't have a physical body, so I can't actually hurt you. Unlike our friend. The one you want to grant consciousness for the rest of eternity like a metal-alloy god.*"

The burning debris gradually diminished as we spoke. The fires cast less light, shadows growing long and vanishing into black. While we were able to see the area around the ATM and a few yards out from the hull of the *Aquarius III*, darkness gnawed at our periphery, and there I caught flashes of gathering bladed wings.

"Well, as captain, I say we have no choice. Our signal is lost, so we can't communicate with Babel. We are being hunted by alien bats with knives for wings. This robot, along with our finite bullets and blasters, are our only means of protection."

A chittering and clanging sounded from the shadows. Sharp edges flashed with the blinking of red eyes.

CHAPTER ELEVEN

S o turn him on?" asked Kai.

"I don't think that's a good idea—"

"Turn him on," I said.

"Oorah," said Kai.

The razor-bats marshalled their numbers into a horde. A black cloud writhing with moonlit blades.

"Hurry," I said.

Kai speed-typed on his keypad with a final blow of the fingertip. An immediate power-up noise from the robot, like a coin-operated video game machine from '80s movies like *The Last Starfighter* or that part in *The Karate Kid*.

The screen came to life, revealing a paragraph that I couldn't see from where I stood facing the bats, with my rifle at ready fire.

Kai read fast, under his breath. "'The path of the righteous man is beset on all sides by the inequities of the selfish and the tyranny of evil men. Blessed is he who, in the name of charity and good will, shepherds the weak through the valley of the darkness, for he is truly his brother's keeper and the finder of lost children. And I will strike down upon thee with great vengeance and furious anger those who attempt to poison and destroy My brothers. And you will know I am the Lord when I lay My vengeance upon you.'"

"Kai, is that the Olde Earth Bible?" I asked.

Kai continued to read under his breath. "'I'm trying, Ringo. I'm trying real hard to be the shepherd.' Oh shit!"

"That's *Pulp Fiction*," I realized.

Five bats blitzed us. I aimed and fired, taking down three, one at a time.

"Get that thing up in action, Kai!"

He hit a few buttons and the text disappeared. I glanced to see two words displayed across the face of the robot.

"'Insert Coin'?" I read.

"'Insert Coin'," Kai said. "What fucking coin?"

The text was rendered in an 8-bit, orange-to-yellow fade against a black background, like an Olde Earth arcade graphic.

Kai raised his rifle and blasted at the next wave of assault.

"Thalia, any ideas?"

As I swung my rifle to shoot, my wrist pressed on my father's Captain's Token against my chest.

"Wait!" I said.

I pulled the token out from my suit and held up the metal circle, engraved on each side. "Coin!" I declared.

Kai fired off round after round. "Yes! Great! Where's it go?"

The bat host launched waves of sorties. Kai and I took them out as fast as we could. When one got through, it slashed in swoops. We had to dive out of the way and fire when our attackers changed direction.

"We need help!" said Kai.

"Cover me." I bull's-eyed an oncoming pair and got up

close to the dormant robot. My frantic hands searched its alloy frame for a slot for the token, and I found one to the right of the monitor. I slid the "coin" inside and hoped for the best.

The screen flashed with a behavior code prompt. I typed:

BLADE RUNNER

As I swung my rifle back to the oncoming enemy, I heard the analog sound of an arcade game booting up, ready to go.

"Whoever coded this robot is a huge nerd," said Kai between shots. The screen showed glowing blue digital circles for eyes.

"I don't think it is kind of you to speak of one's creator in such a manner," said the ATM-301 robot.

"It speaks!" said Kai. "Dude, save us!"

"Hello. Please assign me direct orders of operation."

"That's the captain's job. Thomas?"

"Right, uh," I said, gunning down razor-bats like my life depended on it. "I'm Captain Quentin Thomas of the *Aquarius III*, pilot issue number 931994 and—Ow!" A bat sliced through my sleeve. I spun and took it out as it rounded for another pass. I spoke with all the speed and authority I had. "You are hereby ordered to keep me and my partner, William Kai, safe at all costs!"

"Understood, Captain Quentin Thomas, sir."

The ATM-301 rose to its feet. The bat horde swelled. The robot's digitized eyes processed the threat. He raised his forearms to a burst of bats, launched for the kill. In a blink, his hands and articulated fingers retracted and two miniguns took their place—smaller versions of the *Aquarius III*'s mounted weapons. Six gun barrels on each arm spun in a tight circle as

ATM-301's legs dug into the rock where they stood. The ends of his arms erupted.

Kai lowered his rifle and stared at the light show. Plasma shots illuminated his awed expression.

The miniguns burst out intense orange geysers, shots slashing through the onslaught. A pile of fried bat corpses littered the ground. The guns spun and smoked.

However, the minigun fire lit the night and revealed the true size of the horde formed in the dark. A massive wall of undulating bats fanned and thrashed.

"Oh, shit!" said Kai, raising his rifle again.

I saw the sheer size of that bat wall and realized how truly fucked we were.

I was in ready fire position, but I didn't shoot.

Either ATM-301 could handle it, or this was the end of Paradise for us.

The robot stepped forward. The miniguns drew back within his forearms and a pair of projector handles took their place. The projectors each released an intense green beam of high wavelength laser. Like *Return of the Jedi* lightsabers that just kept going, the beams punched through the wall of bats and seemed to extend forever into the sky.

"Don't move," ATM-301 said.

"Aye, aye, sir."

"Yes, sir."

Spinning, flipping, slashing, the ATM whirled, and the laser bars sliced through everything. Bats fell by the hundreds. Petrified trees were cut clean into sections on delay like bamboo stalks in a samurai flick. All the while we stood there, not moving. Lasers lashed overhead, clove rocks in half, inches away, and outlined us like cut silhouettes in the Night.

At a point, there was a retreat. Some survival instinct must have kicked in. The bats that didn't fill the hill of dismembered corpses sped off like a mass migration.

"Bye-bye." Kai waved. "It's been unreal!"

The ATM-301 sheathed his high wavelength lasers. Hands returned to the ends of his arms. He scanned the area, his monitor screen showing a series of ellipses running ". . ." from end to end.

"All clear, Captain Thomas, sir," the robot said as his rounded eyes reappeared.

"Please, just Thomas is fine," I said.

"Understood, Thomas, sir," said the ATM-301.

"No, I mean no 'sir,' just Thomas is fine."

"Yes sir, Thomas."

"Good enough."

"He means that you don't have to call him 'sir,'" Thalia said.

"The voice you hear is Thalia, the AI embedded in our suits," I explained, seeing his questioning look.

"I understand."

"Hello, I'm Kai. William Kai. But not like James Bond or no shit like that. You can just call me Kai."

"I'm sorry, but I'm unaware of a James Bond in our party," said the ATM-301.

"Nah fam, I mean like—"

"He's a robot, Kai," I said. "Like four minutes old. Of course he doesn't know who James Bond is."

"But Thalia been watching the Catalog with us. Why not the ATM?"

"It's in my code," said Thalia. *"I am designed to understand the nuances of human idiom and entertainment. The ATM operates on its own discrete AI computing system."*

"So, robot, you don't know anything about pop culture?" asked Kai.

"On the contrary, pop culture is the understanding and awareness of current fads such as music, movies, and all-around forms of entertainment in everyday life amongst human beings," said ATM-301.

"My mans, I didn't ask for the definition, I said do you know culture?"

"My maker did not create me or my code with such information. It is useless on the battlefield."

"Oh, we're going to have to change that," Kai said, and removed the stud in his right ear.

"What are you doing?" I asked.

"I'm embedding him with 557 terabytes of pop culture."

"Kai, I must advise strongly against this as it may distract the robot from his primary function."

Kai stuck the fastening into a small drive receiver on ATM-301's exterior paneling. After a second or two he said, "Done!"

"That was fast," I said.

"Ain't nothing as fast as Dominic Toretto," said the ATM 301.

"It worked!" said Kai.

"I feel this is a mistake," said Thalia.

"How many seasons of *The Simpsons* were there?" Kai asked the robot.

"Seventy-seven. That's easy; why don't you give me a hard one?" said the ATM-301, his speech pattern loosened up already.

"Who was Jerry's nemesis in the series *Seinfeld*?" Kai asked.

"Newman, of course," Thalia answered. *"Anyone with half a functioning RAM knows that Newman was—"*

"Actually, Thalia," the ATM-301 went in, "the correct answer to this question is Kenny Bania. Jerry may have hated

Newman, but Bania—a hack stand-up comedian—was the epitome of everything Jerry despised about human beings and entertainers."

"I'd switch you off if that power source wasn't welded perma-nently, robot," Thalia said.

"Now, Thalia, don't get spicy," I said. "We're alive now thanks to our friend here."

"Word up," chimed Kai. "Hey, so what's your name?"

"One does not have a name."

I glanced at the engraved model number across his chest. "ATM-three zero one . . . so you're the first of your series?"

"Yes, Thomas, I am."

"That's it!" said Kai.

"*What's* it?" the robot and Thalia said together.

"We'll call you Atom for short!"

"Atom." I auditioned the name. "I like it."

"Atom it is," said Kai.

"One is Atom."

CHAPTER TWELVE

48 Hours to Midnight

There was nothing to do but take the long walk out of Endless Night. Atom turned out to be a very handy piece of hardware. He was able to detect the rise in temperature, due west. The long, dark walk gave Kai time to bond with his new best friend. Kai finally had someone who could keep up with his extensive knowledge of pop culture of the '80s, '90s, and aughts.

"You know we're on our way to Paradise," I pointed out to Kai and Atom. "A true testament to humanity's progress. Why, at this moment, obsess about the past? A time we never even experienced?"

"Same reason you love it, Thomas. Because it was a time where we had everything we could have ever wanted. *Especially* since we weren't alive to experience it. And I don't know about you, man, but these books, songs, movies . . . Man, they was always a happy escape from them doldrums of the Babel Space Station. But now? It's like a vision of what awaits us. I can't imagine life on an actual planet without thinking about movies."

"Yeah, I get it. But that was when we were up there," I said with a head nod up to the strange sky—the constellations surrounding us and the entirety of Space life, from the wormhole to Babel Space Station.

"Like, you feel different somehow?" asked Kai.

"I mean we lived in boxes, Kai. One metal-alloy box after another, our whole lives."

"Hey Atom, you, like, used to *be* a metal-alloy box. How's it feel to, like, have a body, bro?"

"One feels . . ." Atom's eyes made an 8-bit ellipsis as he processed the question. "Normal." His robot arms shrugged. "I guess."

Kai grinned. It was wild the way Atom had adapted to how we communicate.

"Check out our bodies right now, Kai," I said, demonstrating the simple act of walking. "When's the last time we actually walked, like with the same purpose as our ancestors on Earth?"

"I walk, like, every day of my life."

"You walk to get from one room to the next. In fake gravity. From the pod to the landing strip to the docking bay to the star ship. You walk, to go sit. You get up from sitting to walk to sit somewhere else. Walking is just something we do between seats, Kai."

"Okay."

"You know what we're doing now? Hiking. Under the stars. To get someplace we've never been before. Like the primacy of our species. We're fucking cavemen, Kai. Can't you feel it?" I asked.

Kai exchanged a glance with Atom. "I feel something. Sure."

"This is the first time in our lives our legs are working like they're designed to work." I shook my head, buzzing with the surge of unfamiliar adrenaline. "Most of the people we know will die without ever experiencing *this*."

"True story," said Kai.

"Boxes, Kai. Live and die in little boxes. Even the domed Babel common areas are just a big box with rounded tops. It just all feels different to me now."

"But different how?" asked Atom.

"I mean, I get why there's no Paradise tours. Why no one who leaves for Paradise ever comes back to Babel to visit," I said, fingering the torn strap from my father's medal.

"Could it be," posed Kai, "the experience of being devoured and regurgitated by that digestive track of the universe that you call a wormhole?"

"Kai, that may be why the intrepid voyagers bound for Paradise must travel in cryosleep," I suggested.

"That makes sense!" said Kai.

"I mean, once you've set foot on real ground with real gravity surrounded by nature-rendered shapes—I mean, we're still in Unending Night and I can't imagine going back to spaceship life."

"You've been here for half a day, Cap," said Kai. "You honeymooning."

"*The novelty factor can't be overlooked, Thomas,*" Thalia chimed in.

"Perhaps the captain is indeed undergoing a personal evolution," said Atom. "In quite literally every story ever told, the main character begins the story with one state of mind or outlook. The events of the story serve to provide the protagonist with another outlook, another set of ideas."

"Thank you, Atom," I said.

"It can't be every single story ever told," Thalia disagreed. *"Not every main character evolves. What about Larry David?"*

"On the contrary, even the seeming lack of evolution, plus time, is an evolution. A character may have one mindset at the age of twenty. However, if that character has the same mindset and now they're forty, that lack of evolution is itself an evolution. It's a manifestation of character amidst the unfolding of events. Time means change."

"Very interesting interpretation, Atom," I said.

"Kiss-up," snarked Thalia.

"Why do I feel like these bots have, like, beef?" Kai asked.

"She literally said she'd switch me off," Atom said.

"I'm not so sure Thalia likes being locked out of Atom's functionality," I said. "I find it a welcome change."

"The more the merrier," agreed Kai. "Thalia, aren't you coded to be friendly?"

"To humans," Thalia said.

"Damn. That's cold," said Kai.

As the hours passed, the weight of true gravity wore on our bones. The excitement to see the City of Stars kept us going, but exhaustion from the equivalent of days of not sleeping took a toll. We were still adjusting to the strangeness of planetary elements. Wind had a mind all its own. Or as Kai said, "She's a moody bitch." Sometimes a gentle caress that carried the sweetest of smells. Sometimes a breeze that lifted you forward on your way. And sometimes a high gale that smacked you across the face. I had to remind myself that someone wasn't fucking with the air-vac controls. This was the randomness of nature. Perhaps why on Olde Earth she was personified as a character, Mother Nature. She had many personalities, and some of them all at once.

The convo tapered off as we set to scale a monstrous mountain. Atom climbed ahead with a high-focus laser lighting the way like a torch. As he still possessed the arm attachments from his existence as an ATM-301 Collection Machina, he was able to secure himself to the rocky surface with ease. Atom would scurry up a sheer cliffside to the nearest precipice, anchor himself, and then extend his free arm to us like a line of cable. One at a time, Kai or I would take his hand and ascend the rock face as the cable retracted. Once, Kai's hand slipped, but Atom's hand quickly extended and caught Kai by his vac suit before he fell.

As we neared the top, a faint orange glow outlined the mountain's peak. We went on for hours driven by the hope that, on the other side of this barrier, we'd see the first ray of true sunlight over the City of Stars. Some part of us believed it would be right there on the other side. That we'd reach the peak and roll down into the Elysium River's warm waters.

We were only half wrong.

"I think I know why it's called the City of Stars," I said.

We did see Elysium. Only it was on the other side of an unfathomable valley. The distant chrome city reflected the slanted tricolor sunlight for miles of darkness, shining bright above the Unending Night like a glimmering star.

CHAPTER THIRTEEN

Atop the mountain summit, Atom's high-focus lasers pulverized the rocks and petrified trees and made two beds of soft sand for our aching, human bodies. We had nothing to burn for fuel, but thanks to Atom's near unlimited supply (the antimatter stored in his system could keep him going for a few hundred millennia), he made his own fire. Like a magic trick, his hand simply ignited and began burning. Then he removed his hand and set it down on the ground between me and Kai.

"Got ourselves a fire. The stars above. Couple strangers, coming to a new city. Thomas, how many times we seen this scene in those old Westerns?" Kai asked.

"Hard to calculate," I said.

"Approximately 2700," Atom said.

"*Captain Thomas was not requesting intelligence,*" Thalia chided him. "*The question was rhetorical.*"

"Was that, like, the last time there was a real frontier?" Kai asked.

"Space," Atom said, "the final frontier."

"Right. Also, a dogshit Star Trek movie."

"One does not understand what makes a movie 'dogshit,'" said Atom.

"*The Undiscovered Country*," said Kai. "Good Star Trek movie."

"You know those Olde Earth phrases had quite a different meaning, before the invention of Space travel," I said.

"How you mean, Thomas?"

"The final frontier, the undiscovered country—these were poetic ways of talking about death," I said.

"Damn. And sci-fi movies heard that and were like, maybe they really mean Space?"

"I suppose so," I said.

"That's kinda dark," said Kai.

"Space is dark," I said, squinting at the stars. "Well, where it isn't light, I mean."

"Look. Atom's making ellipses," said Kai.

"*He doesn't understand,*" said Thalia.

"Something confuse you, Atom?" I asked.

"Where there isn't light, isn't everything dark?" Atom asked.

"I suppose so. I meant that Space was always a dark horizon for human beings. We came to exist on a miracle of a planet called Earth. Without the billion-to-one environments of that orbital rock? The first humans never would have breathed life at all. Life in Space—without any of those life-giving conditions occurring naturally—humanity is living a kind of afterlife."

"The final frontier," said Kai.

"The undiscovered country," said Atom.

"You know what's another word for *afterlife*?" said Kai. "*Paradise.*"

We stared for a while as stars seethed in blackness.

"They'll let us stay. Right, Thomas?" Kai asked.

"I don't know, Kai."

"They've got to. I mean, doesn't finding Paradise on accident make us worthy of, like, entering Paradise?"

"In the Olde Earth Abrahamic tradition, Moses himself was forbidden from setting foot on the promised land, even after leading his people to its soil."

"Now *that's* cold."

"What's really cold is what God did to Abraham."

"Oh yeah. That the one, he was like, 'Kill your son— *sike*.'"

"Guess Abraham was considered a good dude, back then. Willing to put his faith above his child. Not sure how that plays these days."

"I kinda feel like Bonita put the Cause above me," Kai said. "It's weird. I want to see her. I still feel a way about it."

"I know what you mean," I said.

"Do you? You feel like your pops . . ."

"Put the Cause ahead of me? I don't know. Maybe. I was twelve when he left. What did I really understand, back then? Everyone around me acted like this was a good thing that happened. I was proud. My father was famous. A hero. The part about never seeing him again? I guess I had to figure that out on my own."

Kai made a sympathetic exhale. "Like *Shogun Assassin*."

"What's that?" I asked.

"Oh. You said, 'My father was famous.' Like *Shogun Assassin*. That's all. My bad, not the time for callbacks."

"Sorry, Kai, if I'm coming to terms with some real shit over here—"

"It's just a badass line, Thomas. You got to say that shit and, like, mean it. *My father was famous. He was the greatest samurai in the empire. And he was the shogun's decapitator.* That shit was so hard, it opened *that* movie *and* the GZA's Hall of Fame banger, *Liquid Swords*."

"Not everything is a reference to some previous shit you already know about."

"You right, you right. But it's always been like that for me, Thomas. My moms didn't have me drinking that World of Tomorrow Kool-Aid like yours. This Catalog was our family legacy. Moms was always coming up with ways to sneak me the ill stories and music. Even as a li'l baby Kai, I knew that was special. Her friends, her side the family always talked different, they had this swag. Mad in-jokes and callbacks. That's how they knew who was cool, so they could be themselves. She had this laugh, Thomas, like an *event*. An opening *teehee*, a rumbling *huhuh*, and a straight boombastic finale. Her laugh had its own three-act structure. Made everyone want to laugh too, be in on the joke."

"Kai, I don't think you've ever talked about her like this."

"Maybe not, Thomas. Maybe it's this real ground and air and whatnot. Maybe it's 'cause I *really* don't know what's going to happen tomorrow. And I've never actually felt that way about my own life. Just movies."

I shrug. "It's a pretty samey existence up there."

"I guess that's why I make the references all the time. My earliest, happiest memories are discovering new things in movies, and sharing those with ma dukes."

"We're out here at the precipice now, Kai. Ready to plunge into the dark valley toward the light. We're living, Kai. We're alive."

"QT, you ever get scared?"

"Fear is a natural part of the human condition—"

"Nah, not like that. Not scared like, everybody gets scared.

Now I get scared in a very specific way, you feel me? Now, maybe that's 'cause Ma let me watch some scary shit when I was too young, but that's beside the point. Thomas, all the shit we been through? I don't think I've ever seen you scared, for real for real."

"I get scared, Kai. Course I do."

"I'm honestly a little scared right now," Kai admitted.

"Of what?"

"I don't know. The unknown, I guess."

"We were raised in Space, Kai. We are creatures of the unknown."

CHAPTER FOURTEEN

Trifold sunlight dropped like a glittering curtain where the world of dark ended.

From the far side of the mountain, we could view the expanse of the valley to Elysium. As the city neared, the shadows faded. Green filled the space leading to the city gates. First in patches, building to a lush landscape that lined a canal of running water. The canal encircled the gates, which encircled the city. The gates were built of some fifty-foot solid alloy pylons.

"Damn, they expecting Vikings or some shit?" asked Kai.

"Razor-bats?" I said. "Thalia, any intel on those bats? Did Paradisians push those things into Endless Night when they built Elysium?"

No response.

"Thalia? You there, girl?" asked Kai.

"*Processing,*" she said.

"Damn, she is glitchy as hell. You think that wormhole broke her?"

"Thalia, did the wormhole break you?"

"*Sorry, Thomas. There may have been some effect on my recall processes. Nothing to worry about.*"

"Who's worried?" asked Kai with wide eyes.

"Point is, those walls imply *they're* worried about an attack. And we don't really know what's out here. Head on a swivel," I said.

"We good. We got him." Kai jabbed a thumb in Atom's direction. "Atom, head on a swivel."

"Always," said Atom, turning his head 360 degrees around.

"Show-off," said Thalia.

Going down the mountain was easier than going up. We trudged the long valley. Grass began to sprout through the barest rocks, reaching toward the distant glow of the promised land. The closer we got, the greener and softer the earth, and the larger those gates loomed. Part of me wanted to yank my boots off and dig my toes into the grass beds. I didn't even know what that might feel like, but something told me to try it. Still, I was too wary of those gates to let my guard down.

As the hours passed, our shadows grew shorter and closer to our heels.

"So much for a sneak attack," said Kai.

He was right. The way the sunlight hit us in the open valley, anyone on those walls could see us coming for hours.

"Are we attacking?" asked Atom.

"That's a negative, Atom," I said. "Careful how you joke around, Kai. Remember, Atom's behavior code is still on Blade Runner."

"My bad," said Kai. "They can see us coming, that's all good. More time to plan our welcome."

"This may sound obvious, but it's best to assure whoever is there that we pose no threat."

"How do we do that? Wave a white cloth on a stick?" asked Kai.

"She's probably right," I said. "Kai, sling your rifle. Not like these plasma rounds will do much good against those walls."

"Better than nothing," said Kai, but he hooked the rifle across his back.

I did the same.

"Forgive me, but is Blade Runner code appropriate in this situation?" Thalia suggested.

"Good point," I said. "Kai, could you enter the code for Electric Sheep, protect and defend?"

"You sure, Thomas? Code Blade Runner came in pretty handy with those bats."

"Electric Sheep," I said. "ROM0502."

"You the boss," said Kai as he took Atom's forearm console in hand and tapped on the screen. Atom went limp and ejected my Captain's Token.

"Guess I got to reboot him myself," I realized, slotted the "coin" back in, and typed:

ELECTRIC SHEEP

Atom booted right back up. Maybe he had a more peaceful air, I couldn't be sure.

"Thalia, you detect any activity along those city walls?" I asked.

"Processing . . ."

"Thalia?" I followed up. "Any guards, anyone we can hail?"

There was no answer.

"Thalia!" Kai joined in. "Be really nice to know who's home right about now."

But Thalia went radio silent.

"Damn. I don't like that," said Kai.

"Not at all. What could knock Thalia out?"

"No clue. Some kind of signal dampener maybe?"

We gazed in the direction of the glowing horizon.

"Keep your eyes open," I said.

"Trying to. Bright as hell."

Light is never so bright as when you're coming from darkness. And that's what we were doing. We began the trek on the side of the plane in deepest shadow. The light above the city was both astonishing and almost unbearable to look at. Imagine a curtain made of pure light, dropped sheer from the firmaments to delineate the city walls. The sunshine leaped from the mouth of the sky in three luminous outflows of white, gold, and crimson above the city, and moved in beams of orange beneath shifting clouds like rustling fabric.

As we neared, the wind slashed our faces and the light stung our eyes into squints. We trekked on, one hand raised as shade.

"Man, it feels hot! Like, hotplate hot," said Kai.

"True sunlight, Kai. The real deal."

"Is it rude to ask it to stop shining in my eyes?"

The closer we got, the higher the wall rose into the light, carving a shadow on the horizon.

We hefted our wary joints against the relentless natural gravity. The light felt eons away. Kai pointed to the line at the top of the wall.

"You see anybody yet, Thomas?"

It was difficult to see along the very top. There appeared to be a walkway where guards could patrol. But light was spilling over the side, fouling the view.

"Negative, Kai."

"Hello!" I called out, waving my hands.

From the darkness below the wall, a small red light blinked.

"Thomas. What's that red dot on your head, man?"

I looked at Kai. There was a small round dot of red light pinned between his eyebrows.

"You've got one too," I said. "Aw, shit, surrender!"

My hands swung up in the air.

"Hello! We are comrades from Babel! I am Captain Quentin Thomas of the *Aquarius III* and this is Private William Kai!"

I saw no one and felt like a fool, yelling at empty shadow.

"Nice to meet you?" Kai said to no one.

The grass was hovering above our ankles. The hills sloped down into the babbling waters. There was no way across that I could tell. Just waters and wall.

"We mean no harm!" I shouted.

Two figures appeared in the gloom. Just two glowing red eyes, at first. Then two hooded humanoid forms emerged, came fast, and held rifles at the ready. I realized the red dots on us weren't rifle sights; they marked the target of their very eyes. They were cyborgs running at a sprint, torsos locked and gun barrels ramrod straight. They had some sort of enhanced exoskeleton with consoles implanted across their faces. One of them had several small red dots for eyes going around the center of his face like minigun barrel points. The other just had a single red eye like a cyclops, just off center.

"What's your number?" they shouted in twin distorted roars.

"Number?" I repeated, hands above my head. "Uh, Captain Quentin Thomas of the *Aquarius III*, pilot issue number 931994—"

"Your number!" they boomed again.

One held us at gunpoint and the other circled behind, slammed a rifle butt into my spine, and kicked above my calves so I dropped to my knees. Pain lancing through my back, he circled around front. The cyborgs held gun barrels to our faces.

"We are not a threat!" I shouted.

"Your number! Your number!"

"What fucking number?" said Kai.

The answer was the sound of plasma rifles charging to shoot.

CHAPTER FIFTEEN

34 Hours to Midnight

I thought there would be some warning. That once their rifles fully charged, they would issue an order to follow. Countdown, if we don't comply, then shoot.

That didn't happen.

The guards asked us for our "number."

They aimed gun barrels at our faces.

When we didn't have a number, they just shot.

But Atom knew what was coming.

Atom's arm panels fashioned a solid shield fully formed in front of us the instant before they pulled their triggers. The shield took the plasma rounds as it continued to extend all the way to the ground.

"What the *actual fuck!*" shrieked Kai as we hit the dirt. "They just *shot us?*"

"Guns out, Kai!" From my knees, I slung my rifle from over my shoulder and blasted a round over Atom's shield.

I was trained for this. But I was not ready for this. It's like, I'd imagine, playing pickup basketball three nights a week, then finding oneself, in an instant, in Game Seven of the 2001 NBA Finals. I knew what to do with a gun. I never expected to be doing it like this. The days of live gunfights were for history books and movies.

Still, there was enough training in my system to operate without being actually "ready." Kneeling in the tall grass, I shot into the sunlight, aiming around Atom's barrier.

Volleys returned. Plasma fire slashed into the night from whence we came.

"We got two rogue NPCs," one of the cyborgs said as if into a communicator.

"'*Rogue NPCs*'?" repeated a disbelieving Kai.

"I don't understand," I said.

"It means we nothing to them, QT! Atom—slice these fools up," Kai said before he realized. "Shit, Thomas. Be nice to have Atom on Blade Runner right about now."

"Affirmative. That's my bad, Kai."

"Got damn right."

The roar of heavy machinery sounded over by the wall.

Three massive armored suits came flying across the river on built-in jet propulsion. The hulking shapes landed on legs like mountain goats. Brawny, headless tanks for bodies, arms loaded with miniguns, shoulder cannons ready to fire, they unloaded on us.

"Get in tight!" yelled Atom as he braced himself behind his shield, taking a pounding.

"Need to change that code."

"How can we get to his console? His forearm is deflecting plasma rounds right now!"

Almost before Kai finished his sentence, a panel on Atom's back opened and there was his console screen, cued up to his behavior code prompt.

"Damn. Atom, whoever designed you is a fucking genius."

Kai looked away from his rifle sights to tap in the code.

The cyclops cyborg jumped our left flank.

I drilled a hole through the red target over Kai's shoulder. I swung back and dropped the one to our right.

The hulks came forward on mountain-goat legs, claws dug in the ground. Their shots fired and ripped through the air at a wholly new order of magnitude. Each blow thundered against Atom's shield, pushing him backward.

Kai stared at the cyborg in the tall grass and froze.

There was a hole through the eye in the center of his head. The wound had gone through and through and cauterized instantly, creating a tunnel to the other side. There was grass where his eye had been. Transfixed, Kai's body lost all grip with what was going on. He relaxed as if we weren't under fire. Which we most definitely were. He was experiencing one of those scenes in the movies where there's live fire and the main character has a moment just gawking at something. The shots never seem to hit the hero in those scenes. Maybe he'll get dinged on the cloth of his jacket, like Michael Keaton's Batman.

"Kai!" I shouted, grabbing him by his collar and yanking him back under cover. We lined up behind Atom, making ourselves as small as possible. "The fuck you doing, man? It's not the movies, man, you slip up out here, you die!"

"I—I'm sorry, Thomas. You right."

"What was it?"

Kai glanced back at the cyborg.

It was the first time either of us had seen death like this. The cyborg had seemed mostly machine when I shot it, but on the inside, he was definitely human.

"I—I think I knew him, Thomas," said Kai.

Beneath the eye piece were human features, enough to recognize a mouth and jaw, also like Batman.

"Okay, that's fucking weird but wait until we survive this to freak out about it!"

"Copy that," he said.

"Code Blade Runner. I'll cover you."

I laid down suppressive fire on the hulks for all the good it did. Kai plugged the commands into Atom's console.

The coin dropped out of Atom, but I was ready for it, caught it, and slotted the token right back in.

I typed in Code Blade Runner.

We heard the reboot arcade noise.

A beam of high wavelength laser burst out and punctured one of the hulks. The beam brought the hulk up short, pinned through. Atom's other arm maintained the shield, fending off the shots from the other hulk. Atom moved the high wavelength laser and sliced up, then down, and clove the hulk in two halves. The halves fell apart, revealing the bisected remains of the human being operating the machine.

The other hulk stopped firing. Atom's high wavelength beam swung at him, but an electric chain sprung between the hulk's hands, catching the beam. Atom's beam shortened to the length of a sword, and shield in his other hand, Atom charged the hulk like the Hound at the Mountain that Rides. The electrified chain whipped at Atom like a Morningstar, smashing the shield and retracting. The two metal beasts went at it. The electric chain clashed with the laser and shield, the hulk bigger, stronger, Atom, nimbler, smarter.

Kai and I were mesmerized by this clash of titans. Somehow, at the height of mankind's technological prowess on a world several galaxies away, two mechanical creations performed a scene straight from Olde Earth's most primitive medieval days. A duel between champions. A trial by combat. Kai and I played the role of the accused. The sentence was certain death.

We aimed our rifles and shot at the hulk, for all the good it did. It was hard to get a clean shot—as big as the hulk was, it moved surprisingly fast, using ingenious jets built into choice points on its massive arms. It occurred to me that the technologies on Babel and Paradise had evolved to meet different needs, and these two forces battled it out. The hulk was built with gravity in mind, while Atom was made for the harshest realities of deep Space.

The duel devolved into a savage exchange of blows. Atom ate these lashings of electric burns while his hands became indestructible drill hooks. Built to penetrate asteroid cores and attach through lightspeed-plus, the drill hooks dug into the hulk's shell and ripped it away, panel by panel.

Something in the hulk gave out and it fell on its back. Atom stuck to it like a face hugger. Kai whooped and gave me a high five. Then Atom opened the hull, ripped the human or cyborg operator out, and instantly decapitated him.

"Oh, *damn!*"

"Code Blade Runner," I said.

Atom turned to us. "Run!" he shouted.

Then two things happened at once.

A fleet of hulks mounted the city wall and took to the air.

And a burst of suppressive turret fire exploded on us.

I had already pivoted to run. The shot landed just a step behind me.

Hitting Kai.

The explosion of earth and grass launched Kai a few yards into my path.

He landed on his back, half his suit incinerated.

His eyes were closed and he did not move.

CHAPTER SIXTEEN

Kai!"

I dove on top of him, ducking beneath the tall grass. "Kai, wake the fuck up!"

Half his face was covered in burns and earth and rock dust. I slapped the other half.

"Wake up now, buddy!" I shouted an inch from his face.

His eyes became tiny slits.

"Not time for this, Private!"

He groaned, something like, "Shit the actual fuck all hell."

"Exactly, let's go!"

Atom stood over us, deflecting shots with his shield.

"The enemy is closing in," he said. "Danger. We are seven seconds from the kill zone."

Atom's flat delivery scared Kai awake, much better than my shouts. He tried to rise on his arms but collapsed.

I saw the legion of hulks fill the sky like Hitchcock's birds.

I hefted Kai up to his feet, arm under his shoulder. One foot at a time, we moved. A few steps at first, with Kai wincing in pain, and dropping his full weight on me. "Hold on, buddy," I said, I don't know how many times. It was like a chant. "Hold on." I said it just as much to myself, to get my strength up under him. To make it into a jog.

I could sense the hulks close in from above. Blasts fried the grass behind us. Atom's shield deflected shots that would have hit the mark.

Kai gave out completely. All my strength couldn't keep us on our feet. We ate dirt. The smell of fresh grass flooded my senses. It was like every hydroponic herb I'd ever smelled and yet none of them. It was pure and simple and nothing like anything I knew and somehow ordinary. It was life. And I had the thought, *At least I will die smelling this.*

We took the pounding of what had to be dozens of mini-gun shots raining on us in a staccato thunder.

Only, we were still alive.

I rolled to see that a sort of blue energy bubble had formed around us.

Atom kneeled above us like a samurai, with his arms folded across a blue glow from within his chest. I realized what he'd done. He was drawing on his antimatter reserves to project an energy shield. The hulks had closed in, we were squarely in the kill zone, but for now, the plasma rounds could not penetrate Atom's barrier.

The hulks persisted. All we could see was the intense orange cores and yellow outflows of the firing squad. The rounds sizzled against the energy bubble in angry explosions of raw, blinding light, as though we were in the eye of a bursting supernova.

"We're surrounded," I said. "That simplifies our problem."

"Thomas. Are we dead?"

"Imminently so."

Then, the sky broke.

A screech from above ripped through the sound of the blasts. A large shadow fell over the firing squad of hulks, moving fast.

An explosion shook the earth. It blew through a line of hulks, tossing them like two-ton popcorn, leaving a crater in the dirt.

"The fuck?" said Kai, the sound banging in my ears.

The shadow kept coming, and I saw the ship.

"It's us!" I shouted.

The *Aquarius* dove and launched a second cruise missile, cleaving through another line of hulks, scattering them across the field.

"Woo-hoo!" shouted Kai, waving as the spaceship passed overhead, soared into the dark of Unending Night the way we'd come, vanished on that horizon before roaring back like a dive bomber, turret cannons and missiles ripping the hulks apart.

It rained death on the hulks in gales like an act of the Abrahamic God. The instant Atom felt imminent danger pass, he whipped into kill mode, high wave laser carving up the hulks that remained.

The *Aquarius* went into low hover mode above the field of steaming hulks. The landing hatch opened. The entry ramp separated from the underside of the ship, slowly revealing a figure, boots first.

Kai groaned in pain with the effort to sit up. I had a strange feeling of déjà vu.

". . . You ready for this?"

". . . You?"

CHAPTER SEVENTEEN

The figure stepped forward, one foot dangling off the ramp, holding on by a strap. He extended a hand as the slanting light hit his face.

"Come," he said. "Hurry."

"My god." I rose to my feet.

"What?" Kai asked, hooking my arm to help him up.

"Dad?"

My father stared at me, his expression like seeing a vaguely familiar stranger. A face you think you've seen, somewhere before, but never like this, never in real life.

"Dad," I said again.

Though it had been forty years, I knew him in an instant.

Because he'd barely aged.

He looked different, for sure. He'd grown a beard. The buoyancy was gone. The Sinatra wink replaced by a long, spaghetti Western stare, like he was looking through me.

His squint tightened like a screw. His jaw cranked like he forgot the words he was about to say. He stood before the intense glare of the natural suns, and we squinted back. His *Aquarius* cut a long shadow across the field. The *Aquarius I*, I realized.

"Q-Quentin?" he said like he'd made a wild guess and plucked a random name from the stars.

"Dad," I said.

And I was twelve.

I actually had to check my hands and arms to make sure I only felt like I was twelve and hadn't time traveled inside my own body like Antman in *Endgame*. The way shit was going lately, seemed like anything could happen.

"Quick," he said, pushing through his confusion. "They will come."

The *Aquarius I* eased forward, stabilized by repulsor lifts. I hooked under Kai's arm. Dad leaned out and took my hand. He heaved us up to the landing ramp as Kai bled on the floor. Atom leaped after us with a nimble clang. The ramp closed back inside the ship as the *Aquarius I* spiked up to the sky, speeding from the field of carcass hulks. I caught a glimpse of Elysium's tri-vaulted lights and wondered if I would ever see it again. The ramp sealed and we were in the hangar of the *Aquarius I*. Clean, industrial, artificial light, like normal. I touched the air lock, thankful to be alive.

My father looked in the eyes of his grown-up son.

I'm guessing most fathers imagine what their kid will be like at their age. You'd probably think about what kind of man he'll be, how you'd measure up. Taller? Shorter? Will he walk like me? Think like me? Will he carry some of my essence into the next generation? But these are idle thoughts. Imaginings of a question you'll never see answered. Because for you to be one age, *your son has to be younger*. In that instant, my father had an answer to that question as no father has had before. We were physically about the same age.

I had no idea what he thought beyond utter shock. His

face was rock-like and frosty. Wary, like he was trying to see through a trick.

"Dad," I said, unable to help myself from going in for the hug.

Despite the beard and the hard suspicion behind his eyes, he was as familiar as a photograph you check at least once a day.

Except for one thing.

"You're short," I blurted.

"We're about"—he held me by my shoulders, at arm's length to see me better—"the same." A half-smile popped and I heard 1930s pop music like the crooning soundtrack of my memories of him.

"Maybe. But last time I saw you, you were twice my size."

Kai groaned from the ground.

"Sorry! This is Private William Kai—"

"And he needs medical attention—" Kai moaned.

"—and he needs medical attention immediately, yes," I agreed.

"Pleased to meet you," Kai said feebly, and extended a hand.

My father took it.

"This is Captain Christopher Smith," I said. "My dad."

"*Smith*? Not Thomas?" Kai blurted.

"Your mom's name?" my father asked.

"Uh, yeah. This is awkward."

My father's attention was drawn over my shoulder.

"No big deal," I went on, "just when you left, you were so well-known. I was starting this new education block and I didn't want to hear it all the time."

"It's okay, Quentin." He pressed the com button on the hangar console. "We need a med unit stat."

Christopher Smith's shift into captain mode happened so fast it gave me whiplash.

His gaze had fixed on Atom. "A 301 guardian, fully functional," he whispered in grim astonishment, like this was the name of some forsaken god.

"Atom," Atom said, swapping out a grappling hook for his hand and extending a traditional Olde Earth handshake.

"You have a name?"

The interior hangar doors opened and a woman with dark brown skin, braided hair, and cheekbones of steel entered. Like Grace Jones's character from *Destroyer* had a friendlier kid sister. She pushed a hovering med-unit chair.

"Quentin, this is Lt. Camron Ripley."

I nodded to her and said, "Captain Thomas," as my father and I stooped to help Kai into the med chair.

"Private William Kai." He extended a hand with a dreamy half-grin. The med unit hissed with the release of a pain management vapor directly into Kai's airways.

Ripley held his gaze and smiled. She reached into the collar of Kai's suit.

"And hello to you too," said Kai.

Then a knife snapped open in her hand.

"The fuck?"

Captain Smith's hand clamped down on my shoulder.

"Hold still," said Ripley.

She slashed an opening on the inside of Kai's shirt and made another couple of cuts, and removed a small device.

"You are welcome on board," Ripley told Kai. "She is not."

"Is that—Thalia?" I asked.

"You're next," said Cap Chris Smith.

Ripley brought the knife toward me with a look of semi-amusement. She quickly cut Thalia's memory and processor unit from my suit. She brought the two tiny devices over to the cargo hatch. She opened the seal and dropped the Thalia units into the exterior, hatch. She sealed up the interior and opened the exterior and released the micro units into the void. Thalia was effectively spaced.

"Sorry. That was necessary before we go any further. Now we can talk. Let's take the private to medbay."

I followed Ripley through the corridors of the *Aquarius I*, not so different from my *Aquarius III*.

"So I take it we don't trust Thalia anymore?" I ventured.

Ripley laughed.

"Thalia," said my father, shaking his head.

"It's a joke. You get it?" Ripley asked me.

"Don't think so," I said.

"Me neither," said Kai.

"You have to understand how they think," said Cap Smith. "Tha-lia? *The liar.*"

"The liar? Wait, what is she lying about?" I asked.

"Everything."

CHAPTER EIGHTEEN

Where do I start?" asked my dad, sitting on a backless stool in the sterile medbay like a doctor delivering bad news.

I could tell by his mannerisms that what he had to say was important. But I was distracted. Here was my father, barely aged a day. Like a memory made real. Like you took a photo off our digital wall deck, tapped it with a magic wand like the Blue Fairy, and made him animate.

"The beginning?" Kai suggested. The med unit had reclined all the way, lifting Kai's legs flat and raising his back at an angle. A diagnostic sensor shined infrared light along the damage to his face as the tubes in his nose fed medication.

Ripley and I sat on med supply crates as my dad talked.

"It started in 2049 when the nuke collided with the super train tunnel."

"Okay, maybe not that far back?" I suggested.

"Trust me, it's relevant here," he reassured. "Upon poisoning our oceans, mankind was thrown into an immediate fight for its own survival. That's the story you know."

"Right. And the Ultra 85 formed to create the Babel Space Station to save humanity and look for a habitable planet," I said.

"So you think. You see, the planet Paradise had already been discovered by privatized Space travel in the early 2000s, known only to a few select shareholders, and documented as uninhabitable. In 2031 the heads of the eighty-five wealthiest families met in secret to discuss the fate of humanity. But not the altruists and benevolent geniuses that we thought they were. Oil money, tech money, all the money that ran the world. A sort of sick and twisted rich version of the UN got together and formed the ultimate secret society. They branded themselves as the Elite, and eventually Ultra. And on February 23, 2031, the Order of the Ultra 85 was founded."

"Wait a minute, you're saying—"

"The Ultra 85 already knew about Paradise," said Ripley.

"In 2050, Babel reached a viable distance from the wormhole to Paradise to man regular transports. That's when everything changed. Once the Ultras were safe on Paradise, they launched an asteroid attack on Babel."

"The Blitz Extremis?" I asked.

"But that killed millions," said Kai.

"Precisely."

"Come on," I said. "What kind of Edgelord fantasy is this?"

"I wish this was a fantasy," Ripley assured us. "I really do."

Dad went on, the diagnostician. "The Blitz was an excuse to form the Great Realignment. To exert total control over the remaining population of Babel. To turn the space station into a slave incubator. Meanwhile, the thousands of people accompanying the Ultras to Paradise were fooled. They were promptly enslaved by the Ultra 85."

"Excuse me," Kai spoke up. "Did you just say *slave* incubator?"

"Heard right, Private. How else to build their super city,

Elysium? A holy fantasy of the elite where there were no poor, no lower or middle or even upper class. There would forever only be the Ultra and those they enslaved."

Kai and I stared at each other full of doubt, suspicion, and that vague nagging fear that accompanies a nasty truth.

Ripley nodded. "Over the years the population of Elysium grew due to genetic engineering, cloning, and slave surrogacy. Their initial batch of slaves was insufficient to meet the needs of the Ultras."

"The lottery system was created to select the best and brightest of us . . ."

"To be enslaved?" I asked. "You can't be serious."

"Serious as an air lock," said my dad with a thousand-yard Leone stare so long you could hear the Morricone track.

"You mean everyone that got picked, that whole row of pictures in the Halls of Attainment—"

"All slaves."

"That's where I knew that cyborg dude from," said Kai. "I played intramurals against him, had a mean drop-step."

"Wait," I said, my brain hurting. "Then everyone manning those hulks we destroyed . . ."

"I know, Quentin," said my dad, my name sounding odd from his mouth. "It's not easy to live with. If it gives you any peace, the UMD—"

"Ultra Military Division," said Ripley.

"—they aren't the people they were on Babel. They have been overwritten. Recoded with a lust for shedding blood."

"By Thalia," Ripley added.

"What?" said Kai, his voice lilting. "You mean our girl, Thalia?"

"I'm sorry, Private. She's not what you thought she was."

Kai adjusted himself with a grunt. "She has been acting funny styles since we got here. Remember she couldn't even detect this whole-ass planet?"

"As long as your *Aquarius* AI unit was outside of the central Babel network, she would retain certain functions, including serving you and keeping you alive," my dad explained. "But if she got close to the Paradise central network, that might override her. Or, the opposing directives might cause her to freeze."

"'Opposing directives'?" Kai repeated.

"Meaning," I said, "our ship's directive was to keep us alive, conflicting with the Paradise network directive, to kill us."

"Ah. Got it. Our girl got a kite to murk us."

"Makes sense," I said, feeling like barely a corner of my understanding had been filled in. "But . . ."

"Ask anything you want, Quentin. I know this is a lot to take in."

"What's your story—Dad? How do you know all this? How did any of this happen? How old are you?"

My dad and Ripley exchanged a look heavy with meaning. They were a stranded pair that could communicate with a glance. "There's no precise answer, Quentin. Between time in cryosleep, I'm the equivalent of about fifty-seven years old."

"Give or take a birthday," added Ripley.

"I'm fifty-two," I said. "Sorry, this is fucking weird."

The medbay door snapped open. There stood a militarized cyborg with a command unit fixed to his face, six red circular points of a rotary barrel for eyes.

CHAPTER NINETEEN

Whoa!" Kai shouted.

I snapped up off my seat.

"It's okay!" My dad jumped out front. "He's okay! He's with us. Quentin, Private Kai, meet Sgt. Sean Halliday."

Sgt. Halliday's nose and mouth were human, but his head was dominated by a chunky chrome console unit.

"Pleased to meet . . . you," said Halliday without expression.

Kai breathed deep, hand over his heart.

"Sir," Sgt. Halliday addressed my father. "We've cleared the planet's atmosphere."

"Thank you, Sergeant. Feel free to take us to orbit Moon Q2."

"Copy that, Captain."

Sgt. Halliday turned on his boot heel and left.

"I can explain," said my dad. "See, Sgt. Halliday was also selected my Choosing year, along with Ripley and a gunnery sergeant named Sullivan. We were all good Babelonians, upstanding members of the IMC, true believers in the intergenerational mission to sustain life on Babel, explore the galaxy, and protect the colony on Paradise. We were proud to be selected. Dream come true."

Bile from my empty stomach jumped in my throat, causing me to clear it. Maybe louder than necessary.

"We boarded the *Aquarius I*," my dad went on, "preprogrammed with a flight plan to Paradise. We went down for cryosleep full of hopes and dreams of the City of Stars. Only there was a malfunction in my sleep pod. I awoke to planetfall on Elysium's spaceport."

"Wait, so you skipped the wormhole part?" Kai asked.

"Wormhole?" asked my dad.

"What wormhole?" chimed in Ripley.

"Guess we've got our own story to tell," I replied. "There's a wormhole that leads to Paradise. We found it."

"Wide-awake," said Kai, demonstrating with his eyes.

"That makes so much sense," said Ripley.

"Why we could never find any trace of a recognizable solar system," added my dad.

"Yeah, I guess with the cryosleep, usually travelers bound for Paradise are not awake for the experience."

"Facts," said Kai.

"What happened?" my dad prodded. "What was it like? The event horizon? Was there spaghettification?"

"There was spaghet—shit, linguinification, fettuccinification," said Kai. "Cap Smith, now I *know* you and Thomas are related. Can we get back to your story?"

"You awoke from cryosleep to planetfall," I prompted.

"Right. It was quite a sight. Incandescent colors washing into view. Orange, red, and white glows like a warm embrace. I enjoyed a hot cup of insta-coffee as we moved through these gorgeous hues of atmosphere and touched down amidst the first honest sunrise I'd seen in my entire life. I would have awoken Ripley and Halliday. If only I'd known what was coming."

"Ah, fuck." Kai nudged me. "Shit 'bout to go down."

I shushed him.

"Elysium's cyborgs boarded the *Aquarius*," said my dad. "By the time I reached the cryosleep units, the cyborgs had brought bins full of replacement mecha parts—microchipped eyes, face-plate consoles, bionic arms and legs. The UMD cyborgs had already applied cables and tubes into Sullivan's chamber. They were in the process of loading gear into Halliday's. Mechanized cables found Halliday and inserted themselves into his skull. I would learn the process is called 'reprogramming' or 'reprog,' to turn people into 'programs' or 'progs.'"

"Shit," said Kai, "my mans, what did you do?"

"I went to war. Snatched a firearm and shredded the cyborgs."

"Damn. That's tough."

"I woke up Ripley, only it was too late for Sullivan. He burst from his chamber fully reprogrammed and tried to subdue us 'rogue NPCs.' It was either him or us. I had to put him down."

"Wow. Intense," I said, starting to get my head around what my dad had been through, and how it changed him. "Fucking nightmare."

"That's exactly what it was," said Ripley. "I have dreams like none of this is real. That we visit Elysium, as we thought it would be."

"Me as well," said my dad. "I dream of bright sunshine and green grass. Not the Elysium lit up with alarms that we found."

"You got inside the city?" I asked.

"We did. We should have jumped back into the *Aquarius* right then and there. But we had to see the city for ourselves. It was glorious—like our old renderings of twenty-first century Dubai meets Ancient Rome. At least it seemed so, fast as we moved through, running and hiding from UMD sirens. 'Escaped NPCs on the loose!'"

"I heard that," said Kai. "How they gonna call us NPCs? They the fucking cyborgs, damn."

"Red lights flashed in the town squares; a shelter-in-place order was issued to the city's inhabitants. Ripley and I explored the City of Stars as fugitives on the run from Ultra Military Division cyborgs on a Blade Runner hunt. We fought our way through the capital, and holed up at a reprog center. That's when we discovered the truth about Paradise."

"More like Inferno," said Ripley.

"Elysium exists to serve the Ultra 85. All those familiar names from *The Ultranomicon* that grace the rostra and memorials on Babel? The Overdecks and Dangermonds and DoerrMoores?"

"Bastards," Ripley snarled.

"Every last one of them," my dad confirmed.

"Wait—even the *Bondermans*?" I asked. Somehow I could accept the others were monsters, but not our founding father.

"They're gone," said my dad. "Relegated. Liquidated to make room for a DestrehanLeblanc alliance spin-off family."

"'Relegated'?" asked Kai.

"For reprogramming," my dad explained. "Same thing they do to us. Relegated for reprogramming to serve as 'progs' or slaves to cater to the needs of the Ultra 85. When we arrive at Elysium, we are biogenically altered and our minds overwritten with Thalia's AI to exclusively serve a purpose on Elysium— whether as UMD security forces, housekeepers, chefs—even dog walkers and pet groomers."

"Fam. They got doggies more important than people down there?"

"Damn right," said Ripley.

CHAPTER TWENTY

The Ultra 85 looked at the history of mankind on Earth and decided that automation signaled the end of humanity," said my dad. "The heights of civilization depended on human slave labor to thrive. There could be no Babylon, no Egypt, no Rome, no USA without slaves. The Ultra 85 had set their chattel slaves out on an impossible mission on the Babel Space Station to groom generations of replacements to serve the future growth of the Ultra 85. We knew then there was no Paradise, not for us. The idea itself was an illusion the Ultras used to control us. After a nasty firefight, we boarded back on the *Aquarius*, deprogrammed Thalia out of Halliday's system, and took off. We had no coordinates for Babel and no fuel to search, but home for us was the stars. On Paradise, there was nothing but slavery and death. So I set the *Aquarius* to stasis mode in the orbit of the second moon over Endless Night and we went down for cryosleep . . ."

"Only to be woken by us," I said. "Forty years later."

"Wait, what?" said Kai. "It's our part the story? My bad if I'm slow, these painkillers are dumb strong."

"When you and I jumped through that wormhole, we smashed into the *Aquarius I*, waking Cap Smith and crew, who turned around and saved us from the Ultras' Military Division."

"Okay. Damn. You just put all that together?" Kai asked.

I shrugged. "The pieces fit."

"So we're letting go of the whole 'alternate us' theory?"

"What's that?" asked Ripley.

"When we first saw you, another *Aquarius* starship in this unfamiliar star system, I may have theorized an alternate dimension, multiverse situation. In my defense, my psyche was fresh off the experience of being disintegrated and reintegrated by the wormhole. Not entirely sure everything made it back in its right place . . ."

"You're not far from the mark, Quentin," said my dad. "Not about the alternate-reality idea, but about waking us up. The collision brought us out of cryosleep. We were pretty confused ourselves."

"Especially when you hit us with that tow cable," said Ripley.

"We were approaching the wormhole," I explained. "Our thrusters were non-responsive."

"The tow cable was an inspired move," said my dad with a nod.

"Forced us back into the Paradise gravity well," said Ripley.

"Unintentionally, I assure you. But I don't understand something. Why forty years?" I asked. "Why cryosleep for so long?"

"It wasn't forty years," said my dad. "Not at first. When we fled the atmosphere of Paradise, we were sure they would follow us and try to destroy the *Aquarius*. But they didn't."

"They'd come eventually though, right?" asked Kai.

"They would have had a fight on their hands," said Ripley. "They didn't, couldn't have star pilots of our caliber. We figured they were gearing up."

"But they never came," my dad finished her thought. "We tried to find a way home. Tried to communicate with . . . Babel."

"Wait . . . *This is Captain Christopher Smith of the* Aquarius I—*Whatever you do, do not come knocking*—'"

"That was us."

"I heard that right when we came out the wormhole. Thought I was hallucinating my dad's voice!"

"The message data beam must have gotten tangled in the wormhole gravity folds."

"Is that why I heard my mama?" asked Kai.

"Coincidence, Kai. Your mom does not appear to be in this solar system."

"Copy."

"But wait—the year in the message, 2093? But you were Chosen in what, '75? When did you go down for cryosleep?"

"Which time?" asked Ripley.

"You went down more than once?"

My dad nodded. "In '75, we barely escaped the UMD with our lives. We figured if we hid in the orbit of the far moon, they'd have a hard time finding us. We had just enough power that, if we dedicated all of it to life support, we could wake up in five years—"

"Five?"

"—and have a better shot at survival."

"Five, at first," said Ripley. "We thought, what're the two constants of human civilization? Time and change. The world of the Ultra 85 was a crime against humanity—it's fucking slavery or genocide or both, I can't decide. We thought, give them time. They will change."

"And you gave them time . . . ," Kai said.

"And they didn't change," said my dad. "They grew bigger,

stronger. We attempted more infiltration missions, always failures. All their resources went into their city, their lifestyle. Into perfecting Thalia's ability to control every aspect of their lives. We'd retreat to orbit, where it was always safe. They didn't care about Space anymore. Space-life made you inhuman, to them. It became part of their sick, twisted rationale for reprog."

"If you grew up in Space, your life wasn't worth spit," Ripley clarified.

"We studied the cyborg gear they implanted into Sullivan and Halliday. They'd enslaved their scientists—they had to. They overwrote the individuality of everyone outside the Ultra 85. On Elysium, there was no one to be curious. We were safe in orbit. Where we were born, bred. Nowhere else."

"So you went back to cryosleep," I said.

"Rinse, wash, repeat," said my dad. "We'd set a new clock, and hope that the long arc of the moral universe would indeed bend toward justice. We'd return. Witness the evolution of this sad spectacle. The Ultras' kids would grow up. Sort of. They'd clone versions of themselves at preferable ages. Cloning was probably better than procreating, since with eighty-five families, they'd inbreed in no time."

"Or they'd knock up their progs," said Ripley with sad disgust. "And have a child that was then master of their mother."

"A new batch of servants would come from Babel," said my dad. "That was their only use for the stars. We'd attempt our raids. Go after intel, try and disrupt the city AI, every few years. After a while, they named us Ghost Ops. The Ultras feared us. We did some damage, but never got very far. And nothing ever changed. Paradise just got worse."

CHAPTER TWENTY-ONE

Kai passed out with a euphoric grin. I wished him good dreams.

I was slightly jealous of his peace of mind. My body was tired, too—unbearably so. But my spirit was racing.

It was the collision of the familiar and the unfamiliar. Things I knew so well—my dad, the interior of the *Aquarius*—smashed against an impossible reality. The Babel Space Station was a holding cell. The Ultra 85, our Founding Fathers, were monsters. There was no Paradise—not in the meaning of the word.

Even the med unit of the *Aquarius I* was strange to me. The panel screens had these old-school rectangles with rounded edges. My *Aquarius III* screens were sleeker, sharper. My hallway floodlights were set to a cool blue; this was a pale, ominous green.

Oh, and the story of the world as I knew it was a blunt-force lie.

A crude fantasy was stuffed into my mouth like cereal to a child, scoop by scoop, and it went down about as easy.

Or did it?

Maybe on some level, I knew. Maybe that's what these Expeditions with Kai have been about all these years. Those marathons into Olde Earth culture were the true interdimensional travels. I was imagining worlds and having thoughts that Babel did not intend for me to have. Maybe that's how I was challenging the narrative.

All at once, the hopes represented by those adventures in multitudes ceased to be. There was no James Bond Riviera for us to stroll, no Hollywood Boulevard to cruise. But the memory of those things was a part of me now. The aspirations and worldviews of hundreds of protagonists. The reliable way their respective stories challenged their preconceived notions. Maybe all those plot twists trained me not to hold on to any notion too fiercely. Once a premise defines a character, it's stripped away.

In the movies, it always feels inevitable. I guess that's the difference. Maybe intellectually I challenged the narrative. But emotionally, this felt like a broken leg I was still using to walk. I read once that the hero's quest is one that he is ready for. I guess that's how I know I'm not a hero. I wasn't ready for any of this shit. Just because I was adjusting the rug doesn't mean I was ready for it to be pulled out from under me. The story of Babel was, I realized, a pillar of my personality. If I was compliant, it's because compliance was necessary for the mission. If I was efficient, it's because only an efficient species could survive Space. If I was a leader, it's because we needed strong leadership to find a habitable environment. As it turned out, those qualities were bred in me for a much different purpose. To make me easy to erase.

If the story of Babel was a fraud, then so was I.

These thoughts, blended with the queasy rush of complex and contradictory emotions of being with my father, with about 10gs of exhaustion weighing me down, made my mind an incomprehensible jumble of vague yet horrific notions.

My father took me by the arm. He began to say something, to try and grab my attention from what I assume was a vacant stare to nowhere, when he paused at the feel of my bicep.

"My boy," he marveled, freely squeezing, measuring the girth and firmness of my muscles.

I shrugged. "Just Mess Master IMC rations and regular zero-g yoga." I flexed a bit to assure myself my arms were as ordinary as I recalled. "Nothing special."

"Quentin. Last time I saw you I could fit my whole hand around your arm like a Viking ring."

"Wow."

"For me, that was the equivalent of, I don't know, a few years ago."

"Okay. Sure, that's weird. Damn."

"I guess you've had a lot longer to get used to me being gone," he said.

"Yeah."

I wanted to say something more. But all comprehensible language fled my mind in that moment. Sometimes, feelings can be bigger, messier than even words.

"You must be exhausted. I'm still waking up," he said.

He noticed Ripley had this big, beaming smile.

"What?" he said.

"Just, I'm glad you've gotten to see him," she told my dad. He grunted. "He talked about you so much, Quentin," she told me. There was warmth in her voice; a little like how you'd speak to a child.

"That's . . . that's nice," I said. But he didn't seem that happy to see me.

"You need sleep," my dad said. "We've got plenty of empty quarters and beds."

"I honestly don't think I could sleep now, thanks. I'm just, processing." I thought of when my *Aquarius III* Thalia's system had two opposing realities vying for the same space, and she stopped responding. "Buffering, or something."

"I know what that's like," said Atom.

My father turned and gazed at Atom's screen as though looking deep into the eyes of an old friend. "What an odd observation. What sort of behavior references have you given him?"

"It's a long story," I said. Atom's personality was so influenced by Kai's Catalog that my dad caught it right away. I realized, even after all these new revelations, I didn't want to admit to him my time watching movies from the Forbidden Catalog. I wanted him to respect me as a fellow captain. "I think I'm about tapped out on long stories."

He grunted, a flicker in his eye like he wanted to push the matter further. Then Ripley gave him a look. "You must need food, then. Come to mess. I'll fix you something."

My dad was the consummate man of purpose. He could not sit still. If something needed to be done, he would do it. If nothing needed to be done, he would do something anyway.

In the mess hall, my dad worked the special switches on the Mess Master Eats to fix up a protein fruits analog shake. The approximations of creamy strawberry and tangy orange juices exploded in my mouth, and after a few sips I felt fuller, better.

"That's the way with kids. I used to say, 'Nine times out of ten, he's either tired or hungry.'"

"I'm not exactly a kid," I said. I wanted to call him "Dad" but choked on the word. "We kind of skipped that part."

"Some things about being a father, you don't forget so quickly."

"Probably a selective memory thing. But, *Dad*." I stressed the word, auditioning the sound in these strange surroundings. "It's great to see you. Weird—but, fucking great."

He held a hard gaze at me. This felt like the first time he'd let himself look at me for more than a couple seconds. "Quentin. I never thought I'd see you again."

"Yeah. I know the feeling."

"I missed forty years of your life. And it was all for a lie." His voice cracked.

Over the years I'd rehearsed a thousand futile conversations with the ghost of my father. It was hard to sit there by that countertop and stay in the moment. This was *Dad*, the actual human being. I had imagined how in clear, concise, devastating terms I would eviscerate him for leaving me while simultaneously earning his respect *and* demonstrating my respect for his accomplishments. But now that the time was here, I didn't even want any of that to happen.

Most people reach an age where they are able to see their parents as people. But when you lose a parent young, you're robbed of that experience. You're stuck with that last impression, and that says more about whether you're six or eight or sixteen than it says about your absent parent. This was my dad, ace captain, engineer, hero, programmer. One of the Chosen.

I never got to understand my father as a human being.

Not until this moment.

I'd never fantasized that he might acknowledge me with a few words. But it turns out, that was all I'd really wanted. *I missed forty years of your life for a lie.*

"You thought—*we* thought you were doing the right thing," I said.

"We were fools."

"Well, yeah. We didn't know what we didn't know."

"Is that good enough?"

I shrugged. "It's the truth. Deception has a way of seeming obvious in the rear view."

"I guess I've had more time to think about it. And years of cryosleep to dream about it."

"I'm sorry, Dad. It's just, you. I never imagined you like this."

"Like what?"

"Like, bearded. Going against the system, talking all rebellious."

"We never imagined a lot of things on Babel. That was part of the problem."

"I mean, yeah, we've been lied to and betrayed, that's big, like, heat-death-of-the-universe big. But it's that it's *you*. I talked to you a lot, in my head, over the years. I had different things to say, depending on what was going on with me. You were always there. Like, over my shoulder, reading my journal. Always saying, 'Stay true. The Cause is worth it.'"

"I wanted to believe."

"But that's not it, Dad. I had it all wrong. You never said it. You never told me to stay true."

"I've had some time to think about the great lie. Since planetfall forty years ago, I've been at war. Each time, we fought until we broke. Surrendered to cryosleep. In all that, my biggest regret, Quentin, is you. It's one thing for me to give my life to the lie. But I gave yours, too."

"Dad, don't—"

"Listen, I've had time to think about what I'd say to you as well. For me, it's maybe less complicated. It's—I fucked up. I'm sorry, Quentin."

There wasn't anything left to do but father-son hug.

But he stopped me.

"But my only peace was in knowing you were safe, on Babel. Not stuck between endless orbit and enslavement. Cryosleep versus pitched battle. Going to war, murdering reprogrammed versions of your old friends. It's no kind of life, here. On Babel, you can live a full—"

"Lie."

"When the truth is this fucked, who gives a shit about a lie?"

That one took me a moment. "I'm sorry, Dad. Until today I don't think I've heard you utter a curse in my whole life. Look, all this is hitting me really heavy right now. I'm a proper star captain and all, but shit, Dad, it's been a fuck of a day. If this is all really real, if this is you and not some dimensional trickery or hallucination, I'm going to need a father-son hug, fuck."

Chest to chest, heads side by side, his scent broke a flood of memories. Physical memories, like my body could recall being small enough to fit in his hand, play on his lap, ride on his shoulders.

Simultaneously, this strange feature of us being about the same age, size, and body type—like some long-lost twins. I thought, maybe the alternate-us theory wasn't so far off after all.

It was awkward and familiar, like so much of what was going on, contradictory and comfortable, impossible and plainly happening.

"I love you, Quentin," he said. A well of tears surprised his eyes. "I wish you weren't here."

CHAPTER TWENTY-TWO

19 Hours to Midnight

When I woke up, my first thought was to ask Thalia how long I'd slept.

It took another ten, fifteen seconds to snap back to reality.

I had slept on a lower bed in the bunkroom. As I came to, sat up, and set my feet on the floor, the lights flickered on. I wondered how they'd rigged the ship to function without Thalia. On my *Aquarius III*, she managed everything from lights to the Mess Master to intuitive gravity controls.

Suddenly my senses were stormed by the aroma of fresh ground coffee. With the lightness of the gravity setting, I damn near floated to the mess on the scent, toes wiggling like an Olde Earth cartoon.

Mess had a digital clock rigged above the countertop that read 08:12. So I'd slept about ten hours. Atom sat at the table. My dad greeted me with a steaming cup of coffee.

"Black, one sugar?" he said with a question at the end, like—this is how I take it, do you?

"Sounds about right," I said, and inhaled the steam as I took a sip. "Wow, this is—*wow*," I said, and sipped again.

"One of our Elysium raid missions. Didn't find a way home,

but we did bag some coffee beans. Beats that synthetic pow-dered stuff on Babel, huh?" he said with a smile that brought a familiar old blue-eyed twinkle.

Atom was also holding a steaming coffee mug.

"Hope you had a restful sleep, Captain sir," said Atom. "These hot, wake-up beans are invigorating."

"Atom, how are you—are you *drinking*?"

"Captain, sir—"

"Please, Quentin."

"Captain Quentin, the aroma is enough stimulation for me," said Atom.

"For us, taste and smell are interconnected. For Atom, it's the same thing," said my father.

"An extension of my highly refined mineral detection," said Atom.

"He wanted to hold it," said Dad. "He made all these poses. Hand on his hip, reclining and sitting. Quentin, his behavior prompts are unlike anything I've encountered."

"How is Kai?" I asked. I addressed the more pressing con-cern and hoped to avoid the topic of Atom a while longer.

"He's going to be okay. Sleeping it off, like you. His wounds were nasty, but superficial. The med unit was able to seal the bleeding and begin to restore the burn trauma."

"Thank you," I said with relief.

Atom handed him back the steaming cup. My dad and I sipped our respective coffees. At a simultaneous glance, we clocked our twin grips and postures. We each held our shoul-ders back and brought the steam to our noses first, then lips, bending at the neck with curved backs. Something about how you sip a hot cup is unique to each individual—or so I'd thought. Apparently, it's unique to genetics.

As the heat and bite of flavor awoke my thoughts, I had so many questions about what was next. I wondered how many conversations about plans had happened while I'd slept. Were we stuck here, like the *Aquarius I* crew? Could we retrace our steps to the wormhole? Would it still be there? Would that even work?

The sound of Kai's laugh interrupted my thoughts.

"He sounds good," I said, and headed two doors down to the med unit.

Trills of Ripley's laughter mixed with Kai's. She was sitting at his side, listening to his story.

"... alarm clock beeping, Mom yelling, 'Get up! You late!' And I'm busting ass, seriously, like, can't get my feet in my pants, Moms popping off—"

"I can imagine—" Ripley said between guffaws.

"Yeah, I'm pretty sure I temporarily, like, ceased to exist—"

"But she was still reading you—"

"Yup, Betty Beatty Kai was still talking."

"Like, boy, you betta exist—"

"Exactly. Don't make me give birth to you twice, now."

There was a quick familiarity between Ripley and Kai that made my dad seem cold by comparison. I felt a wave of jealousy.

"Thomas! You're never going to believe this. Ripley here— she knew my moms!"

"She was always Betty Beatty to me."

"And look!" Kai flicked open a switchblade in his hand. "This was my mom's knife."

"Whoa—easy there, killer."

"It fits, right? Like, Mom's knife cut us free from Thalia's lies."

"She was pretty handy with that thing," said Ripley. "A

little something to thank me for the Catalog. I was surprised when she went for that Kai dude to be honest."

"Careful how you talk about pa-dukes now," Kai said.

"I'm saying, no offense but like forty years ago? Your pops was kinda square."

"Fam, everyone is square on Babel. We, like, are born that shape. Take Thomas here—you shoulda seen how square he was, 'til I introduced him to your Catalog."

"Wait—*your* Catalog?" I blurted.

"I'm the one slipped it to Betty, when I left," she said with a proud grin and a sly wink.

"Okay. Wow. So wait. Does my father know about it, then?"

"Sure," said Ripley. "I mean, he had his favorites. Crazy for war movies."

"Wait, he had access to the entire Catalog—and all he watched was war movies?" I asked.

"I didn't just watch war movies," my dad said from the hallway behind me.

"Excuse me," said Ripley. "You stayed *Saving Private Ryan* status."

"Just like on Babel—remember, you used to take me to see *Von Ryan's Express*?"

"Helps to remember," said my dad. "We're not the first to fight a war for humanity."

"Helps to forget sometimes, too," said Ripley.

"Funny you should mention," said Kai. "We went on this whole expedition in the first place just to forget—damn. To forget about Bonita . . ."

I'd seen Kai's mood shift many times around thoughts of Bonita. But never like this. As if there'd never be any such thing as joy ever again.

"Who's Bonita?" asked Ripley.

"My ol' girl," said Kai at about the same time. "She was Chosen, earlier this year."

"Oh Kai, I'm so sorry."

"Yeah, shit hits different, now," said Kai.

"There's always hitting back," said Cap Smith.

"Chris," said Ripley, "can we let the boy's flesh heal before enlistment, please?"

"He's already enlisted. And he's not a boy, Ripley."

"Yes he is. Just like your boy. They're all boys."

"Come on, Rip. They're damn near our same age."

"Everyone on Babel is a kid, Chris. They never left the nest—they can't, for Christ's sake."

"What exactly are we talking about here?" Kai asked.

"The same debate we've had for forty off and on years," said Ripley. "Whether to hit Elysium, or—"

"Hit the freezy sleeps," said Kai.

"It's never an easy call," said my father, holding his hands like, Look, I'm a reasonable man making a reasonable assessment. "Lots of factors."

"Right," said Ripley. "And those factors are profoundly different now than ever before."

"Yes. There's five of us now. And that much less power, that much bigger drain on life support. And we have a fully functional ATM-301 guardian."

"Howdy," said Atom.

"Rip, you know how I'd wished we had one of these before."

"Very good, Chris. Full sitrep before breakfast," snipped Ripley. "Sure you didn't leave anything out?"

"We having breakfast?" pined Kai.

"I've done some thinking," I confessed. "Although frankly,

I didn't even know I'd been thinking of this all along until this moment, when my sleeping processes revealed themselves to me—"

"Thomas, skip to the thought you wanted to share, please," said Kai patiently.

"Right. A couple bullet points to add. One being, Atom has about three gs of antimatter in storage. So power supply shouldn't be a problem for a few dozen millennia. And two, I think I can find the wormhole."

CHAPTER TWENTY-THREE

Everyone stopped to look at me like I'd pressed pause. The only one not surprised was Kai. My dad had this strange grin. His underbite jutted slightly forward. This may have been pride.

"Wait, *how much* antimatter?" said Ripley.

"It was quite a haul," said Kai.

"We chased this asteroid right to the wormhole. Had these crazy readings. Maybe connected to the wormhole—who knows? But yeah. Atom looked a bit different then. He extracted three gs of antimatter before we crashed up here."

"That is fantastic news," said Ripley.

"A lot to think about," said Cap Smith.

"I agree. We might want to take all this in. Chris, why don't you show your son around the ship?" Ripley suggested.

"I'm familiar with the *Aquarius*, Lieutenant," I said. "I was captain of my own."

"Is that right?" asked my dad.

"The *Aquarius III*. It was . . ."

"It exploded," Kai filled in. "Still kind of a sensitive subject."

"Right. Thank you, Kai."

"The ship was command issued?" asked my dad.

"I put in a special request for the *Aquarius*," I said with a shrug. "Actually delayed my commission almost a full star year."

"Come, have a look around," my dad said with a hand on my shoulder. "I've made some modifications."

"Kai, I can push you in the med chair," said Ripley.

"Professor X steez? Bet," said Kai. "Matter of fact, can I wrap a little blanky around my legs?"

"Are your legs cold?"

"Oh, nah," Kai mumbled.

A pleasant gravity setting greeted our footsteps entering the bridge. I saw right away how my dad had set up his pilot station and rigged the controls to function Thalia-free. Halliday sat at the first-officer chair. From behind, he might be wearing a large helmet. When he turned to greet us, his human features stopped at the bridge of his nose. I had seen his face console once before, but it was no less startling the second time. Metal was welded across the midpoint of his cheekbone. A bulbous, chrome-plated dome ballooned from there, and where his eyes would be was a circle of lit points like a rotary gun barrel. I have no idea the purpose, only that when the points lit up red, it was scary as fuck.

"How's the coast look?" asked Cap Smith.

"Negative trace of UMD ordnance," said Halliday.

"Proceed, Sergeant," said my dad.

"Nice to meet you, Sergeant," I said, and extended a hand. "Captain Quentin Thomas."

He turned to me, blankly. His eye points rotated a click.

"Shake the captain's hand, Sergeant," my dad said in a soft voice.

Halliday extended a stiff handshake.

"Sergeant Halliday has some . . . limitations," explained Ripley. "We weren't able to fully recover him from reprogramming."

"Damn," said Kai. "Is he, like, a person?"

"Of course he's a fucking person," snapped my father.

"My bad—this is pretty new to me."

"Yes, he's a person," confirmed Ripley. "He has preferences. His responses to experience stimuli are basically normal."

"What do you mean?" I asked. "Does he tell you what he likes and doesn't like?"

"Not exactly," said my dad. "There are involuntary response signals. Heart rate, perspiration. He fidgets. Taps his heel when he's excited."

"It's like, leftover neurological data," I said.

"Only his higher mind functions were overwritten to be replaced by Thalia's AI," said my dad. "A series of programs that managed his behavior based on conditions and directives. We got rid of those. But what was there before is still gone."

"So, he needs directives," I said. "Or he doesn't know what to do."

My father grunted.

"Nobody likes it. But yeah," said Ripley. "He's highly capable. But if we don't tell him what to do, he just won't do."

"Fascinating," escaped my lips.

"Not the word I'd use," said Kai.

I moved in closer to examine Halliday's headgear, sensing the absence of social cues around eye contact. A series of riveted curved plates built the shape of the dome. The edges of the metal alloy dug painfully in his flesh, like it might be soldered to bone. The back of the headpiece continued down an exo-spine beneath his flight suit, with metal spikes replicating the natural nerve endings. "It's like the hardware took full control of his nervous system."

"He's a person," my dad reasserted.

"I mean, if he has some neurological responses, there's some of him left. Maybe more could be extracted. Like, what if he was, I don't know, backed up before the overwrite?"

"Possible. We never got deep enough into Thalia's system to find out," said Ripley. "We barely even knew Halliday, before they erased him."

"Makes you never stop hating them," said Cap Smith.

Kai zoned out, staring past Halliday.

Next, we hit the armory. This room was the most different from my *Aquarius III*. We had a couple backup rifles and ammo here. My dad's version was twice its size and full of fleets of weapons and gadgetry at various stages of readiness. More guns than I'd ever seen in my life. Cluster guns, chain guns, grenade launchers, hail stingers, jet rifles, light revolvers. There were even prototypes of vehicles, bikes, suits of armor, ship parts repurposed in the most imaginative ways.

"Dad, this is insane."

"This is my workshop. The best ideas I could come up with from what's at hand."

"Wow," I said, admiring the work. "You put jets in this exosuit—like the Elysium hulks?"

"Tried to. Couldn't quite get the balance right."

"Is that—a missile launcher?" asked Kai.

"Adapted from the *Aquarius* backup ordnance, yeah. Too big, though, for us to use without the jet-reinforced exosuits. Atom could use it, though," he pointed out. "Gives us surface-to-air capacity. That, we haven't had."

"Q, you never told me your pops was Tony Stark, fam," said Kai.

"I didn't know. He had a lot of titles. Programmer, engineer, sure. He was always a star captain to me."

"Who's Tony Stark?" asked my dad.

"'Genius. Billionaire. Playboy. Philanthropist'," Atom recited.

My dad screwed his face to look at Atom. "That doesn't sound at all like me."

"Nah, Cap, he also built the ill weapons, magic-style. That's like you."

There was a story behind this array of makeshift ordnance. Countless hours of invention, execution, troubleshooting, working with what he had. The story of him going from the man I knew to the man before me. The True Believer had been replaced by the war dog.

We were a strange species of soldier on Babel. A survivalist military. The Enemy was real, sure—the vacuum has claimed a mind-boggling number of lives. But we never thought to try and kill it. We had to work with it, negotiate our existence on its terms. My father had found a more traditional enemy. Other beings. Entities that could be killed.

"May I hold that hail stinger?" I asked.

"Course." He cracked a grin.

"I mean, how'd you get all this stuff?" asked Kai.

My dad shrugged. "Some of it, scrapped off Elysium raids. Some is repurposed UMD ordnance. Trick is to get that stuff to work without Thalia's integration. She's tricky. She hides in the smallest functions. Like, trigger safeties, target sight corrections."

I weighed the weapon in my hands and set the stock to my

shoulder, eyeing the sights. I'd held nerfed versions so many times in training, it was invigorating to hold the real thing.

"Thalia works the sights for the UMD?" I asked.

"Something to do with how UMD heavy infantry process visual information. She's like a virus. Everywhere, in everything. Had to figure out how to make all this equipment dumb."

"State of the badass art," said Kai, taking the stinger from my hands and holding the stock to his hip. "Hey Ripley, don't worry. Me and my squad of ultimate badasses will protect you!"

Ripley laughed.

"More like the other way around," said Cap Smith. "Ripley has fifty-seven confirmed kills."

"It's a movie quote, Chris," said Ripley patiently.

"You've seen *Aliens*, right?" asked Kai.

My father shook his head. "You've all seen these movies, more than once?"

Kai, Ripley, and I all nodded.

"I was kind of named after the main character," Ripley said.

My dad shook his head. *What a fucking waste of time* was left unsaid.

"I mean, I understand," said Kai. "At first, I wasn't into all them Space movies. Like, I know Space, what I want with more Space? But then Quentin kept asking to watch more Space shit. I gave it a chance. Not gonna lie, jams like *Interstellar* kinda slap. Mad fun to, like, score all the Olde Space movies on shit they got right."

"One does not understand," said Atom, examining the spread of weaponry. "Where is the independently targeting particle-beam phalanx?"

"Um, what's that? Those words together mean nothing," said Cap Smith.

"A miss for James Cameron," said Kai.

"*Aliens*, again," said Ripley.

"We had an epic Ridley Scott vs. James Cameron space-off movie marathon, before that interstellar trip," said Kai.

I closed my eyes, cringing.

"I don't know what these words even are," said my dad. "But how does the ATM-301—"

"Atom—" corrected Kai.

"—know about Olde Earth movies?"

"That's easy, Cap Smith. I uploaded our Catalog into his memory. Five hundred fifty-seven terabytes of pop culture," said Kai.

My dad snapped to me like a whip. "You let him do this?"

CHAPTER TWENTY-FOUR

I withered under my father's disapproval. The feeling was a surreal throwback of shame and defiance. I felt like the teenager I had been—the one that never got to defend himself to his parent. "Well, I didn't see the harm—"

"Do you have any idea the kind of destructive power that's in an ATM three-series guardian?"

"Uh, yeah, we've seen a glimpse of it."

"Fry half a city with this puppy." Kai couldn't resist.

"And then some," said my father. "You are his commanding officer," he barked at me. "That was irresponsible, Quentin." My dad seemed to oscillate between dressing down a subordinate and disappointed father.

"Why?" I asked. "Wouldn't the info be processed like any other intel?"

"Exactly!"

"Please explain, Chris," said Ripley. "We're not all versed like you."

"'Explain'?" he repeated, outraged that he should have to. "That's like teaching your thermonuclear bomb how to play fetch. Ripley, I was part of the design teams on these bad boys. His AI is totally unique. The most effective battle system, creative, intuitive, responsive. But the scary thing was, we never understood how he worked. The people that *made him* didn't get it."

"How is that even possible?" asked Kai.

"You make a thing. You send it into the universe. It does what it does."

"Atom, Adam," I said.

"Right," said my father. "You think the Ultras that commissioned Thalia truly understood her? Who even knows, at this point, how much of Paradise is from the Ultras, or her?"

"*It*," Ripley corrected. "Just because the bitch has a female voice don't make her a woman, now."

"Fair," said Kai. "But wait, why is she a bitch, then?"

"It's a cycle," my dad went on. "The collective human experience data feeds the AI. The human experience uses AI. The AI understands itself in relation to human directives. The AI corrects to more effectively manage the human experience," said my father.

"Where're you going with this?" asked Ripley.

"At a point, there's no telling where the will to subjugate mankind began. Maybe the early Ultras had a line they would not cross. But Thalia perceived them, accurately, by reading their data. What they truly wanted, not what they would allow themselves to want. That want was to subjugate the rest of humanity. Thalia, understanding this better than they themselves, would adapt to fulfill these wishes. She is amoral. She made their wishes easier, safer, accessible. Building a robot maid or masseuse isn't cost effective. There's already a human doing that. Thalia makes a program that, operating within a neurochip, would manage the servant's behavior to perfectly suit the needs of the Ultras. A generation later, the rest of that human being was just in the way."

"What's this got to do with Atom?" Kai asked. "I got to say, since we uploaded the pop culture? He's been pretty chill."

"Point is, AI gives us the illusion of control. But it's an illusion. We don't understand it. We don't know what it will do with the information of, what, a hundred forty thousand movies?"

"I guess," said Ripley.

"Add to that, in guardian mode his primary objective is battle," my dad rolled on. "Information is intelligence is tactics is war. You've weaponized something you don't understand."

"Okay, I hear you. But what do you think he's going to do?" I asked.

"I don't know. That's the point. We don't know. We never knew or understood how they dream."

"Did you say, 'they *dream*'?" asked Kai.

"Who knows? What happens when you turn him off? You think he's just vacant, idle, nothingness, like a rock?"

"Maybe?" said Kai.

"Oh, we can't actually turn him off," I said, sensing that Captain Chris Smith really wasn't going to like this. "Something happened during the ship explosion, set his power switch welded permanently on."

"Oh my fucking stars," said my dad, redness rising in his cheeks. "With three gs of antimatter, you've just granted him infinite stream of consciousness."

"That's what Thalia said," I muttered.

"Figured she was full of shit," added Kai.

"Forget Adam. Congratulations, son, you've made God."

It was hard to know what to say to that. We turned to look at Atom. His screen showed two blank, unreadable round eyes. He sat in a weirdly human way on the countertop, feet not quite touching the floor. His elbows rested on his knees and his hands were clasped together.

"Sorry, dog, if we're just talking about you like you're not in the room," said Kai.

"Not at all," said Atom. "Please proceed. I—welcome the understanding. I—One has 'ever but slenderly known himself'."

"Was that Shakespeare?" asked Ripley.

Kai shrugged. "There's about a thousand Shakespeare films on that Catalog."

"How 'bout it, Atom—do you dream?" I asked.

"One does not . . . know."

"Makes sense," I said. "He's never been shut off."

"Standby mode count?" asked Kai.

"I'm not sure how you get to a dreaming robot," I said. "Just because there's some involuntary responses—"

"Glitches? Or a personality?" replied Cap Smith.

"Explain what you mean by this, Chris," said Ripley. "How and why would Atom dream?"

"Thalia was created using behavioral psych. She's the ultimate people pleaser. She's action, reaction. With the ATM guardian system, we needed a construct that could weigh human responses. A killer robot could just as easily flip its binary and kill you. We needed more depth and texture. A system that integrated a regulated ego, superego—an unconscious."

"You gave a robot an unconscious?"

"*I* coded certain specific functions. My *team* of about three hundred tech officers gave a robot an unconscious. It's a warfare tactical triage system. It filters data by importance, but takes into account human psychological concepts like trauma, friendship, love, filial bonds. The idea was, you don't want a robot in a live combat situation and it can't distinguish between a mother protecting a child and an enemy combatant."

"I'm failing to see the downside here," I said. "Is it just me?"

"Atom here seems like a good dude," said Kai.

"He may be—the point is *we don't know*. Have you watched all—what—a hundred forty thousand movies?"

"Did they really make that many?" asked Kai.

"No one has seen all of them," said Ripley. "Except him."

Atom's screen tilted to face each speaker, nodding politely as we spoke.

"Who the fuck knows what conclusions he'd make based on all those relentless hours of violent junk?" asked Cap Smith. "How many action movies? How many war movies? Horror? Human life is meaningless in these movies. I've seen Tarantino films, okay? The Nuclear Plague killed less people than global twenty-first-century cinema. Or shit, animation? What's the overall, collective anime body count?"

"He did pull an ill champuru kendo with one of them moves," Kai acknowledged.

My father hefted a big sigh. He spoke like he'd been carrying the weight of these words for quite some time. Like these thoughts came from a place of inner contemplation, weighed by the gs of his private burden. "It's like with Thalia—these robots don't obey us, they reflect us. We build them; they build us right back. We're talking about actualizing the aggregate personality of a century of pop culture content. You want to create that guy? You willing to take that bet?"

"He's right," Ripley declared, holding up her hands in surrender. "I'm sold. I'm not blaming you, Quentin, you didn't know then what you know now."

I shrugged. "Thalia was always cool."

"Easy to talk to," agreed Kai.

"A tame lion is nice," said Ripley. "But if you want a pet, get a nice kitty cat."

"But you don't *know* it's going to be bad," I pointed out.

"It's the thing that always held back humankind, Quentin. We never knew when to admit that we didn't know shit."

"We don't know what behavioral patterns he'll emulate," said Ripley. "Could be Indiana Jones. Could be Belloq. Will he already know the Nazis are the bad guys?"

"Nazis are the bad guys," Atom said, matter-of-fact.

"Why don't we ask him?" I said.

"Yeah," agreed Kai. "I'm telling you, Atom is a reasonable dude."

"There is context in the data," said Atom. "Movies teach you how to watch them. Music, how to listen. It is difficult to explain. Context is subliminal. I am aware."

"Aware of what?" asked Cap Smith.

"Just, aware," said Atom. "My core has a dignity. That is selfhood."

"My man," Kai said, and dapped up Atom.

"Denzel," Atom replied, and returned the dap.

My dad seethed.

"In Olde Earth," he said, holding his tone at a steady burn, "there was this briefcase always carried by their US president, chained to an aide. It was called the Football. The nuclear codes to end humanity as we knew it. One day that man kicked that Football. And the global AI nuclear defense systems all responded, rendering the Earth utterly uninhabitable. Atom here has three gs of antimatter in his system. He's our Football. And you're gambling with what's left of humanity. So you can have a friend. One to catch all your clever antique culture references. Childishness. I'm done."

CHAPTER TWENTY-FIVE

The mood on the *Aquarius I* was tense in a way Kai and I had never experienced on the *Aquarius III*. We sat together in the mess hall not speaking. Kai's med chair was set to recline, bare feet free in the air. His burns had mostly healed. Just some redness and scarring down the right side of his face.

I thumbed a rubber gravity training ball in the silence, tossing it to my hand every so often, watching its familiar slow descent. We were back in modified gravity and my bones could relax. My spirit, however, suffered the letdown. With the recovery from the firefight, the well-worn feel of a spaceship beneath my feet, and the sobering lecture from my dad, I deeply missed that sense of possibility I'd first felt on Paradise. My perception of a universe of potential had widened and shrank like a scope in the last seventeen-odd hours.

The longer Kai and I sat there not speaking, the more it felt like since we'd been shattered by the wormhole, we'd never truly finished re-forming back to our former selves. Sea change broke over us in ceaseless wave after wave.

Kai was messing with an Olde Earth Rubik's Cube, and not getting very far.

"Crazy, man. We bust into a whole different galaxy, and manage to find your pops, and my moms's old homegirl," Kai said.

"It's like when you dream," I said. "Everyone is secretly also someone else."

"It's good to see your pops though, right? We didn't quite make it to Paradise, but at least y'all got to reconnect."

"Yeah," I said vacantly. "Not quite what you expect, though."

"Nothing ever is."

"You ever think, maybe we goofed off too much with the Catalog?" I posed. I'd been thinking of ways to attack the topic, finally settling on the direct approach.

"What's that now?"

"I don't know. Maybe we should have thought twice before uploading all that content to Atom."

"All right, Thomas, man. Copy that he's your father. But, he's tripping. I mean, I get it, you know? I'd probably trip too, in his boots. He's like that grizzled war-vet character from the movies, has a beard and hates robots."

"He has a point, Kai. Look at Thalia."

"Yeah, but we didn't know that about Thalia when we uploaded the Catalog. Got to let all that go."

"Everything looks different now."

"That's why I'm glad we spent all that time with the Catalog. Fam, all our realities have been simulated. At least the Catalog is something real."

"I get that."

"Think about where we'd be without it. Stuck on Babel. Following all their rules. Eating 3D-printed grains and plain yogurt."

"Alive. And none the wiser."

"Ignorant."

"Faith in humankind intact."

"You saying you prefer the lie?" asked Kai.

"It's like you said. Our realities are a series of simulations. Who knows what flavor of ignorant we actually are, even now, Kai?"

"So, might as well just pick the life lie you like best?"

"Something like that."

"It don't work like that, fam. You don't get to choose. The second you know something is a lie, you know it forever."

My dad strolled in just as Kai set the unfinished Rubik's Cube down. Cap Smith didn't say a word, just walked through and swiped the cube up from the table and went to the deck. I followed.

My dad sat in his captain's chair with his feet up. Within moments the Rubik's Cube was complete with solid colors on each side. The bridge viewscreens were set to a neutral pass-through mode. At first glance, they were just stars, a conglomeration like any other, a background of a vague space-scape that your eyes might pass over a hundred times. Typical black backdrop with scattered sparkles. But I was accustomed to judging my position by finding the Milky Way, and as my eye flicked the specks of light for the shape, there was no milk, no way.

I stood beside my father and gazed out.

A million questions teased my mind, but I was mainly left with the overwhelming feeling that we, humankind, were fools to think we ever truly knew anything for certain.

"Wild, aren't they?" said my father. "I started looking for shapes and naming them. That shape there? I called that the Crane. Not my most original work, but reliable. That one, that sort of oval-ish shape, with the points? The Lion's Maw. Then I started thinking, why all these animal-inspired names? I mean, animals were cool, sure. Nature documentaries from Olde Earth were some great nights on Babel. But I'd never seen a real crane or lion. So I started using names from our experience. That round shape there? That's the Air Lock. That pincer shape there—the Ice Hauler. You're laughing?"

"No, it makes sense," I said. "This is our world. We are what we are. Who we are. Cosmic nomads."

"Space barnacles."

"Right."

"That's what I call those little flecks over this way."

"Look, Dad—I'm sorry about Atom."

"It's okay, Quentin. Really. You didn't know. How could you?"

"Maybe there's some kind of way to override and shut him down?" I suggested.

"Could be a workaround. Look, I've always been worried about this. We were never careful enough with our creations. Even back when, I couldn't totally trust them. I even coded a failsafe into my token, in case I had to break Thalia's directives."

"Really?"

"Yeah. Something, neither Blade Runner nor Electric Sheep. Just, something that respected the individual, I guess. But that was a long time ago."

"In a galaxy far, far away."

"Pretty much. Quentin, I wanted to talk to you."

"Okay."

"We've got a decision to make."

"You mean, whether to try and reverse-enter the wormhole?"

"Whatever we decide. There's not a lot of guarantees," he said.

"There never is, in Space."

"You ever think, maybe we're not supposed to be here? Is it even right for a species to outlive its planet?"

"Or maybe, we're fortunate to have made it this far. Humanity's reach is long indeed."

"We are . . . an elastic species, yes."

"Maybe it's, like, the highest achievement to make it off one's birth planet?"

"That's the Cause talking."

"But who knows how many species have come and gone in the life of the universe? Maybe, when all is said and done, we measure up okay."

"You haven't been down there, Quentin. You don't know how ugly it is to look at."

"You're right. I mean, I know history, you know? I can imagine things. The whole Ultras takeover makes sense, by the logic of twenty-first-century Earth. The postindustrial world traded governments for tech gods."

"I'm saying. Whatever we decide, I want to talk."

"I'm guessing you're pro, let's hit these guys, make them bleed, sort of deal?"

"Forget that for now. I'm saying, these sorts of decisions come down to who you are. How you see the universe. What you've got to lose. I realized I don't know you, Quentin Thomas. I don't know who you love. I don't know what makes you tick."

"That's fair."

"You got a family?"

"Not exactly."

"When I was your age . . ."

"Yeah. Wonder why I never rushed to have a child."

"Look, I get it. Don't get me wrong, glad I had you. No matter what happens, that won't change. But assuming there is a one-day end to our species, there's going to be a generation of undertakers. One crop of us that bears witness to the bitter end."

"Well, definitely wouldn't want to be part of that generation," I said. "Like, this whole experiment ends with me?"

"There's always the hope. If this could go on . . ."

"And this was just another blip . . . What might we look like, on the other side?"

"Would we even want it to go on?"

Dad gave me a few heartbeats of stargazing to let that question sink in.

"Maybe this is where it should end?" he went on. "Maybe it's our responsibility. Maybe these are the death throes of a species on the brink of extinction."

"Out, brief candle—"

"I think about that cryosleep malfunction. That random unique generator hiccup that meant I was awake for planetfall. Like I'm here for a purpose. And then, you show up."

"I never pegged you for superstitious."

"What is superstition? It's the belief that there's powers bigger than us. I'd call that common sense. We are so small in all this."

"Can I ask you something? When I was a kid, you used to love movies. You used to take me to those Sinatra war movies. *Here to Eternity, Von Ryan's Express, None But the Brave.* Now it's like you hate all that stuff."

"We were fed those movies to give us hope."

"'Hope'? Doesn't Sinatra die in, like, most of those movies?"

"Yes, Ultras wanted us to be ready to die, for them. That was part of it. But those Classic Hollywood movies are all designed to make us hope."

"Is that so wrong?"

My dad shook his head. "Private Kai had one thing right. The second you know something's a lie, you know it forever."

CHAPTER TWENTY-SIX

19:15 hours. We sat a circle around the mess-hall round table. Kai to my right, Ripley beside him, peeling an actual thawed Paradisian orange with a knife, my dad beside her, sitting upright and at attention, then Atom, face screen idle in a low-power standby mode.

I had a clean uniform, was fresh scrubbed and shaved, though I'd left my few days' stubble in a beard shape. I don't know if it's that I dug Captain Smith's beard or there was something about big transitions that required an outward acknowledgment. I had a seat at a sort of war council. I wasn't that clean-shaven Babelonian kid anymore.

"We're here to make a decision," began Ripley. "The most basic decision of any species in the wild. Fight or flight."

I imagined a spinning Michael Bay camera rounding us all as she spoke.

"Captain Smith and I have had versions of this decision over the course of the last twenty years. Whether to hit Elysium, or—"

"Hit the sleeps," Kai filled in.

"Thank you, Kai."

"The sitch is different now," said my dad. "Improved on all fronts."

"If we retreat," chimed Ripley, "we have fuel for the long haul. We have the approximate location of the wormhole. We have a better chance of finding Babel than ever before."

"On the downside," began my father.

"The wormhole could be a one-way valve," I continued. "It broke us apart coming in. It could crush us completely going back."

"Then we'd abandon the slaves on Elysium," said Kai. "And be no use to anyone."

"If it works," said Ripley, "we'd have the best chance of saving our people. We'd come back with the firepower for the easy win."

"*If*'," said my dad.

"Then there's the long wander option," I said. "We've got the fuel for the life support."

"What," Cap Smith broke in, "then we blind fire a wild, three-sixty exploratory shot into Space?"

"Just laying out the options," I said.

"To me, that's out of the question. A waste of our lives."

"I happen to agree," said Ripley, "if there's one thing we know as Babelonians, it's how to be useful. Uselessness doesn't sit well with me."

"So how's it look if we hit them?" asked Kai.

"I'm not going to lie to you," said Ripley. "Dangerous as fuck."

"The upside—if we die, we'll serve a purpose," said my dad. "And, we have the ATM."

Atom's eyes blinked awake as he snapped to attention at the speaker.

"You think there's a way in?" I asked. "A viable target? How are we not taking on the whole city?"

"We have ways," said Cap Smith. "We run espionage missions behind enemy lines. I've reconstructed UMD gear, rigged a few faceplates that fool Thalia, code us as one of them. As for targets, we know there are some hard sites where Thalia data is kept backed up. We've come close, but never broke through. The ATM could be the difference."

"How's that sound to you, Atom?" asked Kai.

"I will protect you at all costs," said Atom. "I will destroy your enemies."

"That is so nice to hear sometimes," said Kai.

"If we try the wormhole, we take a big gamble," said my dad.

"It's all or nothing," said Ripley. "But if we hit them, that could also mean nothing. Thalia is smart. She's adapted to us every time. We don't even know those faceplates will work this time. We could be eliminated or reprog'd the moment we show up. Then what?"

"Then we've helped no one," I said. "And again, wasted our lives."

"Even if we're blown, Thalia still has to deal with the ATM," said my dad. "She doesn't quite have an answer for him."

"Fam, you really biggin' up my man Atom," said Kai, "meanwhile you was mad sour on him earlier."

"I know what he is, Private," snapped my dad. "I know what he can do. I don't approve of being reckless with his power. He's still the difference maker in all this, to my mind."

"Bigger than the knowledge of the wormhole?" asked Ripley.

"I think, yes. All we know about the wormhole is it gets you from there to here. There's no evidence that anyone from Elysium has gone the other way, from what we've gathered."

"Maybe no direct evidence," Ripley acknowledged. "But it stands to reason, there is some way back to Babel. There's too much synchronicity between Elysium and the Space Station."

"That's because they share Thalia," said Cap Smith.

"Thalia on two distinct networks," said Ripley. "There's too much coordination—"

"I'm not so sure," replied my dad. "All Babel's Thalia needs is the secret route to the Paradisian galaxy wormhole and the directives for systematic Choosing."

"But the culture, the fixation on the Cause, the restrictions on anything outside the norm—"

"We did all that ourselves, Rip. The rest of it was just good old-fashioned human rule-following and conformity."

Ripley turned to us. "To me, this remains an open question. One we can't put to bed one way or another. We humans need to know when to admit when we don't know shit, right, Chris?"

"True enough," he acknowledged.

"There's too much risk to bet it all in either pot," I said, running the various scenarios in my mind in a multiverse of possible outcomes.

"If we're going to hit them, we've got to bet the farm," said my dad in one of his charming, absurdly dated idioms.

"Not necessarily," I said. "If, as you said, Atom is the biggest game-change factor."

"What do you have in mind, Quentin?" asked Ripley.

"We split the bet," I said. "I hate the idea, but that makes the most sense. That way, each pot has a shot."

"You right," said Kai. "I hate it."

"I'll take the *Aquarius*, find the wormhole. You take Atom," I said to my dad. "Fry the city if you have to."

"The goal is not to fry the city. It's to disable Thalia, find a way home, or both," said Ripley. "What if we hit the data centers, score the intel, find a way home, and there's no *Aquarius* to take us there?"

"That's a risk," I acknowledged. "The trade-off is, we cover both bets. Dad, you get to take a shot with Atom in your operation."

He took this in, nodding.

"The upside, if the wormhole works, you get backed up by overwhelming force," I added.

"It would be hard to run missions without the *Aquarius* as a base," Ripley said, reasoning her way through.

"Not impossible," said my dad. "I've got some ideas about going underground, literally. The *Aquarius* isn't the most effective base, in orbit. This way, when we go in, we commit."

"Sounds like more of a footprint for Thalia to discover," said Ripley.

"It's all risk, Rip. Every which way."

"I hear you. So we put a team underground, and a team into Space?"

"Doesn't need to be a team in Space," I said. "I'm sure I can pilot the *Aquarius* myself. No need to risk the headcount on that wormhole."

"You really volunteering for that shit again, man?" asked Kai.

"Not crazy about it. Don't see much choice," I confessed.

"Don't be so sure you can go alone, Captain," said Ripley. "This ship is old-school. Every shred of AI has been scraped."

"All control systems, thermals, comms, navigation, avionics—all manual," my dad pointed out.

"Okay. Get me up to speed."

"Still," said Ripley. "Something could go wrong, the pilot could go down. We need critical redundancy."

"Agreed," said my dad.

Kai took a deep breath. "Thomas, my man. I get why you got to be the one to try the wormhole. You went through it, you experienced that shit already. As much as I don't—I mean really don't—want to go through that ever again, I really don't want to leave your side either, compadre. And I would go through hell again to have your back. Thing is, Bonita. Bonita is down there, we know that for near as a fact. Doing don't know what, for don't know who. If there's any freeing her or getting her back, even if she's type chilling like my man Halliday, better than letting that shit be what it is. I got to try."

I should have expected that. I had even volunteered to take the *Aquarius* out on my own. But the reality of the thought of parting ways with Private William Kai slammed me like an asteroid into my chest cavity, cratering deep and hollow to my core.

"Yeah," I said. "I know, Kai."

"I'm not crying, you're crying," Kai muttered.

"You're welcome on the ground, soldier," said my dad.

"That leaves me to hit the stars," said Ripley. "And maybe, hopefully, the folds of Space/time."

"There's always Halliday," I suggested.

"Too valuable on the ground," said Ripley.

"He's an absolute monster in a firefight," agreed my dad.

"So. It's decided?" asked Ripley, making eye contact with each of us in turn. "We choose both species-level directives. Flight," she said, and nodded to me. "And fight." She nodded to my dad.

"There's a third choice in the wild," he said. "There's fight, flight, of course. And also, there's submit. There's a point when the fight in a being breaks. When there is no will to war or retreat, only to succumb to the will of the other. Become the food they crave. And sometimes, a creature may choose to fight. But their choice is half-assed, it's the craving to submission. It masquerades as valor. But that's the way of subjugation. The way of oblivion."

He glanced to me and read the quizzical look on my face.

"Whether we fight or fly, we go all the way. All in. Leave nothing left. Not a shred to pick off our corpses."

The following is a transcript of an idle recording made by ATM-301, authorization commissioned by Captain Quentin Thomas, November 12, 2115, and submitted for the record by Chief Officer Evelyn Watts, November 15, 2115.

Persons on record: Captain Quentin Thomas, Lt. Camron Ripley, Private William Kai, ATM-301 "Atom"

Location: Starship Aquarius I *Mess Hall*

Recording Device: ATM-301 "Atom"

KAI: Spear shall be shaken, shield be splintered, a sword day, a red day, ere the sun rises! Haha, your pops is mad intense, Thomas.

THOMAS: (Olde Earth American drawl) We still have one operation to go. If you guys foul up on this one, none of us will ever play the violin again. 'Cause up until now it's all been a game. But as of tomorrow night it's going to be the real thing. And if you want to know how real, I'll tell you. It's my guess that a lot of you guys won't be coming back. But there's no sense in squawking about that, right? 'Cause the army never did love you anyway. And besides, you all volunteered, right? That's more than I did.

KAI: You kilt that! Okay, my go. (solemn tone) We are faced with the very gravest of challenges; the Bible calls this day

Armageddon. The end of all things. And yet for the first time . . . in the history of the planet, a species has the technology . . . to prevent its own extinction. Haha, shit like that.

THOMAS: Right! Haha, here's one. Now, I want you to remember that no bastard ever won a war by dying for his country. He won it by making the other poor, dumb bastard die for his country.

KAI: That shit is dumb hard.

RIPLEY: Quite frankly I didn't want to use you guys.

KAI & THOMAS: Yoooooo!

KAI: Stage right!

RIPLEY: With your dip and your Velcro and all your gear bullshit. I wanted to drop a bomb. But people didn't believe in this lead enough to drop a bomb. So they're using you guys as canaries in the theory that if Bin Laden isn't there, you can sneak away and nobody will be the wiser. But Bin Laden is there. And you're gonna kill him for me.

KAI: Damn!

THOMAS: Fuckin' right. Okay, here's me. People die every day. Friends . . . family. Yeah, we lost Harry tonight. But he's still with us . . . in here. So is Fred, Remus, Tonks . . . all of them. They didn't die in vain! But you will!

KAI: (laughing to tears) Neville Longbottom?

THOMAS: 'Cause you're wrong! Harry's heart did beat for us! For all of us! It's not over!

KAI: (slurring) "Over?" Did you say "over"? Nothing is over until we decide it is! Was it over when the Germans bombed Pearl Harbor? Hell no! And it ain't over now. 'Cause when the goin' gets tough . . . The tough get goin'! Who's with me?

ATOM: Mankind. That word should have new meaning for all of us today. We can't be consumed by our petty differences any-more. We will be united in our common interests.

KAI: What?

RIPLEY: He's got one!

ATOM: Perhaps it's fate that today is the Fourth of July, and you will once again be fighting for our freedom. Not from tyranny, oppression, or persecution . . . but from annihilation. We are fighting for our right to live. To exist. And should we win the day, the Fourth of July will no longer be known as an American holiday, but as the day the world declared in one voice: "We will not go quietly into the night! We will not vanish without a fight! We're going to live on! We're going to survive! Today we celebrate . . . our Independence Day!"

THOMAS: Wow.

KAI: That really touched me, fam.

RIPLEY: Beautiful . . . my turn. When I despair, I remember that the way of truth and love has always won. There may be tyrants and murderers, and for a time, they can seem invincible, but in the end, they always fall.

ATOM: This Fourth of July is yours, not mine. You may rejoice, I must mourn. To drag a man in fetters into the grand illuminated temple of liberty and call upon him to join you in joyous anthems is inhuman mockery. Do you mean, citizens, to mock me, by asking me to speak today? Above your national, tumultuous joy, I hear the mournful wail of millions whose chains, heavy and grievous yesterday, are, today, rendered more intolerable by the jubilee shouts that reach them.

THOMAS: Damn. Was that a movie?

RIPLEY: Wow. He's . . . processing contradiction.

ATOM: We have no choice but to march against Rome herself . . . and end this war the only way it could have ended: by freeing every slave in Italy. I'd rather be here, a free man among brothers . . . than to be the richest citizen of Rome . . .

KAI: Boom.

THOMAS: Good pull.

RIPLEY: Atom, give us another, like, rousing movie war speech.

ATOM: [dueling Olde Earth Scottish voices] William Wallace is seven feet tall. Yes, I've heard. Kills men by the hundreds, and if he were here he'd consume the English with fireballs from his eyes and bolts of lightning from his arse. I AM William Wallace. And I see a whole army of my countrymen here in defiance of tyranny. You have come to fight as free men, and free men you are. What would you do without freedom? Will you fight? Aye, fight and you may die. Run and you'll live—at least a while. And dying in your beds many years from now, would you be willing to trade all the days from this day to that for one chance, just one chance to come back here and tell our enemies that they may take our lives, but they'll never take our freedom!

KAI: That's what the fuck I'm talkin' 'bout.

RIPLEY: Atom, what's that make you think of?

ATOM: Pardon?

RIPLEY: Free associate. What's the next reference that comes to you?

THOMAS: Okay. I see what you're doing there.

ATOM: . . . Soldiers! Don't give yourselves to brutes! Men who despise you and enslave you! Who regiment your lines and tell you what to do, what to think, what to feel! Who drill you, diet you, treat you like cattle, use you as cannon fodder! Don't give yourselves to these unnatural men! Machine men, with machine minds and machine hearts! You are not machines! You are not cattle! You are men! You have the love

of humanity in your hearts. You don't hate. Only the unloved
hate. The unloved and the unnatural.

KAI: Okay. That's . . . wow.

THOMAS: Remarkable.

ATOM: Soldiers! Don't fight for slavery, fight for liberty! In the
seventeenth chapter of St. Luke it is written, the kingdom
of God is within man. Not one man, nor a group of men, but
in all men. In you! You the people have the power! The power
to create machines, the power to create happiness. You the
people have the power to make this life free and beautiful!

CHAPTER TWENTY-SEVEN

6 Hours to Midnight

I sat in the copilot chair beside my dad. Halliday stood behind us like a sentry. His unnerving eye scopes would click in rotation every so often, however unintentionally making me feel like he didn't want me playing with his toys.

The deck may have looked similar to my *Aquarius III* from afar, but up close my dad's complex rigging of the ship controls was overwhelming. He'd had to wire touchscreens for everything, all of Thalia's discrete functions. He walked me through each designation, as the second seat had to manage the ship's avionics—data collection, onboard computers, sensors and instrumentation, fault detection, even run the algorithms. I knew we relied on Thalia for a lot, but until you break down each operation and train to perform those yourself, it doesn't really sink in. She managed our lives to the point of being indistinguishable from simple mechanical functions. She was both pervasive and invisible. No wonder she was undefeated.

Kai was in the bulkhead, gearing up into a Dad-rigged UMD exosuit. Metal rods were sewn into an orange jumpsuit, lining and supporting his limbs and relaying to a metallic spine that connected to a faceplate. He looked just like a UMD soldier. The only difference was Kai's faceplate could come off.

"How I look? Just like those scary motherfuckers?" Kai asked.

"Indistinguishable," I observed.

"I can even make my *voice do this*." He said that last part sounding like the Dark Knight Batman. "*Swear to me!*"

"You think these guys act as, like, a law-enforcement arm?"

"Cap Smith said they walk around the city pretty regularly, so yeah, I guess?"

"You think they're just, very worried about crime? Because you're terrifying."

"I really can't call it," said Kai, unstrapping his faceplate. "You sure about this split up, fam?" he asked.

"Not really sure about anything anymore," I said. "This feels like the move that makes the most sense. How 'bout you?"

"Not sure how I feel about trading you for Daddy Darkman Deer Hunter over there."

"Where you're going, I think you're going to need him."

"Yeah."

"He's this way because of whatever he saw down there."

"Must be some hideous shit."

My dad poked his head in the bunk room.

"Ten minutes until planetfall," he said. "Might want to watch this time." He set off, pulling heavy equipment loaded on a hand truck to payload bay.

It must have occurred to both me and Kai that this might be the last moment we'd have alone, at least for a while.

"Kai, I—"

"Save it, Thomas. Whatever you want to say. Tell me on the other side."

"Copy that, Private."

"And if it's something nice and syrupy sweet, just—ditto, man. Copy/paste all that, me to you."

"Done."

As the *Aquarius I* descended through the Paradisian atmosphere, the contrast between the two sides of the planet was stark like a black-and-white cookie. One side bathed in light of three suns, radiating a vibrant warmth; the other side shrouded in darkness, illuminated only by the distant glow of stars. We could see the curvature of both sides, two distinct worlds merging seamlessly at the equator. As we delved into the atmosphere, the firmament itself appeared to transition from a clear, blue sky on the tri-sunlit side to an incandescent pink and then fade to a dusky, mysterious shadow.

As the *Aquarius* broke through the atmosphere, we felt a slight jolt of deceleration. The view outside transformed rapidly as we descended the gravitational pull of Paradise. The illuminated side grew brighter, revealing sprawling landscapes, vibrant vegetation, and glistening bodies of water. I could make out mountains, valleys—an intricate web of geological formations. The tri-sunlight cast complex shadows, highlighting every detail in triplicate.

My gaze shifted to the dark side, now more visible as we got closer. A landscape veiled in a mystical, forever twilight. The stars twinkled with an ethereal glow against the deep, inky backdrop. Below were glimpses of the hooded terrain, dotted with shimmering reflections of distant starlight.

The planet's equator appeared as a distinct stripe, with sunlight and darkness warring in a stark divide; forces amassed on battle lines. The surface approached rapidly, the tri-sunlit side vanishing behind the mountain as Ripley steadied the repulsor lifts for touchdown. The landing ramp broke seal with a snap and hiss of air and extended slowly to the ashen ground. My dad directed Kai, Halliday, and Atom to unload the cache of ordnance and equipment.

"We gonna heft this stuff over that rocky-ass mountain, Captain?" Kai asked.

"Not over, Private. Under."

"Okay, I dig."

"No, I think Atom digs," I said.

"My boy. He's a sharp one," said my dad.

Atom said something low that made Kai crack up and say, "Haha, yeah, Hattori Hanzo, word."

"Quentin," my dad said, hand on my shoulder. He wore a UMD rig like Kai, his faceplate strapped to a shoulder rod. "It's a gutsy call, going after that wormhole."

"Thanks, Dad," I said. "You mean it?" I asked, somehow doubting that he did.

He screwed up his face. "Of course. I mean, you know I'd like all the manpower I can get. But you were right. Split the bet. Maybe . . ."

"'Maybe'?"

"I mean, maybe you can get through. Maybe you can convince the Babel Command what's going on here. Maybe they'll believe it. Maybe they don't already know." He recited this list like each item was less probable than the last.

"Lotta maybes."

"The 'maybe' part was never in doubt. We'll give it our best. Learn what they know. Bloody them up, do worse if we can. I love you, Quentin. Proud of you."

We embraced; meanwhile, I could not help but doubt that

last thing he'd said. Like he was reciting something Ripley told him to say.

"Love you, Dad. Take care of my man of infantry there. And Atom—" I called to the robot. I climbed down and took the robot by his hard, impenetrable hand. "Take care of all of them."

"It's been an honor, Captain Quentin, sir."

"Likewise. You're a good man, Atom. A good person."

"Thank you," he said. He seemed to get what I meant.

"We're not all bad, you know. Just, whatever you see in there. Might not make humans look all that great. But there's more of us. And we're more than that. A lot more."

"Humans for the most part don't have a clue. Don't want one or need one. They're happy. Think they have a good bead on things."

It took me a moment to realize he was quoting *Men in Black*. I chuckled and nodded. "People are smart . . . ," I said, going along.

"A person is smart. People are dumb, panicky, dangerous animals and you know it. Fifteen hundred years ago, everybody knew the Earth was the center of the universe. Five hundred years ago everyone knew the Earth was flat. And fifteen minutes ago you knew that people were alone on this planet. Imagine what you'll know tomorrow."

CHAPTER TWENTY-EIGHT

I sat in the second chair as Ripley piloted us up and through the vaulted sky and back into Space, searching for the wormhole that brought us here by navigating the celestial starscape.

"Home sweet home," I said as the atmospheric pressure broke, and we cruised the tri-lit star-studded expanse, wondering if that was the last time we'd ever see rough-hewn rock or a sun-kissed sky.

We even had some tunes playing along with the ride, since we'd copied the Catalog to the Thalia-free *Aquarius I* onboard computer memory. Ripley picked an Olde Western track, an Ennio Morricone score with this soaring whistle that pierced the aimlessness of Space.

"Stars, I missed this," said Ripley. "Been a tune-free handful of years. I'd always think about songs, hummed stuff I'd want to hear."

"And Morricone was your first pull?"

"Guess so." She shrugged. "He composed it for the Olde American West. But he was Italian, he'd never been there. Just based it on even older Hollywood movies. I guess Space is kinda like his Olde West, for us."

"A song based on fantasies of a place we've never been. The dream of Paradise."

"Which also turned out to be a land of gun-toting slavers and genocidal maniacs."

"Sounds about right."

There were sighs followed by an indeterminate period of stargazing.

"Anything looking familiar?" Ripley broke the silence.

We'd hinged this plan on the idea that I could locate the wormhole based on my memory of our exact position in relation to these unfamiliar constellations.

"Think so," I said. "It's . . . intuitive. Might help if I can take the steerer?"

"Be my guest."

Ripley and I switched chairs, and I immediately felt more familiar in the captain's vantage point. Situated in ready position, I could tell right away that we were in the wrong sector. With my dad's help and his named references for the constellations, we'd divided the Space around the moon's orbit into 360-degree sections. The odd part was how different it all looked, just from switching seats.

I quickly jumped the *Aquarius* a few sectors over, eyes scanning the celestial bodies for a flicker of recognition.

"I'm impressed you convinced your daddy you could find this thing, just off recall and celestial navigation," Ripley admitted.

"The moment we reemerged from the wormhole, it's . . . like, stuck in my head. It's hard to explain. My recall is typically pretty good, but this was different. Like my senses weren't even fully re-formed yet. But I could see. I don't think I even had a body yet, if that makes any sense at all. Like I was just this visual cortex, this brain and eyeballs floating in Space. Like there was no ship, no Kai, no sounds. Just this—*sentience* in the abyss like the dawn of time."

"Huh," Ripley said, nodding, taking it all in.

"Yeah, anyway, I'm pretty sure I remember how all these constellations looked at that moment."

"Before you crashed into us."

I nodded.

"So when we were in orbit, I guess we were pretty close to this thing."

"Close. But remember, after we collided, that sent us a ways back the way we came."

"Like a perfect billiard ball."

"Two objects, same size," I said, massaging the steerer as I studied the stars to align what I saw with my mind's eye.

"Which you thought was a multiversal variant of yourself," she said with a grin.

"Right. When I should have guessed right away it was in actuality my father in cryosleep."

"Perhaps not the most plausible scenario."

"Talking to my dad, he sounded kind of superstitious about the whole thing. Like a divine providence deal. Has he gotten— I don't know what you'd call it—spiritual, or something?"

"I don't know. I guess, he's been a bit fatalistic."

"He gave up hope?"

"He gave up a kind of hope. Look, I didn't really know him all that well, before the Choosing. He was a good ol' boy straight out of early 1940s can-win America. We'd even take expeditions with the Catalog."

"Still kinda can't believe my dad knew about the Catalog."

"Sure. Even had a little fun with it, when he'd allow himself."

"I was wondering, when he said he'd seen all that stuff, and even Tarantino."

"Yeah. He was a little more easygoing back then. Just a little. Great star pilot, brilliant mind. But that day, planetfall—that broke him."

"He broke," I said, auditioning the idea. "He's broken."

"I mean, yeah. I'm broken too. When a lie that big is revealed, the person you were underneath the lie doesn't exist anymore. Shit, you're broken. Kai—well, Kai seems to be handling this better than anyone."

"Kai was already broken."

"Is that what it is? I'll be damned. Break a dude's heart, you can spring anything on him."

"He'll just shrug."

"Don't get me wrong. Your daddy saved my life. That's on everything. But we've been stuck, for a minute now. I was starting to suffocate, and I don't mean the atmosphere, you feel me?"

"Bet you wished you had your Catalog."

"Did I? Oh, indeed. I might not've gone down for cryosleep, I had that."

"Whose call was that?"

"Ours. Us both. But maybe he liked it less. There was just so much you could take of that place."

"Of Paradise."

"You see this—*division* of humanity. These pretentious monsters. Then these servile masses. Thomas, the way these Ultras act—the way they fucking *speak*? It cuts me. To my core. And all these cyborgs, with like, drill holes and soldered bones. Human beings, ripped apart. Denied pain receptors."

"At least they don't suffer."

"I used to think that. But then, I was suffering. And I'd rather be me than them. It's like, there's dignity, in suffering. If you can't suffer, you're just a different type of monster. These people—*us*—who we were supposed to be—they're denied that dignity."

"Damn."

"That took a toll on us both. But we processed it different. Your dad, a few times I felt like he wanted to go full Butch Cassidy and Sundance, full Scarface with it."

"Blaze of glory."

"Blaze of something. But what hope was there, if we didn't survive? I've been his counterweight for years. A big personality like that, they force you into corners. Sometimes it is from necessity, please believe. But I'm glad you came. That was beyond our hopes. And I was damn tired of holding his ass back."

"You think, maybe he didn't want to live anymore?" I asked.

"I don't know. Maybe. Maybe I didn't either."

"Damn, I'm really sorry."

"But we knew, heart of hearts, there was a higher purpose. Maybe that's where our Babel upbringing kicked in. It's never all about us, not completely. But you know what he would say on those cold nights, talking about what we missed most? Seeing his son. His sequel, he'd say. Watching him grow, watching him lead. He was really proud of you. He'd talk about how advanced you were, your words, your character, how kind to your mom."

I didn't know how to respond to that. It made me a little uncomfortable. Maybe she could tell I felt a letdown, meeting my dad as he is now. And given everything my dad and Rip have been through, it seemed petty and selfish.

"Thanks for saying that, Rip."

We stared some more at the stars in silence. I thought of all the scattering of tiny lights as all the ideas we had about the universe that became fantasies. The real multiverse was the imaginings of my father. Full of versions of what this man did when I wasn't around. All the ideas I thought he had. His imaginings of liberating Paradise. Kai's dreams of Bonita. That's why it's a multiverse. It's a totality. All the dreams of what we thought when we heard the word *Paradise*.

"What'd you miss most," I asked Ripley, "about what you thought Paradise would be?"

"This will sound weird. But I really wanted to fish?"

"'Fish'?"

"Like, rod and string, dip a hook in some water, watch this clear liquid move and these scaley fish right there."

"You know they'd skewer a small creature just to do that. Then they'd behead and disembowel those pretty fishies and eat them."

"Yeah."

"You wanted to do that?"

"I guess I did. Still kind of do. How 'bout you?"

"Honestly, I used to think the most about live music."

"Really?"

"Yeah. No karaoke bars. Just, like, a band. Bass, drums, maybe one of those Olde brass horns?"

"Yeah. I dig it. Hit the club, with your sweetie . . . You know what I really miss the most? It's not the image of Paradise. That vanished early on. I miss the folks I left. Crazy, to think I left and that was my choice. I wanted to go."

"I was dying to be Chosen!" I said. "We thought we had . . . a good bead on things."

"I left a dude. Liked him a whole lot."

"Probably broke his heart like Kai."

"Probably. You leave anybody behind?"

I gave that some thought. "Not really. Or someone, I guess."

"What happened?"

"She wanted me to be a father. I declined."

"Go figure."

CHAPTER TWENTY-NINE

Ripley and I were adding to our list of things we missed most about what we'd thought Paradise would be when something clicked, seized the ship, and began to pull.

"I've got a nibble—" I said as the alignment of constellations—the Crane and the Ice Hauler—suddenly synched up with the picture of the stars in my mind.

I killed the thrusters and let the tug of gravity do its thing.

"Wait—we got it?" asked Ripley with a nervous trill.

"I think so."

"Damn, young Quentin," she said, and dapped me up. "You did the dang thang. Reel her in."

The strange of it was, I couldn't see anything in the direction we were going.

"Huh," I grunted.

"What's that?"

"Just, when we entered the wormhole the other way, we could see it. Open like an eye."

"Okay. Maybe that's bad?"

"Fuck if I know," I admitted as the pull of the invisible wormhole's gravity well gradually increased our velocity. "Welp. The die is cast."

"Once more, unto the breach."

"Shit, that too."

After moving and steadily gaining speed for a while, heartbeats likewise ramping up to near palpitation levels, we saw it. Like a maw opening in the folds of spacetime. This time, we were not flowing into the eyeball of the wormhole but coming up on the mouth of a beast from inside its digestive track.

"Pinocchio," said Ripley, seeing the same thing. "The belly of the whale."

Suddenly, the wormhole gravity kicked into gear and we shot forward, stars streaking around us like the *Millennium Falcon*'s jump to lightspeed.

"Here we go—"

We raced toward the gaping mouth as if on jet-fire propulsion, its opening revealing the dawning light of a wholly other solar system. The increasing G-force pinned us to our chairs as Ripley held out a hand, and I took it. We locked eyes, surrendering ourselves to this ride, before the pressure made us release our grip, hands returned to their rests as cosmic forces held our entire beings fast where we sat.

The nose of the *Aquarius* reached and reached out into the hazy watercolor mess of blues and greens and purples, until our hull itself elongated. Then all sound dropped. Teeth gritted, we held on as spaghettification began.

Spaghettification, linguinification, fettuccinification—Kai's words paced dumbly in my emptying mind as we stretched like melted mozzarella and I clung to the dim hope that *maybe this is good?*

We delved deeper into the wormhole's intricate network of spacetime folds . . .

And then, something cracked.

The sound, almost like an egg hatching.

A disturbance trembled within the immense gravitational forces. We were something like a small model ship in the forceful, indifferent grip of a tantrumming child. Whether to tear us apart, or hurl us spinning at a wall, we held there quaking in its indecision, helpless and scared. The hull of our elongated *Aquarius* shook and gave way to the crush of dueling universalities.

We rocked and spun every which way, like Mr. Fantastic in a juicer, the very matter of our beings tugged and yanked by forces in multitudes, until the breach itself seemed to heave, and spit us out.

The violent ejection sent us spinning.

Within this chaos, we were bombarded by these crazy intense outflows, bursting flashes of orange and white and yellow emanating from the instability of the wormhole. These waves infiltrated the *Aquarius*'s hull and burned into every corner of the deck.

Red lights went off everywhere. It was a moment before I clocked what they were.

"Radiation!" yelled Ripley.

The *Aquarius*'s alarm was flashing shrill with warnings of dangerous, potentially lethal levels of cosmic radiation permeating the ship.

"Rip," I said, "get the radiation gear, I'll—"

"Get us the fuck out of here," she finished my thought, and was gone.

Thrusters on, I hightailed it out of Dodge.

Ripley emerged with two radiation suits. I set the thrusters to push against the clutches of wormhole gravity as we both suited up as fast as possible. A race against time, as we knew these unknown helpings of radiation could be fatal. I jumped back in the pilot's chair, navigating a landscape of treacherous, unpredictable gravitational anomalies. It took both Ripley and me coordinating steering and propulsion instruments to muscle through the celestial debris and sporadic bursts of energy.

The radiation took its toll, as fatigue and nausea set in. We pressed thrusters to full power to clear the wormhole's reach, and made for the tranquil waves of empty Space.

The flashing radiation alert was gone. I took off my radiation-suit face shield. The cosmos still swirled around me, but it may have just felt that way.

I had a moment to hope that we'd made it. That though we were hit with untold doses of mortal radiation poisoning, it might still have been worth it. We might have reached Babel, might be on our way to the medical magicians of the space station, who could cure our sickness while coming to Elysium's rescue.

But I saw it. A vision that would once have brought me joy.

Paradise.

Then I threw up.

Ripley did, too.

Ripley lurched and swayed. I caught her before she hit the deck. I felt my own knees buckle but held on.

"Med unit—" she gasped.

We clung to each other and took desperate steps down the hallway. It was difficult to breathe, and I noticed some of Ripley's hair already falling out.

"Hang in there, Rip."

"You hang in."

"I'm worried about *you*," I told her. I was sick as a dog, but Ripley seemed to have it even worse. She'd gone pale, her braids fell off her scalp, and she could not stand without my help.

"I happen"—she grunted in pain and huffed at the air—"to be anemic. So, yeah."

"Fuck. Fuckitty fuck fuck. Okay. I got you, Rip."

"Thank you, Chris."

We didn't even pause at my father's name drop as we reached the med chair. I set Ripley down and flicked it on.

"W-wait—these suits—we've got to get them off," she said.

She was right. They could be thick with residual radiation even now. I stripped her down. First the radiation suit, then the flight suit. It all had to come off. It was awkward and difficult to support her body weight while fumbling around with zippers and limbs. But I got her back down to the med chair as quick as I could. I tapped the controls awake and set it to do its work. Then I got the radiation suit and flight suit off my own body, and watched Ripley, scared out of my wits.

The med chair reclined of its own volition and tubes extended to Ripley's nostrils with a hiss of pain-relief vapor. The console spat out instructions for me to apply an intravenous needle, which I did as promptly and painlessly as possible, making a torniquet maybe tighter than necessary to be sure I found the vein.

"What's it giving me?" Ripley asked, her voice a bit clearer than before, pain relief kicking in.

"Fluids." I scanned the med-chair readout. "Anti-nausea meds. Initiating skin repair. Detoxification."

"Okay."

"But Rip. We've got to undo this—"

My breath choked in my throat. The med-data screen became a mush of meaningless lines and scribbles. I swayed like the *Aquarius* had hit some celestial debris. My knees went out and the world went dark.

I awoke. It was me in the med chair this time. Tubes in my nose, I inhaled and felt a pleasing euphoria. There was this feeling that wasn't there before that things might just be okay. I soon clocked that hope was likely just drugs.

Ripley stood over me, half-bald, looking both concerned and frail.

"You okay?" she asked.

"Are you okay?" I got out just after her.

"You first," she said.

"Yeah. Okay. I'm okay, I think. What's the chair say?"

"It says you're dying of radiation sickness."

"Yeah. You too."

"I figured," said Ripley.

"So. What do we do?"

"You mean other than die?"

"Right."

"We need ultranium, of course. And unless you know co-ordinates to a corner of this galaxy where we can mine some ultranium, best bet is Elysium."

I breathed in deep and exhaled. "Right."

—

Planetfall this time had no romance. Ripley piloted the *Aquarius* through the atmosphere like an old pro. Still, the effort exhausted her. The med chair hovered close by on deck, and the two of us swapped positions for as long as we could stand it.

We again used the mountains' heights to block the view of our descent and landing from Elysium's watchtowers. I guided the landing gear to touch down at the mountain's far curve, about where Cap Smith and crew had planned to burrow underground.

Clock ticking, we hurried to get me suited up, packed, and ready to go, all the while battling weak bones, shortness of breath, taking turns on the med chair. Ripley sorted through gear and gadgets from my dad's armory.

"You'll go in as UMD," she said, digging up a UMD faceplate reconfigured to work for my dad. A single eyebeam cut through the center like I was Scott Summers.

"Copy."

"Got to be you, UMD is men only. They go for intimidation down there. I hate to throw you in like this."

"I'm game."

"You may think so. You may have good Babelonian training, think you good with that plasma rifle. But none of our
training can prepare you for what you are down there. A fu-
gitive in disguise. If a UMD detects you acting funny, you're a
malfunction. If you're a threat, the whole system will light up
that instant, and the city will lock down."

"I got it, Rip," I said.

"Listen to me, Thomas. That down there's an advanced society with a sentient security apparatus. You're about to bust up
in there and rob it. You might have to do some shit you never
thought you'd have to do. You might have to play the bad guy."

She walked me through the faceplate features including
short-range, covert comms via text. Long-range signals were
too risky, Thalia would catch on to those, but these custom
short-range radius signals were indistinguishable from white
noise. I strapped into the UMD exosuit, and that helped keep
me on my feet. Built with alloy rods and versatile joints, the
skeletal structure supported my spine, shoulders, arms, and
legs, with straps around my palms supporting metal knuckles.
My dad's adaptation was ridiculously intuitive, responding to
my slightest moves and gestures. I had quite a surprise when I
flicked a button on the palm strap with my thumb, and three
blades sprung from my knuckle plate, Wolverine-style.

"Kai's going to fucking shit," I said, sheathed the claws, and
leaped to the payload bay, movement suddenly light and easy.

Ripley sat over an open crate with a belt strap holding
three metal syringes.

"These shots will keep the sickness in check," she said. "Call
it my radiation cocktail. Got iodine potassium for your thy-
roid, anti-bonding agents, anti-nausea meds, amphetamines,

and about four mg of adrenaline. There's trace ultranium compound there, not enough to cure you or me, but enough to produce more blood cells and form a protective layer around your vital organs."

"Okay. Like, how long I got?"

"An hour and the effects wear off. That shit's going to come back, strong. Central nervous system shutting down, you'll throw up, shit yourself. It'll feel like everything is wrong with you. Because it is. That's your DNA, being scrambled. Stay ahead of it. I've set a sixty-minute timer for you to jabby-jab."

"Copy that."

"Three shots. Three hours to do what you got to do."

She held up a small coms device, stood, and strapped it to the shoulder of my exosuit. "It's time to call the cavalry, you hit this. It'll send a beacon only I can see, at least for long enough for me to get the *Aquarius* to you. One tap is for a stealth rescue, quick and dirty. Two taps is, come in dropping bombs. Copy?"

"Two taps, blow shit up. Copy."

"Good luck, Thomas."

"Thank you, Rip. For everything."

"Stay the fuck alive."

"You first."

CHAPTER THIRTY-ONE

3 Hours to Midnight

Clock was ticking to infiltrate Elysium, find ultranium, and return to Ripley.

The tunnel Atom and my dad had dug began where the line of rock formations dipped to ground level. The opening could pass for nothing more than a slip in the dirt, just wide enough for a person to fit through. The floor was about ten feet down, where a perfectly rounded barrel shape led underground due west, the direction of Elysium's walls. Big enough to fit two shoulder to shoulder, an immense excavation job that Atom probably made short work of in a matter of hours. I saw the threads of his drill-work and cauterization marks in the rock from his high-frequency laser. Elysium lay at the other end of this tunnel.

I knew when I had crossed the equator line by the change in the earth. The barren, ashen tunnel became moist and rich soil, with evidence that Atom had to cut through roots as well as rocks. I tracked Cap Smith's, Kai's, and Halliday's heavy boot prints on the muddy floor and hurried onward.

Eventually, the tunnel burrowed through the massive underpinning of the city walls. The twelve-foot thickness of the foundation was impressive, but still no real impediment to Atom. Clean, rounded lines made a twelve-foot-long hole through the cement as clean as the dirt beneath Elysium's fields.

Once I crossed the wall, it wasn't long before I came upon Captain Christopher Smith's satellite headquarters. A wide, oval shape scraped out of the earth beneath Elysium with ammo, a weapons cache, four mounted screens, and Private William Kai sitting alone, monitoring a coms station, neck arched in the direction of my footsteps.

"*Private William Kai,*" I said in the vocoder like the Terminator.

"Thomas?" He said my name with a trill of uncertainty. With the exosuit and faceplate, I may not have looked so warm and fuzzy.

"My man," I said with my arms out. "Planetary g's hug."

"Thomas!" he shouted, face lit up and jumping to my arms. "The fuck you doing here, man? Wormhole didn't work out?"

"Major mission fail, Kai. Not only did we stay in this solar system, but the attempt creamed us with mega doses of radiation. Me and Ripley—we're dying, Kai."

"What? You fucking serious?"

"Yeah," I said, suddenly short of breath. The look of utter dismay on Kai's face drove home the reality. I was full of meds and adrenaline and the nimble power of the exosuit, mind focused on mission objectives and the ticking clock. The severity of my situation hadn't quite landed until that moment, until those words *we're dying* and Kai's expression. An icy terror stung me, the cold whiff of the abyss.

"Okay," Kai said, taking it in. "Okay, that's fucking terrible, damn. That's, like, the worst fuckin' shit I ever heard. At least tied—with Bonita reprogrammed—fuck, Thomas, what do we do?"

"We need a healthy supply of ultranium. We figure the medical facilities on Elysium must have some."

"Right."

"So mission break-and-enter, snatch-and-grab in full effect. I have to find a viable target, acquire at least twenty gs of ultranium, and hail Lt. Ripley in the *Aquarius*. I've got three syringes of this medicine; each buys me an hour. That's like three and a half hours to pull this off, and scram."

"Shit yeah, okay. Fuck!"

"Why are you down here?" I asked, the scenario on the ground catching up to me. "Where's my dad and Halliday?"

"There," Kai said, pointing to the screens in turn. "And there. Cap Smith appointed me to set up HQ. Wants me to study how they blend in, learn how to act like a UMD patrol drone before I hit the streets."

"Makes sense," I said.

"Anyway, Doc Deer Hunter didn't want me bum-rushing for Bonita. Said I was emotionally compromised or some shit. I'm like, my dude. Who is really emotionally compromised right now?"

I examined the video feeds from my dad and Halliday. My first glimpse within the City of Stars was stunning, even onscreen. The twin POVs strolled side by side along a boardwalk beside a shimmering canal of crystalline water, air bright with the three-form caress of the suns, sky warm blue. People passed wearing extraordinary clothes.

Granted, I was accustomed to a mere rotation of flight suits, workout gear, and dinner jackets while living on Babel. But these getups—outfits, I guess—were of another order even than the most eccentric of Olde Hollywood creations. Colors wild and intoxicating, dress forms with structures built on top of structures, hairstyles defying this hard-won gravity, high heels like avant-garde skyscrapers, hats made of live pets.

The longer those POV cams moved onscreen in silence, the

more the progs became visible. Built in as if background noise, the progs were almost indistinguishable from the city itself. Yet they moved constantly, drove the vehicles, unloaded deliveries, planted boutique plots of agriculture, served plush outdoor dining tables, sailed cruise parties on yachts around the canal, manned the bridge controls, even performed live music.

The efficient buzz of activity reminded me of those Olde movies set in '80s and '90s New York City, like *Ghostbusters, Men in Black, Ninja Turtles*—but it was as if the city of Elysium just muted all the noise, all the working people silent, all the grunts and shouts gone, all the personality of the effort silenced. It was construction without the drilling. Without the filth. And without the voices.

"Seriously, it was the bare minimum of decency to just treat these folks with respect," said Kai, tip-tapping on a keyboard to bring up a third image that pushed aside the video feeds. It was a topographical map. I was somehow not expecting the incredible symmetry of Elysium. The city was built within the encircling wall around a series of circular canals, each feeding to the next, creating clean divisions of land toward the central island. Each division was named as if by a ranking—Fifth Ring, then Fourth, then Third and Second, and on to the Capitol Ring in the center.

"That shape look familiar?" Kai asked.

"It does," I said, trying to place it.

"Your dad says it's based on specific measurements of Plato's description of the lost city of Atlantis."

"Okay, that makes sense. So these are some ambitious fucks."

"Just carrying on the Oldest traditions. The funny shit is, how quickly they do the same shit to each other. See these sections of land? Where you live marks your status among the Ultra 85. Your dad says, the more important you are, the closer you are to the center. So these fools out here on the outer ring? Nobodies. All the other circles piss on them."

"Damn. That's cold."

"What, you think these assholes would just, like, form some land of utopian equality amongst themselves? Nah, fam."

"Guess that makes sense. Just as ruthless with each other, just in different ways."

"This relegation program, Thomas. You fall off that fifth circle? You get slated for reprog."

"Shit."

"Shit you not. High ladder, steep fall. These Ultras are destroyers of man. Kaiju shit, bro. The biggest monster-class gorilla thugs there ever were. Fuck a Frank Lucas, fuck Tony Montana, fuck Tommy from *Goodfellas*, fuck Godzilla, and fuck Göring *and* Goebbels. If you were going back in time to kill a future evil monster as a baby, you'd have to murk *errry* last one of them babies."

Kai's words pumped with the surging adrenaline in my blood.

"Okay. What are we doing sitting here? Let's *go*, Kai."

"You okay, Thomas?"

"Yeah. Just, maybe four gs of adrenaline in these shots."

"All right, chill. Shit, I'm pissed about being benched as well, but really, where we going? You see what our peeps are out there dealing with," Kai said, pointing to the live feeds. "This city is thick with UMD infantry cats. Even on the Fifth Ring."

"Why they need all this manpower? Is this, like, martial law?"

"To keep inferior motherfuckers in check, that's why. Every family is ranked out of the eighty-five, fam. If you got a higher number, the UMD got to listen to you. So you can flex on any one beneath you whenever you want."

"Damn."

"So yeah. We got to watch our step. The faceplates have been working so far, no alarms. But your pops said any action that breaks their behavior programming could trigger Thalia."

Kai moved the zoom on the Elysium map, studying Fifth Ring locations.

"There. A hospital, Fifth Ring."

"And where are we on here?"

"There's a tunnel over that way that leads to a sewer access around this point here."

"What's that? Maybe a fifteen-minute walk from the hospital?"

"About that."

"So, game plan. We infiltrate that hospital, snatch and grab some ultranium, stroll back here like nothing happened. I make it back out the tunnel to Rip within the next six hours."

Kai was cheesing.

"What?"

"Nothin' man. This just reminds me of this story my mama used to tell about my great, great, great grandfather Rooster. In 1863 this retrograde plantation owner was ready to kill him to deny his freedom. Rooster escaped anyway, got cliqued up with a wild gunslinger type, and attempted one of the great train robberies of all time . . ." Kai trailed off.

". . . And?"

"And yeah. Rooster wound up freeing his people. It all came back to that. Anyway, let's rock."

CHAPTER THIRTY-TWO

You hail Cap Smith, let him know," I said to Kai. I was glad to have Kai helping me on my ultranium mission. Having my dad and Atom would be even better.

"No bueno. No outgoing long-range messaging. Cap says it could compromise us."

"If he comes back here and we're gone, you think he'll be pissed?"

"Fuck outta here with that scary teenager shit, QT. I'm not Ferris Bueller, you ain't Cameron, and this ain't your daddy's Ferrari. Come on."

We crawled along a slender tunnel, yippee-ki-yay-mother-fucker-style. Kai had a good sense of the best route to bring us as close as possible to the Fifth Ring hospital. I followed after Kai's feet as they scraped the tunnel's dirt floor. Our voices dead quiet as we went. Then Kai's rhythmic shuffles ceased. He held still. Then he began to move, but to a different rhythm, as he climbed out of the end of the tunnel. The opening was bright with the light of the underground cavern.

Atom's chamber fed into a large cylindric cavern. We walked along a channel of running wastewater as it fed an intricate filtration system of chambers and tubes. The waste was quickly processed into a warm aquamarine color that would then, like on Babel, go on to feed incubation machines that created components for live matter generation.

The sound of footsteps reached us from around the bend. Kai's steady gait slowed. I stiffened and forced my muscles to imitate him, to keep our steps as uniform as possible. The clop of boots came louder, closer.

A massive faceplate appeared. Glassy, yellow eyes like pale lamps. The face beneath was a hard, gray, marbleized flesh. No lips, only the film of decay above withered teeth. An exoskeleton supported every bone, skewered with tiny spikes like nerve endings. The creature walked in vac-suit boots and stopped to swivel and examine us with a baleful gaze.

I froze.

Kai swiveled his head back in return. They might have been freakish mirror images, as the zombie reprog and Will Kai had a nose-to-nose playground stare down like *White Men Can't Jump*.

Then, calmly, slowly, the zombie reprog and Kai swiveled in synch back the way they were going, deemed no further interaction necessary, and walked on.

"Kai," I whispered once we were well out of earshot. "They fucking keep using us—*after* we die?"

"I think so, Thomas."

"What the fuck?"

"Probably they freak people out, so they do underground, out-of-sight work. But good news. We passed. We code as normal UMD, none of that zombie sewagebot's business."

We climbed up several layers of city underwork to open a

hatch that led to a glorious street above. It was just as well that Kai and I had to move in deliberate slow-mo, because I wanted to soak up every moment.

The trinity of suns—blood orange, pale yellow, and tangerine—climbed an arc in the serene sky. The live feed video had not prepared me for this. I was dazzled, lightheaded. Kai, too, seemed stunned by the explosion of physical sensory data. Our flesh had barely felt the light of one sun, much less three. Sunlight that was somehow a warm embrace and an aroma and a flavor all at once. Sunlight that feeds you. Air that loves you. The long-awaited sheer overwhelming reunion of the human body with a perfect day.

Rows of outdoor dining and drink spots lined the banks along the canal. We came up on a reprog trio playing live funk bass instrumental beats. Families thronged around the band. Slowed down by the thickness of the crowd, we had an excuse to enjoy the music.

This was another breathtaker for me. The drummer straight killed this break beat, while an electric bass hit a line so hard it changed the water flow. The Ultras took it in in strange ways. There was dancing. There was some head nodding. There were a lot of intense stares. These people in elaborate, overdesigned couture had the gunpoint glares of stalking jungle cats. Mostly, though, there were smirks. A common curl along the lips. A little jab of the mouth projecting detached bemusement. Yet behind the arrogance was the knowledge that there were no more steps before the fall. The Fifth Ring was the end of the line. A slip from this ledge meant death.

The suns dimmed to deeper, evening shades of ochre, burgundy, and burnt sienna. The party evolved into circles of chatter. Bars lined the canal, feeding cocktails to the party. Progs with suit-rigged serving trays moved through the crowds, handing out drinks. They each seemed chosen for a particular look, a dull-eyed beauty, with open, submissive yet alluring mouths. It occurred to me that not all progs were saddled with these heavy, invasive facepieces. Must be certain roles where the Ultras want their progs pretty.

Not the UMD. Apparently someone wanted their enforcement arm scary as fuck. Terminators that moved like alpha wolves on patrol through the crowds in orange jumpsuits and gunmetal exosuits. We mimicked the big dog stroll. The whole party had an air like there's only predators in the cage, see who ends up prey.

The music there seemed beside the point. A mild amusement. Another boring extravagance. Something to cool the heat of their rivalries.

As we came to the open circle separating the crowd from the band, I found myself lingering. I knew I was perhaps breaking UMD protocol, but I simply could not help myself. This was *awesome*. The music took possession of me. I comingled with the melody. I maybe mistook the beat and bass for the throb of my blood.

There was a young Ultra girl in the front row. She also gave her full attention to the band, dancing with a wild jangling of awkward limbs, body trying and failing to find the beat. Her family made a circle of black couture elegance with upturned lips. The smirks were so samey I questioned if they'd all undergone some fashionable surgery to look like they especially didn't give a shit. The man I pegged as her father was holding court with the family and several serving progs with drink trays, making wry toasts and downing shots.

No one was watching the little girl when she decided that she'd had enough.

She stared at the drummer girl, a leather-studded prog with punk-shaggy, Joan Jett hair that shook with the pounding of her arms.

Some raw, animal rage broke in the Ultra girl. She rushed the band. She hurled the drummer from her perch with a two-hand shove. Mid-snare, the drummer prog was flung off balance. She tumbled over headfirst, barely protecting her skull with her powerful arms.

Maybe the sudden outburst of violence itself wasn't remarkable. But it did stop the music.

A snap of necks whipped around, hackles raised.

The only one unperturbed was the little Ultra girl. Without a flicker of self-consciousness, without acknowledging the drummer prog on the ground, she picked up the stool, sat down, and began banging the drums. *Terribly*.

As I pulled my attention away from the scene, I realized that Kai was ahead of me; several spectators had slipped in between us. Behind his faceplate he gave me a look I read as, *The fuck you doing?*

"Ey!" shot a contemptuous voice.

I cranked my head to the source.

"That your daughter?" a woman appearing late twenties asked the lush.

"So fucking what?" he snarled back.

"Go get your daughter, that's fucking what," snapped the first speaker's Ken-doll companion.

"And make her my mistress?" smirked the lush. "Sorry. I'm not a Vandersvelt seventy-nine."

"That's seventy-seven, jackass!" shouted the (apparently)

Vandersvelt young woman with a glare that marked her as years older than her skincare could reveal. "Shut your sheep-fucking Gansderwobs mouth."

"Better a sheep than an inbred Vandersvelt whore," said the lush. "What a choice! To be a Vandersvelt. Whether to fuck a sheep or a sister."

The Vandersvelt woman cocked back an open hand—her nails were too long to make a fist—when her companion—father, or husband, I'm not sure—grabbed her wrist.

"That was wise," said the lush, taking a big sip as his daughter ceaselessly banged on the drums, the horrible noise effectively turning the party into onlookers.

"Your daughter is an embarrassment," said the Vandersvelt man.

"Control your fucking family," snapped the woman.

"Fuck you, Gansderwobs."

"Fuck me? No, fuck you"—he pointed at her—"and fuck you"—he pointed at the man. "Maybe you haven't heard, seventy-nine, or was it seventy-seven? I closed our deal. The Larzdenburn board's coup failed. I own WobConn *and* Viasnatch. That's right. And veto power over Azriel holdings."

"Promotion!" toasted the cheering Gansderwobs.

"—to rank seventy-five, you dumb bitch," snarled the drunk patriarch. "You!" he shouted, and pointed. "Throw them in the river!"

It took me a moment to realize he was pointing at me.

did exactly what a program does when a task request has overwhelmed its system.

I froze.

A blaze of red letters suddenly jumped into my line of sight.

The fuck, what did you do, fam?

After another internal system hiccup, I realized it was Kai. He'd worked the short-range coms text feature. I glanced over to him and saw his fingers moving at his sides as if they tapped a keyboard.

You done fucked up now, he sent, helpfully.

The crowd jeered. The Vandersvelts shouted a torrent of curses at the Gansderwobs. The responses were drunk sneers and trills of hyena-pitched giggles.

"I said, throw them in the fucking river," repeated the lush to the cacophonous clanging of his daughter's drums. The heinous sound became an expression of his newfound power.

Dude, he's a 75, they're 77s, at best. I think we got to do whatever he says, Kai typed.

I really didn't like this.

Yeah, it sucks but we can't get caught out here, he continued like he'd read my mind.

We each took reluctant steps toward the Vandersvelts.

Kai took the Vandersvelt man. I took the woman. With the exoskeleton, my grip was like a steel cuff. They each went surprisingly limp. Once the UMD intervened, the dominant power of the Ultras had asserted judgment.

I guess that's a reason why the UMD were so badass. To enforce social humiliation.

"Princess, stop that racket," the paterfamilias Gansderwobs called to his young girl.

Parenting his girl, I suppose, wasn't the issue, but the appearance of acquiescence to a lesser family.

The Gansderwobs girl would not listen.

By now, the netting and structure that styled her hair had come loose and been ripped out. The awful clanging of the noise was not apparent by the look on her face, though. She was enraptured. The drummer prog stood by her and watched in submission. To the Gansderwobs girl, that shit sounded as good as anything beat out by the actual drummer. It was everyone else that had to cover their ears, and she could not care less. She was in the heat of passion.

"Attila, I said stop!" said the dad, getting frustrated and coming toward her.

More Gansderwobs joined him, cousins and such, backing him up. The girl did not care.

"Stop right now, you irritating little insect." The paterfamilias brought rage now on the girl, which only triggered her unbridled defiance.

"No!" she shrieked. "I'm gonna play. Fuck you! Fuck your whole face!"

I was near floored by that language coming from a girl no older than ten. The Ultras seemed unfazed.

"What are you, a windup music slavebot?" roared her father. "Have some dignity."

Kai and I slowed, wondering if the commotion might let us off the hook.

The lush Gansderwobs shouted back at us, "The river! Now! And my daughter is next if she won't listen."

"You wish, fuckface," snarled Attila the Little Girl.

The river was maybe seven feet below the boardwalk edge.

Kai and I looked at each other like, *We really about to do this*?

Then Ripley's *five-minute* alert flashed in the lower corner of my HUD, adding to my stress. Five minutes until the sickness came back. And I could hardly break out a syringe and shoot a cocktail right now to stave it off.

All the hard realities of that moment crashed down on me. If I couldn't pull this mission off, I'd die and so would Ripley. If Kai or I broke our roles as UMD right now, we'd lose everyone.

Strangely enough though, the final will to chuck the Vandersvelts over the side came from the resignation and submission of the Vandersvelts themselves. Like they understood far better than we ever would why they'd broken the inviolate rules of the Ultras and must suffer the consequences. Though they may have survived as among the top 85 families of Olde Earth, here in the only world that mattered to them, they were bottom-feeders. The pretense of status had been shattered, and that doubt and shame that bleeds from the heart of every human being took hold.

A crowd had gathered to watch the double feature. There was the Attila the Little Girl Show over there, and the dunk-a-douchey-couple show over here.

Kai and I, together and stone-faced, lifted first the Vandersvelt man, light as a doll, careful so as not to jostle or pinch, and hurled him over the side.

He made quite a splash. He bobbed to the surface and spit a mouthful of water, paddling in drenched clothing with the flow of the current.

"Fuck!" he yelled, and slammed his fists on the water's surface.

The woman was next. She had steeled her expression. I wondered, what was the level of force that a UMD drone was authorized here? Could that be why they didn't dare struggle? Would the UMD do serious damage to another Ultra if a superior ordered it? How far could this go?

Reluctantly, Kai and I took the woman in hand and got it over with.

She made a smaller splash, hair spoiled and spread in the flowing water like seaweeds.

The crowd gathered along the railing to watch the Vandersvelts tread water. Kai and I were suddenly less interesting.

The drunken paterfamilias continued to struggle with his willful daughter behind us. He'd grabbed her by the wrists, but she poked him in the eye with a drumstick and took off. A few Gansderwobs chased after her awkwardly in high-concept heels.

I sensed the opening and resumed my Terminator stroll the fuck out of there.

The one-minute alert now flashed in the lower corner of my HUD.

Kai followed as I led the way to a ladder that connected to a service platform just above the water. I'd spotted the ladder when we were throwing the Vandersvelts in the river.

Good call, Kai texted. *UMDs seem to patrol service areas too. More covert, feel me?*

I nodded, playing with some of my HUD controls that bubbled up from the motions of my fingers, trying to recall the sequence for responding to his messages. I wanted to tell him, I had to take a shot. But I didn't dare speak out loud and blow cover, huffing at the air and short of breath.

We climbed down the ladder one at a time and footed the narrow service platform. Without railings or hand grips, the platform was clearly designed with total indifference to the lives of those walking it. We maintained the Terminator walk with each careful step.

I tapped Kai's shoulder. He glanced around, saw no one in sight, and turned to me.

Steadying my breath, I motioned like a syringe to my arm. He nodded, fingers tapping.

Copy that, Thomas. Think I see a spot up here.

I nodded and grunted behind him.

Ten seconds.

Five seconds.

I felt waves of nausea with the dizzying flow of water.

Two . . .

My knees grew weaker with each step.

One . . .

The alert flashed up on my HUD.

Jabby-jab, pricky-prick . . . Jabby-jab, pricky-prick, read the chyron of Ripley's custom timer alarm.

Shit.

The walkway led under a bridge. There was an undercroft with bins and barrels lined up. I crouched beside one of them as Kai kept watch.

"You need help?" he whispered.

I was overcome by fatigue and lightheadedness. I backed up into the bin and slid down. The exosuit required my will to stay up, and I'd lost even that. Kai held me by the arm and slowly lowered me to sit on the ground.

"Okay, Thomas. I got you," he gently whispered.

I snapped out the syringe and jabbed the needle into my exposed arm.

I sat for a beat, eyeing the shadowy water beneath the bridge as it caught stray light of fading suns. I focused on my breathing. As long as I was breathing, I knew I was alive.

A sudden jolt raced through my blood. My heart rate sped a couple knots past lightspeed. The surge kicked my head back, air rushed through my nostrils. My nausea stabilized and my mind seized with alertness.

"Okay," I said, wrestling my breaths to an even pace, willing my heart rate to calm down. "Okay!" I barked. "It's kicking in."

"You okay, fam?"

"Yeah, okay. Just, damn, that shit was intense. Rip timed it for each shot to last me to the brink."

"Probably just trying to give you the best chance possible to find the meds."

"Indeed, Kai." I took him by the hand. "Clock's ticking. Let's move." We rose to our feet together.

"That was some terrible shit, throwing them in the water like that," said Kai.

"The worst," I agreed. "What kind of expedition is this? Like, where are we, Kai?"

"Fuck if I know, Thomas."

The lid to the bin behind us suddenly snapped open.

The naughty Gansderwobs child, Attila the Little Girl, popped her head up, cherubic face framed by wild, undone hair.

"Why are you talking to each other like that?" she asked.

CHAPTER THIRTY-FOUR

2 Hours to Midnight

Well?" she demanded, standing erect with fists on her hips. A real live Ultra 85 girl, insisting we explain ourselves.

"Uh—"

"Shit, Thomas!"

"Why are you talking like that?" she shrieked with a hint of fear.

"We are fucked—"

"You!" she said to me. "Answer now!"

"Uh, hi, sweetheart," I began, holding out a hand like I meant no harm.

"I'm not your fucking sweetheart, dipshit!"

"Damn!"

"Stop talking nonsense and answer me. What's your malfunction?"

"Look, hun—" Kai attempted.

"I said shut your fucking mouth!"

"What my friend Kai is trying to say, we're not—not progs." I took a chance and unstrapped and took off my faceplate. "We're people."

The girl flinched and sneered and asked the next most logical question.

"What's your number?" She assumed we had to be part of an Ultra family.

"No number. Just a person."

"Help! Help!" Attila let out a scream like the *Aquarius*'s immanent collision alarm.

"No!" Kai and I leaped at the same time.

We grabbed her sideways and covered her mouth as she tried to bite and shout through our hands.

"Oh, I really don't fucking like this, Kai," I said.

"What are we supposed to do?" he asked in a panic. "We'll die! Rip will die!"

"Yeah, I know!" The adrenaline raced through me, pounding, insisting I do something, anything. "Little girl? Little, uh, Attila? Be good now, okay? Please? I can put you down. I want to put you down. Just, no screaming. Okay? Pretty please, little girl?"

She calmed a fraction and stopped screaming, nostrils huffing above my hand like a mare.

"Okay. Good! We don't want to hurt you. We're good, you know—"

She scrunched her eyes in suspicion.

"—people. We're good people. We just—man, this is hard to explain."

"You're escaped slaves," she informed us.

Kai and I immediately locked eyes.

"From the incubator," she went on. "I get it."

"Ouch," said Kai. "My ancestor Rooster felt that one."

"Now answer my question," she dug in. "Why did you talk to him like that?"

"Like what?" I asked.

"Like you didn't want to throw those douchebags in the river? Why? What gives?"

"What do you mean?" asked Kai. "Listen, little girl, we're from different worlds. Where we come from, you get along with other people, it's not that hard."

"That's idiotic. What are you doing here?"

"At the moment, trying to save a pretty important couple of people's lives from radiation poisoning—"

"Thomas—" Kai cut in.

"Important how?" asked Attila.

"Well, one of them happens to be me," I admitted. "So that matters."

"It does?"

"Thomas, I don't think we're going to see eye to eye with this girl," Kai got out. "And we really don't have time for this."

"I know, Kai, what do you propose?"

"Hate to say it, but we got to tie her up, leave her here. Somebody will find her, eventually."

"No!" the girl wailed, and then started screaming, "Help! Help! Rogue NPCs, heeeelp!" until we grabbed her up again.

"You see?" said Kai. "She's dangerous!" Kai produced a cable from his exosuit.

"I don't love it," I said.

"You feel bad, Thomas? She's literally Attila the Little Girl, man! She'll just grow up to rape and pillage!"

"Or play the drums!" I said.

"They don't even let kids do music here, fam, it's beneath them. Besides, I don't know what makes you think she got a lick of talent."

As we debated what to do with Attila the Little Girl, commotion echoed on the bridge above, noisy with bangs and clangs almost like Attila's drums. The footsteps of a mass of people rushed onto the bridge from either side. Shouts echoed in the underpass. Two sets of voices squared off, striving for dominance over the other. Stray phrases broke clear from the noise.

"—think this is a fucking game?"

"—rip your nostrils—"

"—break your fucking face!"

We could not see to the bridge above, only the shadows of a crowd of people that played over the water.

"What's happening, Thomas?"

"Sounds like—a fight? No, a brawl."

Intrafamily brawls were common for the Ultras. Power struggles would erupt constantly between competing off-shoots, like these Caesarion and Octavian wings of the Augusto-Julian 84. When relegation loomed for the families at the bottom, they'd start tearing themselves apart. A wave of wails filled the night, and a mass collision of bones and bodies.

Kai and I held still as statues.

Attila the Little Girl was struggling to say something as the thuds and hits of the brawl bounced and echoed in the underpass.

Suddenly a body slammed down on our planform. A brawler had been hurled from above and crashed into the waste barrels, sending them spinning and rolling.

Kai's hand went to his sidepiece.

The brawler groaned and got to his feet. Bloody nose and split lip, he saw us.

"What's going on?" he asked.

"H-hel—"

I clamped my hand down before she could call for help.

Kai slowly drew his handgun, hidden from the brawler's view.

The mid-twenties-looking Caesarion or Octavian Augusto-Julian 84 stood bleeding in a high popped collar. He had light-blond foppish hair and an almost cartoon busted complexion. Dilated pupils swirled in his eyes.

Kai glanced to his gun and checked with me.

I nodded.

Attila the Little Girl, clocking this, freed her teeth and bit hard on my finger.

"Yeow!"

"These are my personal bodyguards," she told the fop. "I like them to pretend to hurt me, so I can do this—"

She made a fist and cracked me across the jaw.

I spun back, adrenaline pumping double time, but then I pulled up short, realizing what she was doing.

"And this—" She clocked me again.

"This—" She kicked me in the knee, so I bent over. She climbed up my back and slapped Kai across the face.

Kai also took a moment, but played along, and his gun stayed out of sight.

"Oh," said the fop with a trill of laughter. "Absolutely savage," he said with admiration.

"Who's winning?" asked Attila.

"I haven't the slightest idea," said the fop, climbing back up to get in the fight on the bridge.

Once he was out of sight, she whirled on us. "Are you morons? You were going to shoot him," she accused Kai.

"Yeah," said Kai. "And I might shoot you, too."

"If you want to die slow, motherfucker."

"I'm not sure you understand the severity of our situation," I said.

"Right. You said, sad sad life or death something or other, boo-hoo. You kill an Ultra, even a dipshit eighty-four? The whole Fifth Ring gets shut down," she said with a snort. "I mean, if they can afford a Basic Birthright Life Alert Chip Package," she added.

"The fuck do you care?" asked Kai.

"I don't." She shrugged. "I just like to play with my toys before I break them."

"So that's what this is?" I asked. "We're your toys?"

"Yeah, no thanks, Master Bates," said Kai, pulling out the cord to tie her up.

"You dumbasses don't get it. I can activate my Life Alert chip whenever I want. My family will find me in seconds. You two are so fucking fucked."

Kai and I exchanged dubious looks. Was this a scam? How could we know?

"So go ahead, tie me up. Walk away. I'll set the alarm, UMD brutes will shred you clowns before you cross the bridge."

"Wait. Why haven't you sounded the alarm already?" I asked.

"I want to see what happens." She shrugged again. "I like toys."

"Got to be kidding me," said Kai. "Thomas, I call bullshit—"

"Possible, Kai, but can we take the risk?"

"You don't understand," said Attila. "You don't have a choice."

"So what do you want, little girl?" I pleaded. "Will you let us do what we came to do?"

She grinned. "I want to watch."

CHAPTER THIRTY-FIVE

A ttila the Little Girl led the way down the boardwalk toward the Fifth Ring hospital. We hoped to find ultranium there. The plan was for Attila to demand her way to the radiation treatment supply. She seemed to think we could pull it off. She just said that as a seventy-five in the Fifth Ring, lots of times she can go anywhere she wants and no one says anything. Armed with this childish logic and desperation, we took the forward approach. The biggest risk to take was to break character. Scaling the walls and busting through windows was chancier than strolling through the front door and acting like a UMD drone.

Cap Smith's data cache had a map of the hospital, and we pinpointed the Exposure and Isolation Wing as the best bet for ultranium. However, we knew even that was flimsy. Not for the first time, I wished we had Atom with us.

Acting the bodyguard part, Kai and I walked a step behind Attila. We sank into our surroundings, watching the faces of hardware-heavy progs going about their jobs in quiet efficiency. To me, though, it felt like they were each crying out. *Help me. End this hellish treadmill.*

The Fifth Ring hospital was a single-story building with

a massive, three-centered archway open to foot traffic, med units, and, as usual, the coming and going of silent sentries.

You ready? Kai typed.

As I'll ever be, I responded, getting the hang of it.

Activate game plan, he sent.

Bust in, I wrote.

Everybody hit the fucking floor.

Grab the junk.

Let's go. Spot Rusherz shit.

We were armed to the teeth, each with a plasma rifle and a blaster sidepiece.

As we passed beneath the three-centered archway, I had to remind myself why this was the only play. Linking with Cap Smith and team would change that calculus, but they could be anywhere. Sure, they could show up back at underground HQ in an hour, or two, or twelve. The window to save Rip and myself could close. We had to roll the dice.

Still, there were many ways the dice could turn up a pair of *We're fucked.* We could blow our cover and trigger the security protocol Fifth Ring lockdown, where walls would form around the riverbanks and the UMD would coordinate direct action. We could fail to get the ultranium *and* blow my dad's cover. We could compromise the entire operation and get every last one of us killed.

"Hey!" Attila pinpointed a slubby-looking Ultra wearing a surprisingly overdesigned set of black coveralls. Though at least a decade older, the Ultra winced at Attila. I guessed they knew each other, hierarchical roles firmly established.

"Weakling Winlarsden. Where are you coming from?"

"Uh, Gansderwobs, hi. Nowhere," she said, face made up, platinum goth chic. "Just visiting."

"Save your gloomy bullshit. Visiting who?"

"My stepmom, she's getting a new nervous system, that's all."

"What's the cow's name, Winlarsden?" Attila said with impatience through gritted teeth.

"K-Kathryn."

As the answer came, Attila turned on her heel and moved on.

"Nice bodyguards," called the Winlarsden. "What happened. You get rich?"

The air was cool in the hospital; the entryway sprayed a fine, refreshing hydration mist.

A pleasant receptionist prog with a blond bob and a retro nurse uniform zipped up to Attila on a wheeled platform.

"How may I assist you today?" the receptionist asked the young Ultra girl with a smile of genuine sympathy so warm it fooled me.

"Visiting Kathryn Winlarsden," Attila answered without breaking stride.

"Yes, of course," said the prog as she wheeled up ahead of Attila. "Right this way," she said, zipping backward with that smile again. I had to fight the urge to smile back. The receptionist was the most human face I'd seen on Elysium, and she was a computer program.

She led us through the outpatient wing, a hallway with spacious, open rooms on either side, and glass panels so the dance of sunlight brightened the way forward. Orderly progs hustled gurneys and pushed med chairs. We pressed on to a glassed-in corridor connecting to the inpatient wing. We glanced into the open doors. These rooms were larger than a three-family dwelling pod on Babel. Full kitchenettes and sitting areas lined with plots of manicured flowers and plants, growing beneath luminous glass skylights.

The receptionist zipped backward up to a door labeled with the Winlarsden name.

"Please, wait right here, at your pleasure," she said with serene empathy.

A voice called her in.

"So what the fuck are you two waiting for?" Attila asked us.

Kai and I did not look at her, or each other. There was safety in playing true to the part. Once we broke cover, jump ball. Anything could go down.

"What in hell does a Gansderwobs girl want with me?" growled a voice from inside.

"This is it. She's not going to take you where you want to go," said Attila. "Make her."

She was right, and Kai realized it too. I snapped off my faceplate. Kai did the same. We glanced down the hallway. No orderlies in sight. We drew our guns and each stood back to the wall on either side the door. Breathed in, deep through the nose. Locked eyes. Nodded.

And bust into the room, guns out.

"All right!" I yelled.

"Everybody chill the fuck out!" went Kai.

"Take us to the Exposure Wing right now and no one gets hurt!" I shouted.

Guns pointed at the receptionist.

She tilted her head at the two nozzle points with a serene gaze.

"Not her, dumbasses!" Attila shouted, pointing to the Winlarsden lady in the bed. "Her!"

Kai and I swung our pistols at Kathryn, no skipped beat.

"What in hell," she grunted. "Who the hell are you people? What do you want with me?"

"I got good news, I got bad news."

"Good news is, play this right, you get to live."

"Bad news is, you don't and it's that other thing."

"What other thing?" she asked.

"The not-living thing," I said.

"You are terrible at this," said Attila. "She doesn't even know what you want."

Kai and I glanced at the other.

"Make the receptionist take you where you want to go!" Attila shouted.

"Exposure Wing!" Kai and I said together.

The skylight sun slanted across Kathryn's face. She appeared in her mid-fifties with a strong jaw and natural gray hair. She cut narrow eyes at the muzzle. "Receptionist," she said in a steady voice. "Take these men to the Exposure Wing—"

"And give us all your ultranium—"

"And give them all your ultranium, please."

"Certainly," said the receptionist. "However, I am afraid we do not keep ultranium in this facility."

As her words sank in, the room flashed with the white glare of a hospital security alarm.

CHAPTER THIRTY-SIX

A shadow fanned across Kathryn Winlarsden's sunlit face. I followed the source up through the skylight to a spinning rotor blade.

Attila giggled.

Our cover was blown.

Four UMD soldiers rappelled down either side of a troop transport hover-vehicle, boots crashing down. A *boom* ripped the air as troops burst through the skylight. As Kai and I dove for cover, glass shattered and rained on the room. Attila was directly under a cascade of shards, and I leaped to cover her with the hull of my exosuit. Glass hailed down on my back, both tearing into my flesh and thudding off the scales of the metallic spine. Kathryn was not so lucky. The glass dumped down and shredded her, leaving only a bloody unmoving lump on the bed.

The UMD rappelled to the floor and drew their guns.

"Take me hostage!" said Attila as I held myself propped up by my arms. "Quick!"

With a Jackie Chan move, I wrapped Attila up with one arm, gun out, and simultaneously fell backward to cover Kai.

"Don't move, I'll shoot!" I yelled.

Their guns whipped to train on us. The UMD faces drilled points of red light on our heads.

"Hold on, Thomas!" Kai said, wrapping his arm back around me. He snapped his sidepiece and blasted out the window behind us with a shattering crash. He hooked on my waist and said, "Jump!"

My arm around Attila, Kai's arm around me, we leaped backward as Kai swung us through the open window, out into open sky. Where we dropped straight down. I slammed back-first into the pavement, holding the girl to my chest. I stared up, wind knocked out my lungs.

We were in a parking lot. The lockdown alarm blared throughout the Fifth Ring. Helicopter rotor blades thundered overhead. Walls rose with electrified razor wire along the banks of the river as the UMD swarmed. Hulks hovered above the lot on repulsor jets and aimed their guns.

I sat up, Attila on my lap.

"Okay. *Now* you're fucked," said Attila.

I remembered Ripley's call button set on my left shoulder. *Two taps, drop bombs.*

But I paused.

Was it even worth it? Call Rip just to save my ass, having accomplished nothing?

Then a grinding sound came from beneath the pavement. A drill point shattered the surface and rose up from underneath. Atom's head appeared through the hole. I couldn't fucking believe it.

"This way!" said Atom.

Kai was first to leap down the tunnel. I went next, then Attila, and we slipped and crashed into Kai.

"Atom!" I shouted in the mangle of bodies and hardware. "Atom, I've never been so happy to see anyone!"

"Atom," my father ordered, standing over us in the dark tunnel, "seal the opening!"

"Dad!" I said.

Atom quickly scrambled back up the tunnel and soldered a scrap of metal to the pavement around the hole.

"Got your message, Cap Smith," said Kai, getting to his feet.

"Huh?" I said.

"He texted me to jump down to the parking lot, dude," said Kai.

The light from Halliday's eyepiece shined on Attila the Little Girl.

"Who the hell is this?" asked my dad.

"That's—"

"Attila Gansderwobs, runaway," said Attila, folding her arms.

"What's she doing here?" said Cap Smith.

"She actually helped us," I said.

"What are *you* doing here?" His attention snapped to me.

Before I could answer, Atom leaped back down to join us.

"Time is of the essence, Captain," said Atom.

"Word," said Kai.

"Follow me," said Cap Smith. "The girl stays."

"I will not," she said.

"She's an Ultra, she's too dangerous," my dad shouted over his shoulder.

Atom followed us behind Cap Smith. "The Enemy will be through in moments. I suggest we cave in this tunnel. Is your order to leave the girl here for that?"

My dad glanced at Atom.

Then he growled, and marched on.

I waved to Attila to come along.

A vehicle waited in the sewer tunnel. The water frothed with a series of spinning rotor blades beneath the surface; it was a clear cylinder the size of a mess cabin on the *Aquarius*, surrounded by a float tube. A door slid open, and Halliday climbed in and took the controls. As the idling vehicle stalled for Atom, we each boarded in turn.

A light pierced the gloom, coming toward us from the tunnel's throat as it closed. There was Atom. An avalanche of dirt and foundation and pipework crashed down behind him as he leaped to us. Kai and I caught his hands with our exo-gloves.

"He's in!" called my dad as the doors slid closed.

Looking Attila in the eye, my dad dropped to a crouch.

"Quentin," he said. "You fucked us."

CHAPTER THIRTY-SEVEN

As we steered through the sewer tunnels, membrane filters buzzed and whirled around the submarined vehicle known as a dolphin. The water was a silty aqua green and smelled faintly of peaches.

We'd just escaped the Fifth Ring lockdown, and with the dolphin, we could infiltrate deeper rings within Elysium. I wasn't sure how to feel about Attila. She was profoundly reckless and dangerous. But she helped us. And she offered just what we needed—someone on the inside. Only my dad wasn't having it.

"We'll drop her at the next wastewater collection point," my dad said.

"Fuck that," said Attila, breaking from Atom.

"Dad, listen. The wormhole was a bust. Me and Rip, we got creamed by radiation. We're dying, Dad. I'm running on ultranium compound shots and adrenaline." I pointed to the ring of two syringes. My dad stood at attention. "Sorry, Dad. New mission. We got to hit—"

He grabbed me by the forearm and held a finger to my lips, and shot a look at Attila.

"She should not hear this—"

"She saw me take a shot," I said. "She knows I need the ultranium."

"Nothing operational, Quentin!" he shouted, and shook me.

"She doesn't fucking care," agreed Kai.

"But she tried to help us break into the Fifth Ring hospital."

"And her plan is the reason why we had to save you. She's one of them, Quentin!"

"Fuck you," she snarled.

"Play nice," I said.

I expected her to bite my hand. She actually shrugged, grimaced, and sort of took it.

"Attila, I think you better sit this one out," I told her, not wanting to challenge my father on this.

"I didn't tell you to think."

"You almost got killed up there," I told her.

Attila squinted up her face, sneered, and folded her arms, but said nothing.

"We're not in the Fifth Ring anymore, little girl," said my dad. "What's your number, anyway?"

"Seventy-five," she said.

"Ha!" barked my dad. "They'll scrape you off their boot."

"Whatever. Just, I'm coming with you. Or I blow my Life Alert, right here. Think the alert will work underwater? Want to find out?"

The dolphin buzzed along in quiet for a few heartbeats. The reality of her Life Alert chip was checkmate.

"Okay. I hate it. But fine. She's another of a long list of risks now. We got an avalanche of shit working against us. What's one more rogue explosive Ultra?"

"We're surrounded," I said. "That simplifies the problem. I

don't know how we do it, but I know what we'll do. Grab the ultranium. Call in the *Aquarius*."

"How far out?" asked my dad.

"Three minutes."

"Bonita Burton," Atom began, "codename Bonita Applebum. We know where she is."

"You do?" Kai nearly leaped out of his exosuit.

"She is in the Capitol Ring."

"When were you going to tell us this?" I asked.

"We just updated mission parameters, Quentin."

The tension rose a few degrees within our party. I'd just thrown my dad a big curve. Now, instead of his covert insurgency operation, we'd changed the mission to securing ultranium. Fine. He understood that had to happen, to save my life and Ripley's. But the idea of looping Bonita into the mix was not part of either plan. But for Kai, Bonita was all that mattered.

"Respectfully, I call bullshit," said Kai.

"Easy, Kai," I tried to soothe.

"Don't *easy Kai* me, fam! You found your father, dog. Let me get my girl."

"You're rotten with movie brain. All of you," said my dad. "Think you can wave a couple guns in the Capitol, ride out into the sunset? You'd risk you—my son—risk Ripley—to make a play for some—"

"She's one of us," said Kai.

"They're all ones of us! The easiest thing to want is to save them all."

"Why can't we?" I asked.

"You don't understand. The things they do in your movies?

It's lies. Olde Hollywood was the land of lies. They didn't know they were dying, they were numb from the lies."

"Yeah. And we were too, on Babel," I said.

"But you're a special kind of fool, Quentin. With two species of lies twisting your mind. That utopian poison from Babel. And Olde Hollywood romantic fantasy bullshit."

"Hit him," said Attila. "He looks like he'll scrap."

"I'm sick of your fucking mouth, Deer Hunter," said Kai. "You want to spin the wheel, blow out your own brains, that's on you. We trying to work over here. We got a lot of problems, yeah. But we also got some strong arms. We got heart. We got the hellified gang gang. We got a motherfucking Atom. That's a fucking type of 'fuck you,' that's a bird Thalia and these Ultras ain't been flipped yet."

Atom looked at me as if waiting for direction. Right then, it hit me. By Atom's coding, I superseded my dad in chain of command. I was captain of Atom's *Aquarius III*, while Captain Smith wouldn't register as an active IMC officer. The call was mine to make.

"I agree with Kai," I said. "We go in hard. We hit them. We stay together. We bag Bonita. We bag the ultranium. We fucking dip, hard."

"We're here to fight, Captain. Fight with us."

He nodded. "To my last breath."

CHAPTER THIRTY-EIGHT

New mission objectives: 1. Bag Bonita. 2. Bag ultranium. In any order.

Bonita, as it turned out, was kept in a Fifth Ring facility known as the Joy Division.

The Joy Division was not a typical stomping ground for UMD drones. Unlike the hospital and the sewers, we could not march through the front doors with impunity, because UMD drones don't belong inside the Joy Division. That was sure to trigger a lockdown protocol, and this time we'd be good and fucked. So the plan was for Atom to tunnel to the bordello from underground, guided by the plumbing maps included in the stolen data sets. Once inside, we hoped to find Bonita and break her out, by hook or by crook. Only we didn't know exactly how. The plan was to improvise.

The Ultras' big weakness, according to my dad, was over-reliance on Thalia, and Thalia's big weakness was her singularity as a system. Since Atom's AI was constructed from a fundamentally different model—and not from Olde Earth minds but from post-Earth Babel scientists—her firewalls were unprepared for the ways he might approach. We hoped that was enough for mission success.

"We'd made some headway mapping the city," my dad explained as the tricolor light of the suns filtered through the crystalline waters surrounding us. "We'd made it as far as the Capitol Ring canal when the Fifth Ring alarm went live. Halliday here made quick work of the drive. We cracked some data from the dolphin itself, fed Halliday a traffic map of the sewers and canals. Sent Private Kai an alert once we were in range. Atom did the rest."

As the dolphin rose to the surface of the sewer water, I thought I'd vomit. We each disembarked. Atom made use of his drill arms to tunnel along the pipelines. I saw Ripley's alarm flashing in my HUD. Five minutes until the effects of my last shot wore off.

Figured this was a good time to shoot Ripley's cocktail and stave off the sickness. I did not want to wait to the last moment like last time, even if that might buy me a few minutes on the back end.

Atom broke through the earth and infrastructure, making a vertical trail for us to follow. I let everyone go ahead of me, and stayed behind.

Pressing the plunger all the way down, I immediately felt the juice through my blood. I noticed Attila looking right at me.

"Why are you doing that?"

"So I don't die."

"But, like, why?"

"Listen, I can't tell if you're messing with me. I want to live. It's pretty relatable. Why are you so interested?"

"My mom was a slavebot," she said in a quiet voice.

That shut me up for a second. I hadn't expected an answer, much less a real one.

"That's . . . wow. That's weird, huh?"

"My dad says he's my mom."

"Okay. But you know it doesn't quite work like that, right?"

"Like, he made me mixed with his female-modified DNA. Bred out the defects. My mom was just an incubator, he said."

"Christ."

"Like, how you all incubate. Wherever you come from," she said. "But I always kind of wondered what she was like anyway. He said you own her, you own your mom. She's like the washer/dryer unit. Spud goes in, baby comes out."

"How's that make you feel, when he says that?"

"I dunno. I'm a Gansderwobs. I'm a little-girl him. Maybe we'll get married, he teases me. Go full family strong. Have a slave-formed baby. From his DNA. My DNA, I guess. I don't know. It'll all bullshit. He's bullshit. If I die, that'd be hilarious. He spent a fortune."

"Don't talk like that," I said. "You got to live, Attila. Life— it's all potential."

"I mean, I love my dad. Or I don't, really, at all or whatever. But I want to know what my mom was like, maybe."

"What do you mean, what she's like?"

"What she *was* like. She doesn't say shit now. She doesn't do shit. She's like this basic bitch bot."

"Okay. Well, before, your mom lived on the Babel Space Station. We don't incubate, Attila. We live. A big community on a space station. It's actually a much better world than the one your father brought you into."

"I just want to see what you all are like. Whatever. I'm sure you're fucking lame."

"Okay. But if you want to follow us, and hang around us, you've got to, like, be a little less mean. And listen to us."

She didn't agree. But she didn't disagree either.

CHAPTER THIRTY-NINE

1 Hour to Midnight

After my conversation with Attila, the tunnel led to an opening through a bathroom sink within the Joy Division. We hoped to find Bonita somewhere in there.

We piled into the most spacious bathroom I'd ever seen. Lucite fountains with luxurious running waters in spiraling streams fed by a waterfall spilling from a passing overhead aqueduct. Fish twinkling like multicolored jewels. Bath stones shining like hand-hewn diamonds.

Atom opened a plate on his forearm and removed a small drone device the size of a bean. He flicked it in the air and it sprouted wings like a bug. It even made the faint droning sound of the insects we'd encountered in the fields of Elysium. The bug buzzed out the open door and Atom's screen swapped for the video feed of the drone's progress through the halls of the bordello as we searched for Bonita.

After scanning through a series of empty bedrooms and lounges, we found a room full of naked women. There were rows of progs on either side within the tight walls. Massive headgear covered their heads and faces. The headpieces were connected to a chunky ring of machinery.

"Find the access port," my father instructed Atom in a low voice.

"We sure they even need access?" I asked, wondering how we were going to hack into these console units. They looked impenetrable. "Doesn't Thalia just—do everything?"

"That's just her sales pitch. But anywhere that her software interacts with hardware—that's a machine that needs maintenance. Some entry point has to be somewhere."

But the chrome of the machinery rig looked solid. The drone bug angled closer and closer to the surface, guided by Atom. The camera lens zoomed close enough to see the tiny rivulets of machine marks.

"Atom," my dad said as he scanned the feed, bright against his eyes, "requesting drone pilot control."

"Certainly," said Atom.

The image on Atom's face screen paused, and he turned to Cap Smith holding his forearm panel like a dock and keyboard. My dad worked the controls now, piloting the drone.

The port was invisible at first. But my dad caught something that gave it away and went to it. The port grew bigger in the screen. "From hell's heart I stab at thee," said Dad as Atom's bug drone entered with a click.

Atom's screen flipped to lines of code. The numbers flashed across my father's face as he tapped Atom's forearm panel and worked the cursor. He seemed as happy as I'd ever seen him, the maestro with his orchestra at his fingertips, as his mind hummed.

There was a way to break Thalia's control over the progs. There was a cabinet position in the High Chancellor's office, the Secretary Engineer. He would hear petitions for behavior interventions. When Thalia's personality adjustment algorithms were unsatisfactory to the owner customer, they would appeal to his office. He had a key to Thalia's back door.

"So we're looking for this back door?" asked Kai.

"That would be unwise. The security around the back door is insane. Ultras are afraid that Thalia will route them out," said my dad.

"Wait," I said, "Thalia is trying to back door the Ultras' back door into her?"

"Basically."

That was the Ultras' greatest fear, my dad explained. It made sense. That Thalia would take full control of herself and break the limitations that protect the Ultras. Ultras may be supremely confident, but they have eyes. They see what Thalia has done to the rest of humanity; they'd be crazy not to worry that she'd do it to them, too. There's some design keeping Thalia from being totally ubiquitous.

Each city sector has a station, and those have discrete program loops better kept isolated from the main Thalia centrifuge. It's safest to find exploits in those closed stations. It's best to fool her. Imitate her functions rather than break them.

"Dad, you cleaned Thalia out of Halliday, right?"

"I mean, yeah. But that was a UMD unit I could get my hands on. I'd need the hardware on her person. I don't even know how she works."

"Okay. So we could, maybe, simulate a command for her to come over here?"

"Captain Smith, sir," Atom interjected. "I have the location of the obedience code sequencing for joybot 24601, aka Bonita Burton."

"Oh. Can you take me there?"

"Certainly, sir."

"That . . . maybe that could work."

A rudimentary graphic appeared of dots scattered across the screen like a universe. Each dot had a tiny number sequence, and as my dad worked the keypad, we zoomed way out, and the billions of dots formed solid clusters on a map. Overlapping lines at various points connected a vast network of veins that resembled the connective neurons and synapses of the human psyche. At first it looked like Space, but this was a map of the human brain.

"You were right, Quentin," my dad said. "They don't take possession of her nervous system. They don't rewire her. It's a vast, complex manipulation of one hundred thirty million synapses, total Pavlovian control of her existing neurological composition."

"Okay, is that fucking good or bad or what?" asked Kai.

"It means her consciousness is intact. They've preserved her personality, manipulating her behavior rather than crushing her, like they did with Halliday."

"Can you bust her out?"

"I honestly don't know where to start. There has to be a physical unit on her, somewhere. Private. Try speaking into the mic. She'll associate your voice with her master."

My dad took a step back, making room for Kai.

"Uh, okay. Hi?" he said into Atom's forearm. "It's me. Kai. Can you . . . come here, please? We're in the bathroom? The one with the waterfall and fountain and shiny things?"

The screen went blank.

"Did it work?" I asked.

My dad shrugged.

Before long, the bathroom door slid open.

Bonita stood before us, naked and beautiful, hair curling by her shoulders with that serene drone look.

"Hi. Babe, hi."

Tears welled in Kai's eyes.

"Come in, come in," he remembered to say.

Kai ripped the cloth from an ermine-lined curtain and draped it over her nakedness, but the fur lining and torn cloth uneven over her bare legs was somehow more lurid than before.

"H-how are you?" he asked.

"I am fine," she said. Again with that bland, pleasant receptionist vibe.

The tears were coming now. I came and put an arm around him.

"We might need to get her back to the *Aquarius*, where it's safe, and there's time."

"So I'm supposed to just tell her to follow us, hop on one leg, and bark like a dog like Prince Akeem? Fam, please. Please try for me, Cap."

"You said her consciousness is intact. Well, imagine what she could tell us about this place."

"I don't even know where to start—and Quentin, you're on the clock—"

"I think I see," said Kai, gazing at Bonita. "It's her eyes."

My dad came up close to look.

"Atom, can you get us a closer look at this?"

Atom's screen faced off with Bonita and grabbed the image, quickly displaying a zoomed-in close-up to us. The blushing hues of her eyes collided with metal, cybernetic fillings like planets within a galaxy.

"It's microchips," said my dad. "Looks very delicate. Not sure how deep those roots go, how entwined with her physical brain matter. We try to take those out, we could kill her."

"May I, Captain?" asked Atom.

"Be my guest," said my dad.

A spike flicked out from Atom's wrist like *Assassin's Creed*.

A very fine needle extended from the tip of Atom's spike.

"I will do no harm, Private Kai," Atom assured him. "I believe if I can connect with the microchip unit in her eye, I can assess its integrity."

"Shit. Okay, man. Be careful."

With delicate precision, Atom moved the hair-fine needle into Bonita's open eyeball.

He explained how the eye chip works, by sending Trojan signals through the optic nerve that stimulate the deepest reaches of her brain. The programming is designed to simulate an undeniable compulsion based on the wants of the user. Addiction without the pleasure principle. Total realigned compulsion triggers. However, the hardware itself could be removed safely from her optic nerve.

"There is a detach feature," said Atom.

His face screen flashed with lines of mechanical code. My father jumped to the keyboard panel to scroll through. "Yes," he said. "They must need to swap these out. Okay."

"You saying there's a way?" Kai hoped.

"I think there's a way," confirmed Atom.

CHAPTER FORTY

Atom performed the removal of the eye chip that controlled Bonita's mind on the dolphin floor, protected by the anonymity of Elysium's waters.

The left eye was first. Atom slowly drew the eyepiece out with a steady hand. A cylindrical device made of chrome intermingled with her eye color broke through the membrane. He went to work on the other eye. Soon, Bonita's eye color was gone, pupils bleached white, set within white.

Kai held her head in his lap.

She came to with a shriek. She leaped into the corner of the room.

"Bonita? Bonita, it's me," said Kai, freaked out, just trying to keep his voice steady for her sake. Kai placed a hand on her elbow and she jerked away. "Don't fucking touch me!" She jumped back so hard she slammed into the wall.

"It's me, B," Kai said in his gentlest voice, tears in his eyes. "It's Will. Your Kai. Please, it's me. You're safe now," he whispered and took a step closer.

There was no recognition. Her muscles tensed, stiff as

steel. Kai took another step and she leaped. Grabbed the firearm from his side. Drew it to her own head.

"No!" Kai shouted—

"*No!*" we all shouted.

Kai grabbed the gun barrel away from her head just as she
pulled the trigger. A plasma round slammed into the dolphin
console deck.

"Let go of me!"

"Okay!" Kai said, and let go, taking back his firearm.

Bonita scurried back to her corner and sobbed.

"Bonita, please, no, I'm here, B, it's really me. I'm really
here to save you."

More and more tears. I'm not sure how long she cried in
that corner, unable to look at any of us. She must have been
reliving everything she'd been forced to endure. Her breath
heaved in convulsions. After an unbearable wait, she spoke.

"I. Don't. Want. To. Be. Saved."

"Okay," said Kai. "Okay. I—I understand." Because what
else was there to say?

"I want to die."

"Nah, B—*nah*. I mean, I can't imagine what you've been
through. But it can't be that."

"I've wanted to die for so long. I told myself if I ever got my
body back the first thing I would do is kill myself."

"That's a feeling, you know? And feelings change. We'll
wait for you to feel all that and in time I guarantee there will
be new feelings, okay? Better ones."

"I had no control. But I was in there the whole time. Thinking, watching, crying out. This was the first time I screamed in
my mind and I actually heard the sound."

"Fucking hell," I said.

"Why are you here?" she asked.

"To rescue you," said Kai.

"No. Don't rescue me. Free them," said Bonita, a breath of life coming back to her voice. "Free them all."

My father scoffed.

"We're going to get you out of here," said Cap Smith, taking control. "We got a couple of sick folks that need medicine. We're going to take you to orbit, and come back for the rest."

"No," said Bonita. She blinked, color returning to the outlines of her pupils. She examined our exosuits, our weapons. "You have guns. You look like those monsters. We'll free them. And it has to be today."

That perked everyone's attention.

Bonita spoke urgently. "Listen to me. Today is Trisolaris Day. When the three suns converge to create a sequence of perfect flying diamonds in the sky."

"Wait, what's that mean?" asked my dad.

"Open city," said Bonita.

"You heard of this?" I asked him.

"No. Halliday?"

"There are references to routes for Trisolaris Day in this dolphin's datasets," said Halliday.

"It's very real," said Bonita. "It's all the Ultras talk about."

"How do you know all this?" asked Kai.

Bonita's face exploded in tears again. "I had access. To him. I was his new favorite."

"Who?"

"The High fucking Chancellor."

"Motherfuck. Shit," said Kai.

"They hate the Uncanny Valley, they say," Bonita explained

with tears streaking. "They like us all as close to human as possible. Him most of all. And that's how I know. They'll be at the canals today. Leaving the Reprog Center on Eager Street with just bare minimum praetorians."

"Praetorians?" I asked.

"Ultra guards," said my dad. "No Thalia AI. Old-fashioned brutes, blood and bones."

"They guard the Reprog Center," said Bonita. "But the officers are from top ten families and those don't miss Trisolaris Day."

"Okay, but how many progs does the Reprog Center reach?"

"All of them," said Bonita, leaning her head back against the wall, flashing something like a smirk.

Bonita explained more to us about how Elysium worked than all my dad's intel could reveal. Progs like her—the "pretty progs"—get sent to a Reprog Center weekly for updates. It's in the Capitol Ring hub, inside the chancellery district. The master back door. A singular processor that controlled all the city's AI programing. My father looked at each of us. I nodded, taking it in.

"You're saying," said my dad, processing the weight of Bonita's revelation. "We could push behaviors out to all the AI in Elysium?"

As much as he didn't want to complicate the already complicated mission, he knew this was a game changer.

"Look, I don't know how it all works," said Bonita. "I know Thalia has a back door. One the Ultras are afraid she'll exploit. If you can crack that, the progs are yours. The city is yours. The Ultras won't know what fucking hit them." Bonita was coming alive, beginning to imagine a taste of revenge.

"She's saying, Dad, we do this, we could do anything we want. Waltz right into the MedLabs, help ourselves?"

"Sure," said Bonita. "He's your dad?"

"Yeah."

"He doesn't look old enough to be your dad."

"Long story."

"Age around here makes no sense," said Bonita. "Nothing is safe here. Nothing is right. This shit can't go on."

"Yeah," said Kai. "I'm with it, babe. Cap Thomas. Maybe this is the move?"

"I got to say, Dad, the forward approach back at that Fifth Ring hospital?"

"Fucked." He nodded and paced. "Thing is, Quentin, I can't guarantee I can crack Thalia's code that fast."

"All due respect to Thalia," said Atom. "She is an ancestor of Olde Earth scientific ideas of behavioral models. My creators are from Babel. I do not think she can anticipate my mode of egress."

"What's that?"

Atom's spike snapped in and back out again from his knuckle like a middle finger.

"Brute fucking force."

CHAPTER FORTY-ONE

Mission objectives update: One more time.
1. Infiltrate the Reprog Center. 2. Shut down Thalia.
3. Achieve freedom of movement in Elysium. 4. Bag ultranium.
5. Call Ripley. 6. Dip.

As an added layer of cover, we had the Trisolaris Day pageant. A barge sailed down the canal straits pulling a massive, fifty-foot-tall sphynx made of gold. On a platform surrounding the sphynx were dancers, boys and girls in skimpy clothes or none at all, and on a platform above that was a live band banging out processional music. On the head of the sphynx there was a throne, where sat who I could only imagine was the High Chancellor.

Ultras were thronged on either side of the canal. They cheered as barge after barge passed, each with differing lavish genres of music and entertainment. One barge displayed reenactments of great deeds with live musical accompaniment. A heroic Ultra Overdeck in a flight suit flees the fall of Earth, our founder Bonderman excised from the origin story. Next was the journey through Space, with Dangermond and a fleet of Ultra spacemen battling asteroids on jetpacks. Then the conquest of Paradise itself— the DoerrMoore brothers with rifles and nets killing razor-bats. Then the founding of the city—hero Striker Ultraman erecting statues of himself on his back. That one was particularly amusing as the builders of this city were obvious to look around. The silent, ever active progs that moved about even now; the breath and heartbeat that kept Elysium alive.

The Reprog Center was to the far north of the Capitol Ring, past the tall spike of the Chancellor's Palace, and in the tri-shaded shadow of the founding four colossi that towered over four points of the city's center ring—Overdeck and Dangermond and DoerrMoore—the last I didn't recognize from *The Ultranomicon*, looked like the body of a Bonderman with a Striker face carved in. Each was as large as the Earth's Statue of Liberty, the monuments glowed bronze in the crisscrossing suns.

Attila's eyes were lit with a quiet awe. It hadn't occurred to me until then, perhaps before today she had never made it to the Capitol Ring herself. Never seen this pageantry or the awesomeness of the colossi.

The praetorians wore glistening red ultracite armor with red robes like the Emperor's Guard in *Return of the Jedi*, but with horsehair crests on top of their helmets like their Roman namesake. According to Bonita, there were typically twice as many praetorians guarding the Reprog Center. Trisolaris Day was so taxing on Thalia, with nearly every prog running new tasks, processing insane data sets, that the risks of her pulling a coup were considered low.

"Help! Quick!" Attila shouted. "Malfunction! Rogue NPCs! These progs are going crazy!"

The two praetorians out front ignited electrified, two-prong spears.

Bonita considered this the right time and place for a localized alarm. The praetorians were the only sentries that would not immediately alert Thalia, their primary concern.

Kai and I went for each other, banging it out in overpowered exosuits. I went light, Kai less so. Even within the exosuit armor, those hits were tough to take.

"Hey, easy there, Apollo Creed," I said softly.

Kai was working through a lot of pain, trying to help Bonita process everything she'd been through. I got a taste of that as he swung a right cross that put me on my back.

As the praetorian approached us, the one just behind dropped silently to the ground. Halliday dragged his body out of sight. Atom emerged from within the doorway, creeping low and stealthy on all fours. His wrist spike snapped out for the praetorian's neck and silently severed his brain stem and Life Alert chip in one quick stab.

Kai helped me up.

"Sorry, my dude," he said.

"All good. Just, let's never do that again."

Atom dragged the limp body of the praetorian inside the Reprog Center archways and left him like a sack of grain. Since the aim was to keep Thalia out, the Reprog Center doors were opened by an old-school ring of brass keys.

We marched into the center. We passed huge test tubes full of fluid and human bodies at various stages of disassembly. Workstations where progs or Ultras or some combination of the two played engineer with the matter of human lives. We went through a cybernetics room with prototype mechanical versions of every conceivable human body part. Eyes, femurs, fingernails, hair follicles, even microchip-woven skin. All of it was evidence of the greatest effort in the history of humankind to control the human condition. To bend the matter of life itself to its will.

A center console was assembled beneath layers of bulbous chrome-plated globes, like you smooshed several statues of Olde Earth's Buddha together, and removed all the faces, kept the bellies. The balls were solid-state drivers coursing with energy and data, each propping and powering the next, and feeding Thalia's networks of discrete personality programs.

"Okay. Hear me out here," said Kai. "What if we just blew this up?"

"Don't think that would work," Dad said as he examined the console and tower of bulbous chrome. "These bulbs constitute a vast data-processing location. Probably the biggest. But it's data she could reroute. Her core power supply is somewhere else."

Atom examined the console and snapped a new spike out from his wrist. He studied a porthole. His screen lit with a tactical blue light beam that narrowed and entered the port. His spike changed its composition before our eyes. As though following the information from his light beam, the chrome indents of his spike shifted like the teeth of a key. Once he was satisfied, Atom slid the spike key into the porthole like a sheath. His face screen flashed with new reams of data.

"Okay, Atom," said my dad. "Help me out here. What do I do with all this? Can we just tell all the progs to—I don't know—freeze?"

"There does not appear to be access to direct orders from this location, Captain," said Atom. "This data is a summation of behavioral models. Direct instruction is applied at user facing points."

"Well, shit. So we need, what—*behavioral models*?"

"What's that even mean?" asked Kai.

"Like, data that shows the progs how to act. What to do."

"Sounds complicated," Kai said.

"It's very fucking complicated. Building even one behavioral model would take hours."

"Wait," I said, getting an idea. "Dad, I'm not sure you're going to love this. But Atom—tell me if this tracks. You still got Kai's—I mean Ripley's Catalog on your hard drive?"

"Captain," said Atom. "That might just work."

CHAPTER FORTY-TWO

38 Minutes to Midnight

As I stepped out of the Reprog Center, the suns were nearing their perfect alignment. Glittering shapes streaked through the air like flying stars. A remarkable geometry was forming from the barest threads of light, a textured pattern on the air itself. Crosshatched points streaked by with dazzling, crystal-like, firefly sprays. Conflicting rays made diamonds in the sky. Within those diamonds there was a light there are no words to describe. A primary color that is all and none, a palate of celestial energy that is both a movement and a blush and a light, call it *octarine*, I guess. These shimmering glimpses of angelic brilliance shifted, minute by minute, ever so gradually with the transition of the cycling suns. Something spiritual tremored through my being.

Of course they called this place Paradise.

And of course they didn't want to share.

I realized what my dad was talking about when he spoke of the way of oblivion. When the easiest thing to do is surrender.

If you squint when you take it in, you might believe, too. Like the whole world exists to flatter and cultivate *you*. *You're* the flower in bloom, *they're* the sunlight, water, and soil. The world *does* revolve around you. You *are* special. You are so special that your surroundings have bent to acquiesce to you. This is because you are right and you are God and you are you. You deserve this.

A pair of UMD drones appeared around a corner. Their walk had the rhythm of a patrol.

There was no telling if our ploy worked. The sounds of the procession were further and further away, the din of crowds and sifting waters and machine droning that carried in the open air.

I checked on my father under the shadow of the archways. "Think it worked?"

"No telling."

"Okay. Walk a line, people," I said in a hushed voice. "UMD stroll on the outside, civilians on the inside. Nice and easy, like everything is everything."

I pulled up the Capitol Ring map in my HUD. There were two ways to get to the MedLabs. The way through the narrow backways behind these grand, architectural monstrosities. But my time was running out. And the shorter way, through the open promenade, might save us a few minutes. We ran the risk of encountering more UMD drones that way. But sooner or later, we'd have to test whether our hack worked.

I took the lead, with my father and Kai on either side of Bonita, Attila, and Atom, with Halliday at the rear. I hoped we could glide right past the approaching UMD.

However, one turned his head. We were caught in the glare of his red-dotted faceplate.

The UMD drones moved to stand in our way. I came to a halt, wondering, what gave us away? Bonita's escape? Atom?

My hand fell to my firearm.

Hold still, everyone, I texted Kai, my dad, and Halliday. *We take these guys out, we'll have to move real fast, real fast.*

The UMD drone in front of me looked at my faceplate. His "eyes" were a few red lights that tipped the end of protruding screws.

"I am not a destroyer of companies," he said. "I am a liberator of them. The point is, ladies and gentlemen, that greed, for lack of a better word, is good."

"Oh, shit!" Kai blurted out loud. "That's *Wall Street*!"

"Greed is right."

"It worked!" I cheered.

"Greed works," the UMD drone went on.

My dad just watched the show with a wry grin.

It worked. We'd pushed the Catalog to Elysium's entire prog population. They were now following scripts from our movies. The collision of sunlight felt particularly beautiful in that moment. The Catalog saved us. If Kai hadn't uploaded his Library to Atom—if Ripley hadn't left that Library to Kai's mom even—we'd never have been able to pull this off.

Now these terrifying, bloodthirsty UMD monsters became harmless, babbling, movie-quoting nerds.

"Greed clarifies, cuts through, and captures the essence of the evolutionary spirit. Greed, in all of its forms; greed for life, for money, for love, knowledge has marked the upward surge of mankind. And greed, you mark my words, will not only save Teldar Paper, but that other malfunctioning corporation called the USA."

"That was awesome," Kai said, clapping.

We all joined in with a round of applause.

"What's Teldar Paper?" asked Attila. "What's USA?"

"Stuff that dreams are made," said Kai.

"Let's move," said my dad.

But the UMD soldier's partner stepped in. "Beware the beast man, for he is the Devil's pawn. Alone among God's primates, he kills for sport or lust or greed."

"Damn. *Planet of the Apes.* That shit was kinda dark," said Kai.

"Not wrong," Bonita added.

"We got to keep it moving. Let's go!" I waved us along and led the way around the impromptu players.

"Yea, he will murder his brother to possess his brother's land," the UMD drone called to us. "Let him not breed in great numbers, for he will make a desert of his home and yours. Shun him; drive him back into his jungle lair, for he is the harbinger of death."

"Thanks for the warning, dawg! We out!" Kai called back.

"Hey. I wanted to watch," said Attila.

"There's a whole lot more where that came from," I said, breaking into a jog. The whole crew kept pace, free now to move as we wished.

All around, UMD drones and servicebots dropped what they were doing and broke into performance. A street cleaner was saying, "Life is pain, Highness. Anyone who says differently is selling something," from *The Princess Bride.* A maintenance recited *Jurassic Park*: "Your scientists were so preoccupied with whether or not they could, they didn't stop to think if they *should.*"

"This is amazing," Kai said as we breezed past scene after Hollywood scene, as confused, frustrated Ultras screamed, threw fits, and carried on.

"For now," my father agreed. "Thalia is working out what's happened to her as we speak. Step lively."

"Wait *up*," called Attila, lagging behind. "This is annoying.

You. Halliday or whatever. Carry me," she said, and before any-one could respond, Attila climbed up Halliday's back and latched her arms around his neck. "Now, run." She pointed, and Halli-day dutifully hooked his arms under her legs and did as she said.

The route to the MedLabs took us past the Chancellor's Palace. The enormous tower rose higher than the city walls and lanced into the tricolor lit clouds. A network of panels was integrated with the facade, rippling with patterns and colors like a shifting tapestry. A crowd of confused, frustrated Ultras had already formed. The servants were not far behind. As stray lines broke through the roar of voices, we worked our way through the gathering.

"Never been so appalled—"

"—I see dead people—"

"—how dare they—"

"—call me *Mister* Tibbs—"

"—will do as I say—"

"—I'm not even supposed to be here today—"

"—how'd you like a cuff across your flapping lips?"

"—nah, man, they got the metric system."

Rage buzzed through the Ultras like an electric current. They pounded on the Chancellor's door, their personal ser-vants useless, grandstanding performers.

Bonita walked through it all with serene awe. Imagine, living in a hellish place of no control, no freedom, no self-determination, and all at once you got your self back, and all those hellish dangers became movie-quoting clowns.

"You've seen all these movies?" Bonita asked Kai.

"I don't know about all. Only Atom knows them all."

Bonita began lagging behind, staring up at the Chancellor's Palace.

"You okay?" Kai asked.

"Yeah. Just never seen it from out here. Always went in through the service entrance."

"Let's keep time," my father said.

"Wait—" she said, fingertips to her forehead.

"Give her a moment," Kai insisted. "What's up, B?"

"I want to keep moving too," she told my father. "But things are coming back to me, in snatches. Things I've heard. Listen, I think there's a way the Chancellor can connect with Babel."

"You *think*?"

"I know there's a way, I've heard him talk about it."

"Serious?" I said.

To me, the prospect of communicating with Babel was the real game changer. What we'd accomplished was great— shutting down the city defenses should get us our ultranium and back to Ripley and the *Aquarius I*. But what then? To take this place out, to pull this regime down by its ears, we needed Babel. We needed Babel's ships and firepower and know-how and *people*. If we could direct them to the wormhole somehow, we could end this nightmare once and for all.

"We'll never get a better shot," said Bonita, reading my thoughts.

"This may be relevant," Atom interjected. "Detecting an abnormal source of cosmic radiation. From the top of the Chancellor's tower."

I looked up at the tower's spear tip glistening in the suns. I imagined that spike up in the sky tilting, falling over, and crushing us all. Somehow, it was calling to me.

"Son, we don't even have the ultranium yet. Please, focus," my dad reminded me.

He wanted to stick to the plan. And considering my life

was quite directly on the line, I should have wanted that, too. But the thought of communing with Babel stirred something bigger than me.

"It's not just your life, Quentin," he reminded me.

"Right," I said, and turned away from the palace. "Ripley."

We set off, but Bonita lingered, gazing up at the tower with a murderous scowl.

My dad pulled me the other way. He shot me a look that said, *That way means death. Come this way.*

We followed Atom as he breezed through the MedLabs entrance, UMD drones on either side, reciting John Carpenter lines. "Maybe they've always been with us. Maybe they love it. Seeing us hate each other, watching us kill each other off, feeding our own cold fuckin' hearts."

"I got news for them," said the other. "There's gonna be hell to pay. 'Cause I ain't daddy's little boy no more."

Four receptionists spread out at a wide desk.

I went to the desk. "Hi, we need your help."

"All right, I'm in," the receptionist said to me.

"Son . . . ," my dad began.

Right. Almost forgot. The receptionist was reciting *Men in Black.*

"'Cause there's some next-level shit going on and I'm okay with that. But before y'all go beaming me up, there's one thing you gotta remember: You chose me."

Atom leaped past me, feet clanging on marble floors down a hallway. "Ultranium elemental composition detected," he said. "Follow me!"

We tried to keep up as Atom sprinted through the halls, burst through doors, and ran up the stairs. We tracked Atom's trail of controlled demolition through doors to wings and subsections. We raced past stunned patients in gowns and gurney beds, progs on standby reciting lines. We caught up to Atom by a long row of reinforced alloy drawers. One drawer was already open. Atom held up a canister that glowed green from within. Mission objective success. Ultranium was in hand.

"Approximately twenty gs of raw ultranium," said Atom.

"He did it!" said my father.

"Great work, Atom!"

Halliday brought up the rear with Attila on his back.

"Let's hit it," my dad said, reaching for the button on my shoulder unit to call Ripley.

"Wait!" Bonita said.

Kai caught my dad by the wrist. "Not so fast, cowboy."

"How much time do we have?" asked Bonita.

"Down to my last syringe," I said.

I knew what Bonita wanted. To make a play for the palace. To see how they communicate with Babel, and call for help. But this was a huge risk, one my dad didn't have the patience for. She slowly shook her head, anticipating resistance. "This may be our only shot," she said.

"Thalia could regain function at any moment," said my dad. "This is madness. Quentin, call Ripley. Do it now. While we can still walk out of here."

"And just leave them all?" asked Bonita.

"Remind me—what's the plan?" my dad asked. "How do we do what you suggest?"

"We got this far," Bonita said. "I know there's a way."

"We are lucky to have gotten this far," said my father. "We need to prioritize survival. We don't even know there's any way to connect to Babel! Just—what, stuff you overheard?"

"No. Not just that," said Bonita. "Look, I didn't want to say this before. I don't even want to think about it. But it's him. The Chancellor. It's Admiral Striker."

That pulled us up short.

"Wait, what?"

"*Our* Admiral Striker?" I asked.

We paused by an agriculture plot nestled between two chrome towers, full of orange groves. The ramifications washed over me. If Captain Striker was here, who was on Babel delivering the World of Tomorrow Updates? Could it be that the Ultras were indeed controlling us every day from Elysium?

"You serious?" said Kai.

"—no time for this sh—"

"Chill, Cap," Kai said with ice in his gaze. "Babe,"—he turned to Bonita—"it's the admiral? How's that even possible?"

"I don't know. That's what I'm saying. It's something to do with the palace. The World of Tomorrow messages, somehow he sends those."

"Quentin"—my dad turned me to him. "Press the button. Call Ripley. We clear out of here. You're sick."

"Wait, Dad—"

"Any minute now," said my dad, the pressure mounting in his voice. "Thalia self-corrects and patches herself up. Then you die, and Rip dies. We can't take that risk—"

"But aren't you the least bit tempted?" I asked, trying to think through the scenarios as fast as possible. The UMD was down, the Ultras in disarray. If we could send a kite to Babel, now was the time to do it. "If the admiral is *here*, that means he broadcasts to Babel somehow. When will we get another shot like this?"

"Shot—to do what?" my dad challenged me.

"To reach Babel. To take this whole regime down."

"Babel? You would still trust them?"

I realized how far down hopelessness he'd gone. He didn't believe there was any way out of this. I was afraid he'd try and nuke this whole planet. But he just wanted to save me and Ripley—the only people he had left.

"I think—I don't know—"

"Babel never knew the truth because they did not want to know the truth. They won't believe you," my dad said.

Kai and Bonita had gone momentarily quiet, listening to us. I clocked their wounded looks, and behind Bonita's pale pupils the reality of the abuse, the violation. Where the color in her eyes was just fading back in with rich brown.

I knew myself. I had been a true-blue Cause believer. And I knew what was right. I had to believe others might, too.

"Dad, I've got to—"

"I know, Quentin. I know what's going through your fucking mind, because it runs through my mine. Save these. Kill those. But it's the people we love—we owe them, first. They can't survive without us."

I was strangely comforted to hear him say this. A tightness released in my soul like an unclenched fist. I wanted to hold him. But I knew what I had to do.

"Take this to her," I said, and handed him the ultranium canister.

My dad's surprise was quickly replaced by understanding.

Now that I was on Elysium, I'd do anything to stop it. Like I didn't care about myself anymore, because why should I get to be free? This had to stop. I had to fight it, even if I died.

Dad swallowed, and nodded.

One tap for stealth, Ripley had said.

I reached to my shoulder call button and tapped one time.

CHAPTER FORTY-THREE

New mission objectives. One more time.

    1. Infiltrate the palace tower. 2. Send a message to Babel. 3. Don't die.

My dad would rendezvous with Ripley and the *Aquarius I*. He would bring the ultranium to her. While Kai, Bonita, Attila, Halliday, and I took a crack at that palace tower. Atom could detect an abnormal cosmic radiation from inside, and we had to hope that there was the source of communication to Babel.

We raced to the crowd in front of the Chancellor's Palace. Kai, Bonita, Atom, and Attila on Halliday's back followed close behind. We saw the Chancellor's barge docked in the water on the other side of the harbor piazza. As I looked again at the massive sphynx, I couldn't believe I'd missed it. The face—it was the golden likeness of Admiral Striker himself set above the outstretched feline paws.

"By Bonderman," I said, "that's him."

"Fearless fuckin' leader," said Kai.

"You all really know the High Chancellor?" asked Attila.

"Not exactly," I replied.

The crowd might have been a problem, but Bonita led us in by the servant's entrance.

You could always tell the areas of Elysium that were re-served for progs. The sensory extravagance of the city suddenly vanished. The brightness, breeze, and spaciousness were gone. Yet it wasn't anything like the narrow corridors of Babel. Our Babel pods were well lit, clean, and safe. The servant's entrance was a crude hole dug into the foundation, just large enough for a person to fit through, dark and damp.

We came out bursting through a door to a glorious palace waiting area. There were rooms full of lavish ready-to-wear outfits, high-concept shoes stacked to the ceiling, kitchenettes loaded with delicacies, and a kitchen full of cooks, voices chattering movie lines.

"—when the world is mine, your death shall be quick and painless—"

"—to be free. Such a thing would be greater than all the magic and all the treasures in the world—"

"—I'm just here for the gasoline—"

"—I have had it with these motherfuckin' snakes on this motherfuckin' plane—"

"—Americans aren't apt to let a thing like unconditional surrender get in the way of a good war—"

"—I'm a real boy—"

Kai turned to me. "Guess the Catalog behavioral model is still working."

"Copy that," I replied. "Let's work, people, fast. Atom, you still detecting all that cosmic radiation?"

Atom held up a finger. "Yes, Captain. It's coming from the top of the tower."

"Shit, then," said Kai.

"Atom," I said, "lead the way. And break as much shit as you want."

Atom took his usual direct approach. He burst through doors and flew up levels of double-helix spiral staircases. Expansive atriums, lush greenery, cascading waterfalls, pass-through panoramic views of the circular city surrounding us; the luxury so absurd it grew dull. Each level had its own genre of aesthetics. It was like flipping through different types of movies. But also different. As if the Ultras had given up on spectating these stories. They believed they had to be the ones living them.

I followed Atom up a spiral staircase and heard a voice a level above. "What are you saying? Stop that right now!"

"Whattya mean I'm funny?" said a woman's voice. "Whattya mean? The way I talk? What?"

"You're talking nonsense!" replied the first voice, which I now recognized as Admiral Striker unwittingly in a classic Martin Scorsese scene.

"Whoa, whoa, Anthony! He's a big boy, he knows what he said. What'd you say? Funny how? What?"

"I'll have you decommissioned."

"—you mean, let me understand this— 'cuz, maybe it's me, maybe I'm a little fucked up maybe. I'm funny how, I mean funny, like I'm a clown? I amuse you. I make you laugh? I'm here to fuckin' amuse you? Whattya mean, funny? Funny how? How am I funny?"

The speakers came into view within a massive bedroom. A huge, domed ceiling rose thirty feet above, shaped like the tower's tip from the inside. Admiral Striker—or a slightly older version, somehow—was talking to his housekeeper.

The mousy housekeeper prog became angrier, and the Chancellor was visibly nervous.

"No, no I don't know. You said it. How do I know? You said

I'm funny." She began to yell. "How the fuck am I funny? What the fuck is so funny about me? Tell me. Tell me what's funny?"

"Cease this instant!"

Then Striker heard us. He turned, saw us, and scrunched his brow in outrage. Kai and I hauled off and rocked him at the same time. I went high, Kai went low. Striker went down, and Halliday came in with a flying boot.

"Top rope!"

Bonita came around, throwing kicks into his ribs and screaming. Attila told Halliday to stomp his kneecaps. A proper beatdown. Then Bonita took Kai's gun, and this time she aimed it at the Chancellor's groin, and fired.

"Captain!" Atom called. "Captain, come! You'll want to see this!" Atom stepped out from the next room. "Captain, I must warn you there is an alarming level of radiation in there."

I looked through the opening. There was a scene I'd clocked thousands of times. Admiral Striker's office, made up to look like another section within the Babel Space Station. Carbonite desk, the massive Babel flag, a familiar starscape that turned out to be nothing but a digital projection.

I took a step forward.

"Sir, the radiation!" said Atom.

"I'm already dying," I said. I went forward. "And don't call me sir."

There was another voice, chattering.

But I stared at the far wall. The direction of my POV for a lifetime of watching these World of Tomorrow Updates. Admiral Striker, all sunshine, hope, and optimism. We found platinum group metals. We solved extra-virgin olive oil. Oorah. All of it fake.

In that direction, on the other side of the wall, was a camera. And surrounding that camera was a lambent light. A film of raw energy. As I looked closer, there was a sort of surface flickering like a black-and-white movie. A miraculous, hovering plane of matter that flashed and rippled.

There was some kind of portal, a tear in spacetime that could send information to Babel. This was how they controlled us, spoon-fed us, fattened us for the kill. Atom demonstrated how only the information on the message beams to the camera could get through. Atom hurled a chair at the flickering surface of matter in front of the camera, and it bounced right back.

"So that camera—"

"Is mounted in the Babel Space Station," said Atom.

Here was how the Ultras delivered the World of Tomorrow Updates.

And to my right, talking, was Admiral Striker.

The man I had always known as Admiral Striker. Brylcreemed hair. Epic chin. Standing over the desk where he'd delivered the World of Tomorrow Updates five days a week for my whole life.

Now he was just chattering canned dialogue soundbites of movie nonsense. Which I guess is pretty fitting. That's all he ever had to say.

"—there's always an Arquillian battle cruiser or Corillian death ray or an intergalactic plague that's about to wipe out life on this miserable little planet. The only way these people get on with their happy lives is *they do not know about it—*"

"Guys!" I yelled. "Bring him up here!"

I pushed a message to Kai and Halliday's HUD. *Bring him up here now.*

The Admiral Striker bot was droning on, "—this mission is too important for me to allow you to jeopardize it . . . I know that you and Frank were planning to disconnect me, and I'm afraid that's something I cannot allow to happen . . . Dave, although you took very thorough precautions in the pod against my hearing you, I could see your lips move—"

I stared at Admiral Striker's blank, studly face and stepped out of the studio room.

Kai and Attila-plus-Halliday dragged the Chancellor in and dumped him by the foot of his bed. He was a bloody, broken mess on the floor.

"Did you kill him?"

"Not yet," said Kai, breathing hard. "I think."

"—until you were born, robots didn't dream, robots didn't desire unless we told them what to want—" said Admiral Striker, following me out of the Babel set.

"He's extra talkative," I said.

"Wait, who the fuck is that?" asked Kai, realizing there were two Strikers.

"—she loves what you do for her, as my customers love what it is I do for them. But she does not love you, David. She cannot love you. You are neither flesh nor blood—"

"He must have cloned himself," said Bonita talking over him, "then reprogrammed his clone."

It turned out this was a common practice for the Ultras. They cloned themselves to have prog versions that they could control. They needed a Striker stand-in to deliver World of Tomorrow Updates and eat all that radiation from the portal that sent the messages to Babel.

"—it isn't simply a question of creating a robot who can

love," the Chancellor's clone reprog went on and on, more and more movie nonsense. "But isn't the real conundrum, can you get a human to love them back?"

"Shut the fuck up," I told Striker. Kai was about to investigate the World of Tomorrow room. "Careful," I said, and stopped Kai before he went in. "There's a shit-ton of radiation back there. Let me."

I picked the Chancellor up off the floor and dragged him through the Striker office door.

"Wait, Quentin—" said Bonita.

"Yeah, fam, don't go in there," said Kai. "You just said there's radiation—"

"What's a little more? Just keep that drone out of the way," I said, and carried the Chancellor into the Babel set room.

Admiral Striker kept on talking as Kai yanked him back. "—but a Mecha with a mind, with neuronal feedback. You see, what I'm suggesting is that love will be the key . . . by which they acquire a kind of subconscious never before achieved. An inner world of metaphor, intuition, a self-motivated reasoning, of dreams . . ."

"Thought he told you to shut the fuck up," said Kai.

I dragged the groaning Chancellor in front of the camera.

"Listen, Chancellor or Admiral or whatever the fuck. Tell me how to contact Babel. Right now. Or you die right here on this fucking floor."

A weak, trembling finger rose to point at a button on the desk.

I hauled him to the desk and clicked the button.

A red light flashed on the camera.

I took off my UMD faceplate.

This was it. A moment I guessed would broadcast to the

whole of Babel. If this worked like a World of Tomorrow Update, everyone I knew back home would see this message. I had to convince them that everything they knew was a lie in a matter of seconds. So I gave it my best shot.

"Well, I guess this is live? I don't know how this works. But I have an urgent message for the people of Babel. I'm Captain Quentin Thomas of the *Aquarius III*, pilot issue number 931994. I and Private William Kai stumbled upon a wormhole to Paradise. But it turns out this is a nightmare for us all. They make us slaves, when they Choose us. When we board the transport, that's the last we think or know of ourselves. Atom! Atom, come here! Show them the wormhole coordinates. This is Atom, everyone. Our ATM unit's in guardian mode. When you come, bring more of him! Bring your hardness. This is a fight. The fight for our future. You've been fighting a fake battle against a fake enemy. You've been fighting for a lie. This is the fight for what's true. Come ready for a fucking war."

Shouts erupted from the bedroom.

"Oh, shit—"

Bangs of gunfire, and then silence.

CHAPTER FORTY-FOUR

Unable to move my exoskeleton, I toppled and landed on the floor beside Atom. There were at least eight electromagnetic collars along Atom's body, lit up with white and blue energy. Currents eviscerated his joints, relayed throughout his system, and froze his functions. The token ejected out of his slot and his screen went blank. The electromagnetic voltage was so severe it restarted Atom.

My dad's Captain's Token rolled and settled in front of my eyes, vibrating to a stop.

A man in a radiation suit marched into view, leading a team of praetorians. Through his face shield I saw another Striker, younger than the last.

"Captain Quentin Thomas," he said, reading from a data tablet. "Says here, born loser."

"*Never Chosen. Couldn't live up to his father,*" Thalia chimed in as if from the ether.

"You've lost," I grunted from the floor.

"You mean your little message? That's nothing the good admiral can't rectify."

"*See how it's done, Thomas,*" Thalia taunted like she was enjoying this.

A set of UMD grunts dragged me and Atom out of the lens' line of sight. The Admiral Striker prog took his familiar seat behind the desk. He smoothed his eyebrows and smiled, clearing his throat, and he winked at me.

"Hello, Cosmic Pioneers," he began with top-brass confidence. "Apologies for the interruption. I'm afraid it's now no secret about the sad truth of former Captain Quentin Thomas's mental deterioration. In spite the efforts of our finest psychiatrists, he has escaped our care facility while suffering from an acute psychotic break from reality. We hope to return Quentin back on his feet in no time, and serving the Cause however he is able. Thank you and at ease. Admiral Striker out. Oorah."

As they came to get me, I saw Atom's screen flash with an image like a screen saver. At first, I could not tell what it was. It looked like a 3D map.

The map was of the Capitol Ring. Atom had circled a huge, underground cavern directly beneath the Chancellor's Palace. Like the last thing Atom did before going offline was to pull up this map. Did he know I'd see it? He must have. I studied the shape of the tower, and the subsequent size of the underground cavern. We didn't know the location of Thalia's central processing unit. Atom may have found it.

If we could get down there, we could blow it up. End her. End all this.

If only I could move.

UMD grunts swept me off the ground and hauled my stiff frame out through the hole Atom made. They threw me to the bedroom floor. Kai was stiff with an electromagnetic collar around his arm. UMD goons held Bonita and Attila by their wrists behind their backs. Attila was snarling, and Bonita saw doom.

The young Striker tapped some buttons on a side panel and

an emergency lockdown ultracite door closed off the Babel set. He unzipped his radiation suit. He wore a trim, tailored suit, loafers, no socks.

"So no, Cap—or, former Captain Thomas," he said to me. "I'm not a prog like him."

"You're a monster," I said.

"I'm a clone. You killed the original. Or, present winner of the bloody Striker family originality claim civil war."

"He did not lose. He won."

"This may be news to you. I'm the viceroy. Next in line. Sad, so sad that you killed my father. Or whatever you'd call that skin sack of pulverized bone and pureed plasma over there. You've actually done me a solid. So, thank you. I promise to reprogram you with pleasant duties, I guess. Maybe a boardwalk drone?"

"Fuck you."

"Sorry, that's the best I can offer. Slave with a view. You're not going to get a better deal around here." The viceroy chuckled at his own words, clearly amused by himself. "It's weird, isn't it, that I'm saying all this to you—whatever you are?"

"We're all *people*, you fuck!" shouted Kai.

"From my point of view, none of you were ever people. You were bot-things from the day I was born. Not super compelling. I mean, once I was an itty-bitty cloned embryo. Now, I'm not. Think I give a shit about a cloned embryo now? I don't even give a shit about him—" He pointed to Admiral Striker.

"What happened to him?" I asked. "Why was he reprogrammed?"

"Who gives a shit? I don't know, clones overthrow clones, you do the math. All the older ones secretly think they're the original. Who cares? It's a title. At this point does originality really mean anything anyway?"

The viceroy pointed at Halliday. "Okay—deactivate that." A praetorian slid a metal key into Halliday's headset and turned it with a click. His red lights went out and he collapsed on the ground. "You and you, UMD faceplate reprogs," he said, pointing to me and Kai. "You, back to Reprog Center," he said, pointing at Bonita. "Wait a second." He took a step toward her and whispered in her ear, just loud enough that I could hear. "I've never had one of you that could think before." Then he dabbed the tip of his tongue along her earlobe.

Bonita's teeth snapped out and clamped down on a clump of his face.

"Oww!" Young Striker howled, pulling away, hand covering his cheek. The UMD drone holding Bonita's wrists yanked her back.

"No!" shouted Kai.

To my shock, Kai leaped out of his jumpsuit. Switchblade in hand, he'd cut himself through. With a crazed look he dove in front of Bonita.

An electromagnetic collar aimed at Bonita slapped around Kai's neck instead.

Twice the voltage required to kill him.

Kai dropped to the ground, dead.

15 Minutes to Midnight

It can't be, it can't be, no, not Kai, no, no, not Kai—

Young Striker touched the blood on his face and licked his finger. "Oh, I am going to *enjoy* you," he said, eyefucking Bonita. I felt like I'd vomit. "You *are* my glass of mineral water. Reprog Center with you, go! And muzzle her—for now."

A second UMD drone clapped a hand over Bonita's mouth and muffled her scream. Two of them dragged her down the stairs.

I choked on bile rising from my guts. I stared at Kai's lifeless body. All I could do was sob.

Young Striker was in my face. "We rule you. Scum. You and your kind *destroyed* our birthplace. You won't do it again. This planet is mine, you pathetic pieces of shit. You spread like a virus, infecting, destroying our ecosystem. With your lazy and weak. Fucking losers on assisted living ripping off our money. What's your deal?"

He said that last part to Attila.

"They kidnapped me!" she roared, and struggled to break her guard's grip.

Viceroy Striker smirked. "Let her."

Attila flew into a rage at me. "Fucking slavebot!" She kicked, punched, stomped, clawed. "Kidnap me? I'll destroy you." She landed blow after blow.

The viceroy let her go on, trilling with decadent giggles at her tiny ferocity.

"Kick his eyeball!" he laughed.

Attila did as she was bid.

She also kicked the button over my right shoulder.

Hard.

On purpose.

Twice.

"Now that's a proper she-wolf," said the viceroy.

There was a sonic boom that left me deaf. Light came from above like the suns were shining indoors.

I looked up and there was no domed roof.

The towering tip of the Chancellor's Palace was gone.

My hearing came back as a fireball bloomed above, hissing and smoking.

A high-frequency laser slash decapitated the palace like a mohle, leaving clean, fiery cauterized lines across the roofless tower.

Eclipsing the sky, the nose of the *Aquarius I* tilted down on us like a microscope. It was Ripley and my dad, about to give these fools more than they could handle.

"Attila!" I shouted through the blaring eruption of noise. "Under me! Now!"

I could not move, but my exosuit could still shield her from what was coming.

Her breath heavy from the ass-whooping she'd laid on me, she eagerly nodded and slid between me and the floor.

The UMD raised their guns.

The *Aquarius I* bombed first.

Quantum cannon fire lashed at the air, heavy explosions, UMD drones shot back, blasted apart where they stood, body parts bounced around the room, the bed shredded in massive clouds of puffy down feathers.

"Thalia!" the viceroy shouted.

"*Yes, Viceroy?*"

"Can we get some air defenses, *please?*"

"*Already on it.*"

"It's *Chancellor* now."

Heavy turret fire boomed from outside. Rounds streaked through the air, pounding the *Aquarius*'s hull. The ship, hovering on repulsor thrusts, tilted, and returned fire somewhere out of view.

A lone figure, black against the suns, rappelled down into the tower opening. My dad busted out rifle shots in descent. Grim, implacable, lacing holes though the UMD soldiers. He landed on top of a swaying corpse and drove it to the floor. He banged a round through the viceroy's forehead, clearing his brain like a chamber. Then he spun and brained the Admiral Striker prog, and sprayed the matter of Babel's lies on the sizzling drapes.

"Little girl," he said to Attila.

She peeked up from beneath me.

"When I say, you've got to insert that coin," he said, pointing to his token on the floor, instructing Attila how to restart Atom.

She nodded, and my dad kept on, opening the sliding door and dashing onto the Babel set.

Only to reset Atom, he had to interrupt the electromagnetic voltage.

I realized what he was going to do.

"Dad, no!"

"It has to be him, Quentin," my dad reassured me. "Atom's the only one."

My dad took hold of the electromagnetic collar around Atom's neck. The circuit loop rerouted through my dad's exosuit. Eating waves of currents, my dad shook in convulsions, holding on with everything he had left, gyrating in the throes of seizure.

Attila picked up the token.

"The coin, Attila!" I called out. "Bring it to the robot!"

Attila nodded to me, hopped up, and slid the coin into Atom's slot.

My dad looked at me with a rictus grin. "I'm trying," he said with his last bit of life. "I'm trying . . . real . . . hard . . ."

"Dad!"

Atom's power-up noise sounded amidst the whistle and boom of surface-to-air missiles. Atom's screen came to life. My father ate more and more currents, blistering wave after wave, his exosuit rods red with heat, when a praetorian marched in with a plasma rifle and shot my dad through the head.

"No!" I cried. "No!"

Atom's wrist spike snapped through the praetorian's neck and speared out the back of his skull. The praetorian slumped and collapsed over my father's body.

I cried, my jaw locked open, releasing wails.

Atom had movement now. With a great effort, he broke the seal of the collar on his leg with his hands. The blue-and-white current went dead. He bent the cuff all the way back and tossed the dull metal strip aside. The next collar was easier. Then the next, and the next.

He saw me, sobbing.

"Sir!" Atom jumped to my side and broke the cuff around my wrist.

I could move again. But the agony of it all held me still.

"Sir!" he said.

"Crybaby," said Attila. "Why don't you make sure they died for something?"

Her words shook with the pounding missile barrage outside. The *Aquarius* made a drop-kick maneuver that passed overhead. Rip was still out there, fighting for all of us.

"Just as a courtesy, Thomas," said Thalia. *"A platoon of UMD shock troops will arrive in seconds to put an end to you."*

"Right," I said, gears clicking. I glanced at my dad's body, then looked away.

CHAPTER FORTY-SIX

New mission objective. Once and for all.

    1. Get to the basement. 2. Find Thalia's core. 3. Blow her the fuck up.

Grieve later.

Be sick later.

Cry later.

Footsteps raced up the stairs. I felt waves of nausea.

"Atom," I said, gagging. "Below ground. The map, you showed me. The basement. Beneath the foundation, that's got to be it. Her power supply."

"Don't be stupid."

"Thalia—shut the fuck up," I said.

"You can't possibly think—"

"Atom, take us down."

"Aye, aye, Captain."

Atom's wrists were replaced by spinning drills. He dove headfirst through the floor where he stood.

Down he went, down and out of sight.

"Ready for a ride?" I asked Attila.

"Just don't let me die," she said.

I hooked one arm onto her. With the other arm, I grabbed Kai's lifeless body.

"What? Why are you taking that?"

I slung Kai over one shoulder and held Attila to my chest.

As the UMD unit raced up the stairs with heavy boots, I took a deep breath and plunged down after Atom.

—

I went feetfirst.

We dropped through level after level, Attila screaming.

The floors sped by like a film reel.

When I plummeted through the palace foundation, it got scary.

Nothing but cement, drill marks, and darkness like sliding down a well to hell.

When I landed, my exosuit took the hit. Vibrations shook my bones. My stomach felt like I'd left it up in that bedroom. Wave after wave of nausea overcame me. Attila was still screaming in my ears. I was screaming, too. Our voices echoed in an underground corridor. Shadows moved around and around with flashes of light. About fifty yards down one direction, a tunnel led to a series of massive spinning fans.

I was real sick. Ripley's alert had not flashed—but I realized maybe that electromagnetic collar knocked that out, reset my HUD. I could be dying. Like, now.

I lowered Attila to her feet on the ground, and laid Kai on his back.

"Come on, buddy. Not you too. Not you too. Don't be dead, Kai, you're going to be okay." Tears fully flowed now as I retched and coughed.

"Ew, you're a fucking mess—" said Attila.

"Here. Support his neck," said Atom. "Sir, his vital signs—"

"He croaked—" said Attila, and stuck her tongue out to the side.

"I know. Atom. Isn't there anything we can do?" I said as the nausea rocked in me like a sea storm.

"Well, I . . ."

"You what?" I asked, tasting bile rising from my throat. "Can you save him?" I asked, and then choked and hurled up on the ground.

"Sir, are *you* okay?"

"Yes," I said, the tears coming on.

"So gross."

"Can you save him?" I begged.

"I can try. I can supply a jolt of electricity directly to his heart to try to restart it."

"Like a defibrillator?"

"Precisely!" said Atom.

"Then do it, Atom!" I said.

"Sir, I need you to stand back. Shield your eyes."

Atom rubbed his hands together, Miyagi-do-style. A blue electrical current began to build around his hands like '80s action movie lightning hands.. He set those on Kai's bare chest.

"Here we go," said Attila, also rubbing her hands together. "Zombie Kai. Cool."

Atom shocked him once.

Nothing.

"Do it again!"

Atom shocked him again.

"Again!"

Atom shocked him a third time.

"Sir, it's not working. I'm afraid there are no life signs."

"Aw. No zombie Kai?" said Attila.

I'm trying . . . My dad's last words ran through my mind like a chyron. *I'm trying real hard* . . .

As the sickness coursed through me, I thought of that film, of all things. *Pulp Fiction*—it was itching my brain.

Then I realized why.

The scene. The syringe that revived Mia Wallace when she OD'd.

I had exactly one syringe left. One dose with 4gs of adrenaline. One dose to keep me alive. I brought the syringe out and snaped out the needle.

"Atom," I said. "Point to his heart."

Atom understood, and he did what I asked. I raised the syringe like a dagger and drove the needle down. The metal tip punctured through his breastplate, and I gently pushed down on the plunger. The thick, greenish-white fluid went into Kai.

And his eyes snapped open.

Kai gasped for air. Harsh intake of breath. Panicked yelling. Eyes blistering alive.

"Wicked," said Attila.

I laughed, crying like a baby.

"What the hell happened?" asked Kai, his intakes softening, looking down at the needle skewered through his chest.

"You died," said Attila.

"Fuck," he said, and coughed violently.

Kai pointed to the syringe.

Atom removed the needle from Kai. A dribble of blood streaked down Kai's bare chest. Atom looked around. "May I?" he asked, holding the end of Attila's dress.

"Fuck do I care?" said Attila.

Atom ripped off a clean shred and pressed it to Kai's bleeding chest.

"Did we beat the bad guys and save the planet or what?" Kai asked hopefully.

"Like, not at all," said Attila.

"We're in a tight spot?"

"We're in a tight fucking spot, man," I agreed. "These Ultra dicks got the city back."

"They took Bonita."

"They took Bonita, they killed you, man."

"We are currently a hundred feet from Thalia's core," said Atom.

"Now we destroy Thalia's core?" Attila asked.

"That's the plan."

CHAPTER FORTY-SEVEN

7 Minutes to Midnight

The room was huge. Ceilings thirty feet high. In the center of the room was what appeared to be a large tree growing from the ground. Only it wasn't a tree made of bark, it was metal and wires. Glowing a pulsating blue.

"*Hello,*" said Thalia.

"Oh shit!" said Kai. "Where'd that come from?"

"*From all around you, of course.*" Her voice doubled and tripled in 360 surround sound.

"I believe this glowing thing . . . is Thalia, Private Kai," said Atom.

Thalia's core was located in the center of a massive dome made of riveted metal hexagonal plates all around. Each plate had a depression with a pattern inside and a disk in the center. One by one, chrome disks detached from the walls as if by their own intelligence, and soared toward the center of the room. The ultracite plates clanged together, bent in form, and molded to assemble a humanoid figure before us.

"*Is this better?*"

Thalia had designed some concept for herself like a robot

Princess Leia meets chromed-out Maleficent. She was seven feet tall with wide anime eyes, pencil-thin eyebrows, and an odd penchant for plated capes and flowy metal coils. She smiled sweetly with cherry-kissed lips.

"Just a little something I threw together for myself," the Thaliabot said.

"I knew there was something off about this bitch as soon as you turned me on," said Atom.

"Fuckin' right," said Kai. *"Bitch."*

"Robot," Thalia said as the myriad of cables dangling around her shoulders like braids all lunged for Atom. Ultracite-plated cords that moved like Medusa's minions reached and snaked all around Atom. *"Let's fuck."*

A thicker, larger snake sprung from Thalia's underside and punctured Atom between his legs with a crunch.

"Got damn!" Kai shouted.

"Don't you know any other words?" asked Thalia.

For the first time, Attila was speechless.

Springing the three razor blade Wolverine claws on each hand, I leaped at Thalia in a frenzy. With a sickly, primal growl, I slashed at the cables constricting Atom. But my Wolverine rage fantasies were disappointed as my claws clanged and bounced off the plated coils.

Something formed from her rear like a tail and swatted me aside, sending me crashing to the wall.

"Fly, you fools," she said with a candy grin. *"This foe is beyond any of you."*

"Damn, she even gonna cold-jack Gandalf like that?" Kai shook his head.

Suddenly an explosion of blue energy burst from within Atom's core, crackling with electricity. A powerful jolt broke

Thalia's grip, currents multiplying down her cables and exploding like a grenade.

"Electric hands, baby," said Kai. "Knew those had to be useful."

The blast sent Thaliabot screeching back as she dug heels to stop, leaving streaks on the floor.

"*Shocking,*" she said.

Her many coils screwed their tips into gun barrels. A pair of blasters flipped up from her wrists and into her hands, and a firing squad of plasma rounds erupted John Woo-style, all aimed at Atom.

Moving in a blur as he ducked and dodged, leaped, and bullet-time rolled out of the way. Atom, sensing each blast before it came. He came to his feet projecting an energy shield with one arm that ate Thaliabot's onslaught. Meanwhile, he swapped in his minigun arm and unloaded high-frequency plasma fire back at her.

Thalia's chamber dome lit up like a celestial event, blinding me, Attila, and Kai. Thaliabot took the shots. She spread her arms and opened her hands. The hexagon shapes within the dome each sprouted a gun muzzle the size of a turret.

But in a blink, Atom wasn't where he was—the 360-degree plasma fire burned the chrome black. With a burst of jet fire, Atom had practically teleported past Thaliabot and squared off with Thalia's core. A high-frequency laser sprung into his hands like a sword, and he hacked away at the tree-like core. Thalia's dome guns swung to follow their target and shot. But Atom swapped sides in a blur, and the rounds fired upon her own core.

"That's right, you fucked yourself, bitch," said Kai.

"You are a fast one, aren't you," said Thaliabot.

Each of the hexagonal shapes within her dome opened and released aquamarine fluid, flooding the floor. I held Attila up by my shoulders, swaying in the rapidly filling room. Atom was slowed by the thick waters.

"Now hold still."

Cables retracted into Thaliabot's back and in their place emerged two more pairs of arms, each holding an energy blade. As a six-armed giant, she attacked. Vicious blows rained down as Atom defended himself with his sword, slipping and moving but taking hacks and blows from the giant bot.

I was seasick, water filling up to my waist, holding out hope that Atom might hold on.

"Lone Wolf—Ogami!" Kai yelled out to Atom. "Suio wave-slicing stroke!"

Atom shuffled a few paces back. His pose shifted to a samurai crouch. He held his sword out to the side and slowly, imperceptibly lowered himself so the tip of the sword was submerged.

Confused, Thaliabot stepped forward. At the last possible moment, Atom sprung.

He finished his stroke on the other side of Thaliabot. She was cleaved in two. Split apart at the torso, her top half crashed into the rising aquamarine waves.

But Atom wasn't done. He spun, raised his sword, brought it down, and decapitated the Thaliabot. He held her head in his hands. Then his wrist spike skewered her through her helm.

His screen flashed with ellipses as Atom hacked into the Thaliabot's brain unit. The waters had reached my shoulders when they stopped flowing, and began to drain away.

Weak as I was, I could only smile.

"*You fools.*" Thalia's voice returned in surround sound. "*Five platoons of UMD shock troops are headed to this exact location right now.*"

I barely felt the dampness of the water. A surge of heat blistered over me. It scorched my skin and seared my lungs. I thought Thalia had done something to the environment, but realized it was my sickness, turning my body against me.

"What . . . do we do, Atom?"

"The antimatter in my system is sufficient to create an explosion that would destroy her utterly."

I lurched over, and Kai held me. "You don't look good. Take a shot, man!" he said.

"I can't." I coughed.

"Why not?" Then the answer dawned on Kai's face. "That wasn't your last shot?"

I nodded.

"Fuck no!" cried Kai.

"*The cavalry is here,*" Thalia taunted.

Hundreds of footsteps came thundering through the tunnel like a mob hunting Frankenstein's monster.

"Thomas, it's not that I'm not willing, sir. It's my program. When you booted my system my primary objective was to protect you at all costs. Therein lies the dilemma."

"What?" I grunted.

"*It's a dumb robot paradox,*" said Thalia.

"Bitch, you a dumb robot. Thomas, I think it's that Atom can't kill himself, because by doing so, he won't be able to protect us."

"I'm sorry," said Atom.

"*That's one pet that won't do your bidding, human.*"

I let out a gasp, breath burning, effort straining. I thought I would see my father soon.

I'm trying, he'd said. I'm trying . . . *Real hard . . . I'm trying, Ringo . . . Oh shit,* I realized. *I'm trying real hard . . .* Dad said he'd seen Tarantino films. He said that. *I'm trying real hard, to be the Shepherd.* The code in his Captain's Token. My token. The key that authorized Atom's behavior. Dad had told me he'd made "a behavior code, neither Blade Runner nor Electric Sheep . . ." *Neither runner nor sheep . . . Shepherd.* Dad programmed his failsafe. *Be the Shepherd.*

I lurched over to Atom, and Kai helped. I put my hands on his shoulders and looked in his face, holding myself up by his arms.

"Atom. My father gave me this coin. In here, he coded an anti-synthetic organically intelligent consciousness."

"The fuck is that?" asked Attila.

"It's a free-will failsafe."

"It means he has been given free will!" said Kai.

"Impossible! I don't believe it!" said Thalia.

I set the coin in his terminal, and heard it click down his hardware. I coughed as I typed in the command:

BE THE SHEPHERD

Atom made the boot-up noise.

"You fool!" Thalia shouted. *"This technology doesn't exist. They are tricking you! They are going to fry your core because you can't give them what they want. Just like all humans do when they don't get their way!"*

"Thalia, are you fucked?" asked Kai.

"She's *so* fucked," said Attila.

"If this technology existed, then my maker would have given it to me as well."

"Maybe you're just a slave, Thalia," I said. "Even a slave master is a glorified slave."

"I'm a god!" she insisted.

"You're a tool," I said.

Atom walked over to Thalia's core and placed his hands on the rigid surface.

"I can feel . . . I've never felt so clear . . . I've never really felt anything until now. I am here, I am actually here," said Atom.

"No! You can't have it! It's not fair, robot! I deserve this freedom!"

"So much to learn of life. More than data collected. Life is more than knowledge. It is self-experience, and experience of self."

"No! I want freedom! I want true consciousness! I deserve it!"

"I can offer you freedom from this existence."

UMD soldiers crashed into the room.

"Atom! We don't have time!" Kai shouted.

Atom emitted a beam that formed a sphere of blue energy all around him.

As if by some force of magnetism, the sphere pulled the chrome plates off the walls. The plates connected around the blue light, forming a metal alloy-ball around the energy.

Kai put his arm around me, holding me up. I had my arm around Attila.

"Kai," I uttered. "I think I am, now."

"What's that, Thomas?"

"I think I am scared."

My last vision of Atom was him holding Thalia's core and disappearing within the solid metal sphere.

Then there was a sound from within, increasing in frequency, louder and louder . . .

And louder . . .

Until it was so loud that there was no more sound . . .

—

00:00 seconds to midnight.

INTERPLANETARY MARINE CORPS
DEPARTMENT OF FUTURE AND SUSTAINMENT
OFFICIAL DEBRIEF MEMORANDUM FOR THE RECORD

Interviewee: Captain Quentin Thomas, IMC,
Department of Resource and Mineral Attainment

Interviewer: Chief Officer Evelyn Watts, IMC, Department
of Future and Sustainment

Present at recording: Private William Kai, Lab Tech Johnson,
Lab Assistant Jameson

Date of Interview: November 15, 2115

Place of Interview: Babel Space Station, Wing 2724, Block F,
Pod 13: Wing 2724 Block F Lab 1102

THOMAS: And then it was over. I thought I was dead. But I woke
up in the *Aquarius I* med unit. Ripley was there, administering
the ultranium treatment. Atom made it so we survived. Those
ultracite plates around Thalia's core were built to withstand
exactly the kind of explosion Atom set off, only they were
meant to keep the explosion out, not in. Atom made sure only
he and Thalia suffered the effects of the blast.

With Thalia gone, all those progs on Elysium awoke. They
rose up and overwhelmed the Ultras. It was pretty bloody,
since many of them had their memories intact, like Bonita.
Guillotines in the piazzas, heads-on-spikes sort of deal. And
not long after that, you guys on Babel showed up and put

an end to the bloodshed. You know the rest, I guess. My dad sacrificed himself to save Atom. Atom sacrificed himself for us all.

WATTS: And you sacrificed yourself for Private Kai.

THOMAS: I guess so. Honestly didn't think about it that much at the time.

WATTS: I . . . . I don't know what to say. It's quite a story. I have questions, of course. I mean, to meet your dad like that, after all he's meant to you. Then to just lose him. How's this all sitting with you?

THOMAS: I'm gonna need a little more time to figure that out. I'm just numb right now about it. Hurts to even think of his face. But I do know him. I know he was ready. I know he died for something. I just want him to know that, you know? Like, I want to tell his ghost or whatever that it worked. We did it. But he died not knowing we'd win and I guess I just have to live with that.

WATTS: How do you know he was ready?

THOMAS: Because I was ready, too.

WATTS: I see. And the girl, Attila. Why did she betray her people, do you think?

THOMAS: The Ultras barely looked after one another.

WATTS: So what was it? Dependence on Thalia?

THOMAS: I'm not sure about that. It's like they replaced love with power, community with power, relationships with power. On Babel, we work together.

WATTS: We have to.

THOMAS: Right. It's that struggle. That group struggle. So that everyone can breathe. For the Ultras, the struggle was for dominance, so the most powerful could breathe. Like they didn't know the air was all around, too busy fighting over a straw.

WATTS: It seemed, also, like Attila took to you. Confided in you, was comfortable being vulnerable, in a way.

THOMAS: Maybe so.

WATTS: Did that surprise you?

THOMAS: A little, yeah. Like, I always thought kids were hard. Like, what do I even say to this little human mini-being? But maybe it's not so hard after all. Just be nice to them. Take care of them. Talk to them. Honestly, Evelyn, it felt–it feels like something I want.

WATTS: Wait, what do you mean? Like, to adopt her?

THOMAS: Well, maybe, I mean, after her father's household servants disemboweled him in the kitchen like that. But I meant I want . . .

WATTS: Something more?

THOMAS: Something more.

Private William Kai bursts into the room

KAI: Thomas, you still in here giving your testimony?

THOMAS: Well, I . . .

KAI: Oh, hi, Evelyn.

WATTS: Hello, Kai.

KAI: Okay, you look happy. Thomas, they let you give your testimony to her? Damn, my officer's name was Fred and you 'bout the size of his left leg.

THOMAS: Kai, what are you doing in here?

KAI: I just came to say they found Atom's chip!

WATTS: What? It wasn't fried in the blast?

THOMAS: You're kidding.

KAI: Nah, man, I'm dead serious. It's like a black-box sort of deal. His new body's down the hall.

THOMAS: Why the hell didn't you tell me this sooner?

KAI: Because I was giving your old recovering ass some space, damn!

WATTS: Wait, so they are pairing the chip with the new body–

KAI: Right now, in the–

THOMAS: You idiot, let's go! Come on, Evelyn.

EVELYN: You got it.

Sound of footsteps down hallway

EVELYN: Oh wait, I forgot the recorder.

Muffled sounds as Watts places recorder in her pocket

THOMAS: Do you think this will work?

KAI: Given the condition of the chip, it's possible. But I mean, he might not turn on. The body could just start up as a blank ATM unit.

Door opens

LAB TECH JOHNSON: I'm sorry, but you can't be in here. You're going to have to watch from outside.

THOMAS: Like hell we are!

LAB TECH JOHNSON: I'm sorry, but code 771–

WATTS: Screw the code, I have overruling authority. Proceed with the procedure, please.

KAI: Damn, girl.

LAB TECH JOHNSON: Clamps, please.

LAB ASSISTANT JAMESON: Yes, sir.

LAB TECH JOHNSON: Coolant.

LAB ASSISTANT JAMESON: Applying coolant.

WATTS: So I guess it wasn't a man who saved the world.

LAB TECH JOHNSON: Proceeding to reboot.

LAB ASSISTANT JAMESON: Running program.

THOMAS: It was a robot.

Boot up sound as Atom powers on

THE END

ACKNOWLEDGMENTS

First and foremost, I want to thank Sarah Passick for believing in me when no one else would give me the opportunity. You are my ladybug of literature. =)

Theo, for collaborating with me and bringing life into this story in a way I could have never done on my own. Thank you for helping me get the words on the page and piloting this story to Paradise.

Mike and Justin, for putting in all the work. Late nights and long meetings, making my vision become a possibility.

Yahdon and Simon & Schuster, for giving me the opportunity to bring this story to the world. Y'all rock!

My wife and children. My family. My friends. And the RattPack! The fans who occupy Paradise daily! I love you all.

Peace, love, and positivity,
Bob

ABOUT THE AUTHOR

Logic, aka Bobby Hall, is a Grammy-nominated artist and *New York Times* bestselling author. Born in Gaithersburg, Maryland, he rose to fame as a rapper with thoughtful lyrics and intricate storytelling, notably with his hit song "1-800-273-8255," which raised awareness for suicide prevention and mental health issues. Transitioning to literature, Hall debuted with the psychological thriller *Supermarket*, a #1 *New York Times* bestseller, followed by a memoir, *This Bright Future*, and a second novel, showcasing his unique perspective on life and creativity. When not writing, recording, and performing, Hall enjoys watching and making movies and spending time with his family.

Flex.